Ascension

Felicity Heaton

Copyright © 2011 Felicity Heaton

All rights reserved. No part of this publication may be reproduced, stored in a retrieval system, or transmitted, in any form or by any means mechanical, electronic, photocopying, recording or otherwise without the prior written consent of the publisher, nor be otherwise circulated in any form of binding or cover other than that in which it is published and without a similar condition being imposed on the subsequent purchaser.

The right of Felicity Heaton to be identified as the Author of the Work has been asserted by her in accordance with the Copyright, Designs and Patents Act 1988.

First printed April 2011

First Edition

Layout and design by Felicity Heaton

All characters in this publication are purely fictitious and any resemblance to real persons, living or dead, is purely coincidental.

CHAPTER 1

Taig closed his eyes and released a long low groan of unexpected pleasure as Lealandra's warm mouth fused with his. Her tongue slid between his lips, a delicious and familiar hot velvet caress that swept across his teeth and drew another hungry moan from him. Without considering the consequences and forgetting his anger, he twisted her long black hair around his fingers and tethered her to him so this breathtaking fantasy wouldn't end before he wanted, and he wanted it to go on forever.

He tilted his head and pressed harder against her mouth, his tongue brushing hers, delving in deep to taste her. A shiver of desire and need shot through him, and his breathing turned rough as he reacquainted himself with her sweetness and warmth. He hadn't imagined things turning out this way when she had walked into the bar tonight, but he wasn't about to push her away now that she was kissing him again, rekindling passion whose embers had burned deep in his heart all the time they had been apart. She moved against him, her lips soft and grazing his, slowing the kiss until he wanted to groan and pull her against him, wanted to thrust his tongue back into her mouth and show her just how ravenous she made him. It coiled tight in his gut, pushing for control, urging him to act on his desire.

All too soon, her lips left his but she remained close. With a soft puff of air into his mouth, she spoke.

"Are they gone?" Her quiet voice trembled along with her body, telling him that the kiss hadn't only affected him. His heart pounded for more and his blood rushed through his ears, dampening his awareness of their surroundings.

Taig glanced around the dim emptying bar. The two men were gone. He stared into her eyes, refreshing his memory of every fleck of silver against stormy grey. It had been too long since he had seen her, and felt even longer since he had kissed her. A tortuous length of time and an absence he couldn't easily forgive, even when her kiss made him forget it.

"Not yet," he whispered the lie against her lips, a split-second before his mouth claimed hers, dominant now that he was ready for the kiss. Desire became a raging inferno within him, burning away the anger that blazed back into life whenever he had a moment to think. This kiss was the only thing that mattered right now.

This time, Lealandra loosed a deep breathy moan. The sound sent his blood rushing ahead of his thoughts. He hardened instantly against his tight black jeans and wrapped his fingers around the nape of her neck, pressing them in and dragging her closer still. The heat of her kiss reawakened lost passion and a need for her that could never die. Six years of separation disappeared in an instant, erased by the fact that she had finally walked back into his life. He wasn't going to let her go this time. Even if this kiss was only a decoy, it still meant something to them both. He knew it did.

Her fingertips grazed his neck and pushed into the shorter black hair at the back of his head. He groaned internally at the feel of her nails against his scalp, declaring her growing hunger, and furrowed his brow as he brought his hand forward to claim her jaw, holding her in place. He burned at the feel of her soft satin skin beneath his fingers. Her touch was still electric, sending waves of hot sparks dancing along every nerve in his body, bringing his cold flesh to life. Tilting her head back, he thrust his tongue into her mouth and slid his free hand around her waist at the same time, pulling her so close to him that her breasts pushed against his chest with each gasping breath she drew. He eased his hand lower and caressed the patch of bare warm skin between the bottom of her short black strapless corset top and the waist of her long black skirt. Lealandra tensed. Too fast.

Taig braced for impact.

The flat of her hand slammed against his chest, forcing him backwards in the curved padded seat of the booth and tearing her from his grasp. Her gelid gaze stopped him dead.

"They're gone, aren't they?" Lealandra's tone was pure venom that matched the ice in her pale grey eyes.

Taig held his hands up, surrendering with a seductive smile that confessed every sin he had been considering. Lealandra wasn't the kind of witch you lied to. With such strong power flowing in her veins, it was easy for her to read everyone. Everyone but him. His blood saw to that. Her ability to see through him didn't come from magic. It came from the divine six months they had spent locked tight in each other's embrace. Six heavenly months he would never forget followed by six hollow years he wished he couldn't remember.

Lealandra looked around the bar, flicking her straight dark hair over her bare slender shoulders. His black gaze raked over her in the same hungry way it had done when she had first appeared in front of him tonight. She had grown a little thinner in their time apart. Her partner hadn't been taking care of her. Taig curled his fingers into fists at the thought of another man touching what was his. Anger blazed in his chest, ignited by the idea that the man she had chosen over him hadn't been looking after her needs. Had the idiot failed to see what she truly craved?

The magic that inhabited her body drained her and made her hungry. She needed to feed often and he wasn't talking about food. Magic as old and potent as hers demanded the highest price and had the basest needs. If it didn't get what it wanted, it was hard for Lealandra to retain control. It only proved the point he had tried to hammer home to her when she had been on the verge of leaving him all those years ago and disproved hers.

Taig didn't give a fuck about the rules of her kind. A witch was no match for a witch, especially not one who needed blood to sustain her.

Demon blood.

The thought that Lealandra had been struggling with her power these six long years stoked his anger into blind fury. Every muscle itched with the desire to find her pathetic excuse for a man and teach him a lesson he would never forget for making her suffer. The kind of lesson that would satisfy Taig's own deep dark cravings.

"I can't believe you'd take a cheap shot like that," Lealandra muttered in his direction, her eyes meeting his. "No. Wait. Actually... I can."

With his best sexy smirk, Taig leaned back into the grotty dark brown leather seat and stretched his arms out along the top. He shrugged and held her gaze.

"You kissed me first. I just returned the favour."

Her tongue swept over her lips, as though she wanted to kiss him again and was contenting herself with the lingering taste of him. If she wanted him to kiss her, he would. He would kiss her so hard that she would forget that idiot she had left him for and her own name in the process. She would forget everything but the feel of him inside her where he belonged. He would ruin her to everyone but him.

"That's not the kind of favour I need from you." Lealandra casually rested her elbow on the back of the leather seat and propped her chin up with her hand. Her head tilted to one side, her dusky kiss-swollen lips curving into a smile. His heart thundered, beating hard with the rush of desire that flooded him.

That smile had made him want her the moment he had laid eyes on her all those years ago. He still wanted her.

He tamped down his desire and got a grip. Her kissing him hadn't changed a damn thing. Whatever they'd had, it didn't exist anymore. She had trampled it on her way out of the door and it was going to take a lot more than a kiss to get her into his good book again.

"A favour? Tell me, why should I do you any favours? Last I checked, you were shacked up with another bloke. Why don't you ask Loverboy to help you out? I'm sure he could do something... unspectacular." Taig picked up his shot of whisky from the table and necked it. The liquid burned his throat as it slid down, heating him through. Sometimes it was nice to feel something other than cold. Alcohol and hunting were the only things that did that these days. His gaze ran over Lealandra. She used to make him burn hotter than Hell on a summer's day. She still did, but he wasn't about to let her see that. "I guess that's why you're here. Loverboy just doesn't cut it when it comes to handling demons. That pair of weaklings would have him inside out and back to front before he could lift a finger to cast whatever impotent half-assed spell he could muster."

Taig held her gaze, cool and steady, watching the hurt surfacing in her eyes and feeling like a bastard for it, but on some twisted level, it satisfied him.

He narrowed his eyes and casually placed the glass down. "Well, you're shit out of luck, Lea. I'm not interested."

Her only reaction was to look away from him. She flicked the small silver bells on the ties of her long skirt and her shoulders lifted in a sigh. That was unsatisfactory. He had expected a better response than that. He had wanted her to argue with him about it. Perhaps even fight him. A good fight with her might go some way towards releasing the anger that was burning like acid in his veins, eating away at him and filling his head and heart with acrid memories.

Memories that drove him to kill.

He quirked a dark eyebrow and waited for her to say something. It wasn't like her. She looked up at him through her eyelashes.

A hint of fear surfaced in her beautiful eyes and rippled across her pale skin in a wave that only he could detect. He sat up, all sense of casual lost now that he had realised that she was frightened and it wasn't of him. His anger faded. Something was very wrong. Lealandra didn't do frightened. No witch as powerful as her did, at least not when they had their Counter-Balance, their other half, the one who could temper their magic and help them maintain control of it.

"I'll pay you... whatever you want... just name your price." She coughed to clear her throat, as though such a pathetic attempt to cover her turbulent feelings would fool him.

It was there in her body and her power, and he knew her well enough that he could easily read both. She was scared, and he was an idiot for not noticing it the second she had approached him, and the moment those thugs had walked into the joint. They had been out of place and suspicious, and he had sensed their demon blood, and then Lealandra had kissed him and he had lost track of them and her feelings. She had tasted purely of hunger and desire. All sweet with arousal. It had been enough to throw him off her underlying fear.

"You know my price." Taig's eyes narrowed on hers, intent and showing her that he was being serious for once. His voice dropped to a low whisper. "I want you, Lea."

She swallowed and blinked. Once. Twice. "No deal."

When she moved to stand, Taig grabbed her wrist, locking his fingers tightly around it. She looked down at his hand and then into his eyes. Her startled look added to her natural beauty, her eyes round and her rosy lips parted. A blush stained her pale cheeks, deep enough that he noticed it even in the low light of the bar. He wanted her more now than ever and he wasn't about to let her walk out on him again.

"You knew what I'd ask for so why come to me with your problems if you were going to refuse?"

Lealandra pried his fingers off her and frowned. "You saw those men. I need a demon hunter. You're the best I know."

Demon hunter. The job title neglected to mention the fact that his father had been one of the most powerful demons to walk the Earth. He stared into Lealandra's stormy eyes and saw the same calm acceptance that they always showed him. Had his mother looked at his father that way? She had dared to be with him after all. That union had spawned himself—half demon hidden behind the mask of man.

Taig tapped his fingers on the dark table, torn between rejecting her request unless she agreed to his terms and kissing her again. His eyebrows knitted tight together. This wasn't easy. What they had shared six years ago wasn't the kind of everyday passion that most people found at the start of a relationship. It had gone beyond that. The dark and hungry craving had consumed them both, had pushed them to the edge and had almost tipped them over it a few times. It had been unbridled passion—the sort that was rare in this world—and it still flooded him whenever he looked at her, whenever her beautiful eyes met his and dared him to make a move. He could deny it all he wanted, pretend that he no longer felt a thing for her, but she still tied him in knots and had him on his knees with only a smile. She licked her lips again, a nervous sweep of her tongue that reminded him that something was wrong.

What could be so bad that she wasn't asking her precious coven for help and was instead looking him up after six long years?

Was it just the demons that had her scared or was there more to this than she was telling him? Witches and demons got on like a house on fire but usually they kept well clear of each other, sticking to their own world. It was unusual for a demon to go after a witch, but he couldn't deny that the two kids earlier had been looking for Lealandra.

And now she was asking him for help.

What reason could demons have for going after her?

Taig looked deep into her eyes, focusing on them as he tried to get a hold on her feelings. There was anger in her now, aimed at him, but the fear was still there too. It echoed in the unsteady beat of her heart and danced in the depths of her eyes. She was in trouble, big enough that she had sought him out even when she knew that he would be pissed off at her and that he would demand a high price for services rendered. Either she was desperate or she truly believed that he was her best choice.

Or maybe she just wanted to see him again and this was the perfect excuse for her to waltz back into his life.

Still, his ineffable charm and attractiveness aside, parts of it didn't make sense. Lealandra was powerful enough to take care of a couple of weak lower demons and her bastard Counter-Balance and dear coven should have been able to protect her if she couldn't fight them for some reason. Taig had never met them, but the coven was probably strong enough to take on a demon of his strength. Two weaklings would be nothing to them. Like swatting flies.

And why was she here anyway? Alone too. Her Counter-Balance would have a tantrum of galactic proportions if he knew that Lealandra had come to her ex-lover for help.

In fact, none of it made sense.

Taig's head ached from trying to figure it out. It was just like her to send his mind in ten directions at once. There was only one way to find out what the hell had Lealandra walking back into his life. He never had been backwards about being forwards, after all. It was one of the qualities that Lealandra had liked about him.

"Why do you need me?" Taig sensed the deep spike in her feelings, the rise in her desire that struck him hard and sent a jolt to his groin, reigniting his own hunger.

Her eyes widened and her cheeks coloured.

He hadn't considered the possibility of a second meaning to his words but now he was. His suspicions had been right. He wasn't the only one the kiss had affected. He wasn't the only one who felt this need burning deep within.

His eyes narrowed on hers in both a challenge and a command. He was damned if he was going to let her get away without answering, and damned if he was going to let her walk out on him again.

"Tell me."

CHAPTER 2

Lealandra slumped onto the cracked leather seat and placed her hands between her knees. She stared at them. They were pale against her black skirt and she could see the veins marking the back of them in the low light of the grotty bar. Her gaze drifted to Taig's left wrist.

The rolled up sleeves of his black shirt revealed thick toned forearms that stated he could snap a man's neck with ease if he felt like it. She had witnessed proof of that declaration more than once. His strength and his ability to dispatch demons without breaking a sweat was incredible and exactly what she needed right now.

Numerous thin silvery streaks marked a haphazard path up the inside of his forearm, closely packed together at his wrist and growing more distant towards his elbow. A rich metallic scent filled her mouth when she remembered the taste of his flesh. She trembled inside, hunger stirring in the depths of her as her power cried out for blood. Her hands shook.

Six dizzy months of passion with him collided into one pounding thought in her mind. She needed him still. It wasn't just about the blood that he offered so freely but also the mindless desire that consumed her each time she saw him, each time they touched. She had craved that for six long years, an age in which her Counter-Balance had forced her to keep away from what she needed most. He never had understood her needs, and his ignorance of her hunger and denial of its existence had cost him dearly.

"Charlie is dead." No trace of emotion touched her voice. She had mourned the loss of her Counter-Balance for as long as her heart would allow. Now it demanded that she protect herself. "I thought they were after him. I was wrong."

"They want you." Taig leaned further back into the seat and her gaze leapt to his body.

Her pulse trebled over his limp, ready for anything pose. Memories of him naked and hard sprung to the front of her mind and her fingers itched to retrace the paths they had taken across the delicious muscles of his broad torso, to tease his pebbled nipples and rake down his back as he filled her body with his own. Her tongue wanted to taste his flesh again and lick every inch of him. A shudder of pleasure wracked her when her eyes found his arm and the marks there. Marks for her. Cuts made in the wildest throes of passion when she craved his blood the most—when she craved him like a drug and needed him more than air.

Her heart fluttered in her throat, driven to a wild beat by her passionate thoughts.

Lealandra swallowed it back down. She was here on business, not because she needed a fix of Taig. She was over him now. Those first few months without him had been Hell but she had made it through.

It was over.

She faltered when her eyes met his black ones, their endless depths entrancing her and warming her right down to the marrow of her bones. A hot but empty feeling filled her chest and she resisted the temptation to touch the spot over her heart and rub it in the hope that the feeling would go away. It was pointless. She had never realised it before tonight, before seeing him again, but she had missed him and she had been lonely without him. A part of her had been missing. Her heart. Taig held it in his grasp, clutching it so tightly that it hurt, nails poised to puncture it. One wrong move and her heart would break all over again. It was a fool's game to come to him and risk so much pain but he was the only one who could protect her now, and as much as she would hate herself for it, she might even stoop to pay the price he was asking.

"I don't know why," she confessed with a nonchalant shrug that drew a quirked eyebrow from him. It was redundant to try to cover the desire that crept through her whenever she looked at him but she had to keep a lid on her emotions so he wouldn't see how vulnerable she was and take advantage. She had to at least try to get him to take her offer of payment and not insist on his.

Taig reached across to the full shot glass beside the one he had emptied not minutes ago. His eyes closed when he tilted his head back and swallowed the golden liquid. The glide of his Adam's apple made her swallow along with him. Her tongue pressed against her teeth, eager to trace patterns on his neck and to feel him biting her throat so hard he would leave a mark.

This wasn't going well.

One midnight-black eye opened and slid to her. The corner of his deliciously curved lips tugged into a smile. She cursed his demonic senses and how flustered he was getting her. This wasn't about sex. This was about her life. The quicker her libido got the message, the better. Still the thoughts of their naked bodies entwined and writhing filled her mind. They were impossible to shut out. Just being near him had been bringing everything back. When she had kissed him to disguise herself from the men, it had opened the floodgates of pent up desire and need, and left her aching for his touch.

"They killed Charlie to weaken you."

Those six words sent fear into her heart, each an icy spear that froze her to her soul. She hadn't considered that they had meant to kill Charlie too.

"I thought they'd messed up and got the wrong person. It was dark in the apartment and the shot that killed him came through the window. They could only have seen our silhouettes where we were sitting on the couch." Her hands shook for a different reason. Panic erased any desire to touch Taig. Was he right? Charlie had been far less powerful than she was and the coven had chosen him as her Counter-Balance for that reason. He had been perfect for the job. His magic had craved the strength of hers. It had absorbed some of her power, making it easier for her to keep control. Without him, she was in danger of her magic consuming her. It was building inside her, growing stronger with every passing second. Soon it would push for control and, if that happened, it would force her to seek out what it wanted most. She shuddered.

Lealandra had seen witches turn. Her own mother had lost herself to her magic. If her father hadn't been so powerful, none of them would have survived. Who would bring her back if the magic took control? No one at the coven was strong enough. Not even Gregori, the New York City coven's leader. If the magic seized her, it would take all of them to join forces in order to save her.

Her eyes wandered to Taig. Would he help her? Could he help her? She studied his handsome face, watching the flickers of his thoughts cross his pitch-black eyes. He was as beautiful as she remembered—the kind of gorgeous that could win him any girl he wanted, even her if he tried hard and turned on the charm. She wasn't strong enough to hold out against him forever. Something would give and it was likely to be her heart. He rubbed a thumb down the line of his defined jaw and then paused, his expression turning pensive.

"The curtains were closed?" he said and she found herself savouring the sound of his deep voice. She had never forgotten how he sounded, with his mixed accent, not quite American but not quite another unknown country either, or some of the things he had husked in her ear during making love with her.

Lealandra nodded. "They're thin enough to see through when all the lights are on, but we only had the table lamp lit. They could have only seen our heads above the couch back. When they shot Charlie his—"

The memory of seeing her partner's head blown wide open stole her voice. Her throat closed and she struggled to breathe, clinging to the last shred of calm inside her. There had been so much blood. It had covered the apartment. It had covered her. One second Charlie had been there, the next she had been sitting beside a corpse, still talking as though nothing had happened. It had taken almost a full minute for her senses to fall into order and make her realise that he was dead.

Taig's large hand covered hers and she jumped and looked up at him through her lashes. The concern in his eyes made the tears in hers tremble on the brink of falling. She placed her other hand over his, completing the tangle, and closed her eyes. Focusing on their hands, she unleashed a fraction of her magic, giving it more rein but still keeping it under tight control, and drew strength from him. His power seeped into her hands and crept up her arms until it suffused her entire body, sending a heady rush through her.

"You're hungry," Taig murmured in a voice laden with sensuality.

No denial left her lips. Right now, she was more than hungry. Kissing him had been a mistake. It had given her a taste and made her remember how things had been, and how he had made her feel. Her magic had latched onto those memories and it didn't want to let go. She held his hand tighter and stole everything that she could from him in an effort to calm herself and restore the balance of power inside her. Taig had once provided her with a substitute before she had found her balance in Charlie.

His own power.

His blood.

"It'll cost you extra," Taig said and she realised she was staring at the scars on his forearm.

She took her hands away from his, unwilling to pay the price he was asking for his help, let alone the price he would place on his blood now. What he had once given to her freely would now cost her everything. He would make her pay dearly for it just to spite her, and part of her couldn't blame him for doing such a thing. She could understand why he would think that she deserved such punishment.

He gently brushed her long dark hair behind her ear, his touch comforting and speaking volumes, telling her that the desire she felt wasn't one-sided. He was still attracted to her.

"He didn't look after you properly."

Lealandra didn't have an answer to that accusation. Charlie had neglected her need for sustenance through blood. He had thought he had been doing the right thing, when in reality it had been nothing short of torture.

"He said I didn't need it," she said in a small voice and then straightened and found her strength. She didn't want Taig to see her weak. It had been her decision to leave him and go with Charlie and the coven. She had to accept that and the things that had happened. She had to take responsibility and stick to her decision, even when she now felt it had been a terrible mistake. "You know he didn't believe in that kind of thing. None at the coven do."

Taig laughed and toyed with the two empty shot glasses. "He was more of a fool than I thought."

His laughter died in an instant when his eyes locked with hers. Their fathomless black depths sparkled with intensity. Her breath shortened and her palms sweated with anticipation. She subconsciously leaned forwards, eager to be close to him, desiring to feel his hands on her again and have him continue to look at her with such need and hunger.

"I should never have let him take you." His expression darkened with his frown, his lips compressing into a thin line that conveyed the anger flowing from him and through her.

Lealandra got the better of herself and picked up her own shot of whisky and downed it. The fire as it slipped down into her stomach did nothing to dampen her desire or boost her courage.

"You didn't have a choice." She leaned back into the seat with a false smile that covered her fear and her feelings.

He shifted forward and stared into the far reaches of her soul. His eyes lightened. The black melted to reveal a red inferno that flickered and licked around the wide chasm of his pupils. She drew a deep steadying breath, refusing to let him fluster her.

"Believe me," Taig said on a sneer, "if I'd decided not to let him take you, he wouldn't have. He would've died a lot sooner."

That was no idle threat. A sweep of pin-pricks chased across her back and down her arms, and a wave of fury swept over her, so intense that her magic retreated, bowing to Taig's superior force of nature. As powerful as she was, she was no match for him when he was angry.

Taig rarely let his demonic side come out to play and she had only witnessed the gruesome aftermath when he had, but it had given her a glimpse of the devastation of which he was capable.

Lealandra didn't need to see the true form he held locked beneath his skin for her to know that any decision he made was final and he was willing to resort to bloodshed to ensure that.

It was half the reason she had come to him.

The other half?

Lealandra looked down at her chest and the intricate mark between her breasts visible only to her. A circle within a circle about the size of her palm. Runic symbols filled the two black bands around the outside. Within the central circle were a series of patterns that marked her fate and the role specific things had to play in it. A little off centre within this circle was a mark she recognised. Her gaze drifted to Taig's shoulder. Hidden beneath his black shirt on his left shoulder blade was the same mark. It wasn't a tattoo. It was a brand of his demonic bloodline. A birthmark.

"So... you lost your partner and now some demons are out to kill you but you won't pay the price for protection. You've got to have a pretty good reason for hunting me down if you'd already made up your mind to refuse my fee." The cocky smirk was back, tugging at the dusky lips that knew her intimately, every inch of her.

Finger-length strands of his black hair criss-crossed his forehead, messy and seemingly out of control as always. The feel of the short back had been like silk beneath her fingers, bringing forth memories of raking her fingers through it, of clutching it tightly to keep his mouth fused with hers. His dark eyes narrowed on hers and his smile widened. Her heart thumped in her throat at that look—all hunger and need. He hadn't changed a bit since she had last seen him. Still so handsome that he would never have a problem catching a girl with his otherworldly masculine beauty but still a loner who refused the company women offered him. Still a negotiator gunning for the right price before he would do anything but still itching for a fight so badly he would gladly hunt demons for sheer fun.

"I think I'd like to know that reason now."

Before she had come out tonight, she had vowed to keep this hidden from him but now it might just be her trump card.

Taking hold of his hand, Lealandra ignored his raised eyebrow and moved towards him on the curved leather seat so she was within reach. She took a deep breath, held it and brushed his fingers across her chest. The mark there shimmered rich red and sparkled into life. The glow lit his face, dancing in his wide eyes.

"You've started the ascension," Taig whispered with the barest glance into her eyes before his gaze fell to her chest again.

His hand left hers and he touched the ascension mark, tracing the circle with a light caress. Her breasts tingled and her nipples hardened against the black strapless corset top. She tried to ignore the delicious feel of his hands on her but it was impossible. It was Heaven to have him touching her again, even if it was only so he could see her mark.

His fingers paused against her, cool points on her burning skin.

Lealandra knew what had arrested his attention. "It's your mark."

Taig lowered his hand until his palm rested against her right breast, the weight of it making her ache for more as her mind raced forwards to imagine him removing her top and caressing her. She rolled her eyes closed at the thought of his lips latching onto one of her nipples and tugging on it, teasing it with his teeth. Her groin throbbed in response to the fantasy.

"And this is supposed to make me help you?" Emotionless and deadpan. His response was the exact opposite of what she had expected.

"In a few days, possibly less, I'll be vulnerable, Taig. I need you to protect me. I'll pay you with money, everything I have. It's over twenty grand." Her eyes searched his for any sign that he would take it. He had to help her.

The mark on her chest meant that he was going to play a role in her ascension. Without him, she might not make it through. It was rare for a witch to go through the ascension, a process in which their power matured and reached its maximum level, and even rarer for one to survive. Normally the power became too strong and seized control of its host, eventually destroying it. Lealandra didn't want to die, not during the ascension, and not before it, and she knew that she would if Taig didn't help her.

"You know my price." Taig's flat expression gave her the distinct impression he wasn't about to change it any time soon.

"Your price is too high." Part of her again said that it wasn't. She would do it, even if the ascension weren't a factor.

Six years without him had been hollow and hellish, living day-to-day, stuck in the coven and doing nothing but learning or practicing. Not once had she needed to fight. It had been dull, empty, and she had grown so used to it that she had never realised. Not until now. She had missed him. Her time with Taig had been thrilling, and not just because of their passion. They had hunted together and the danger had been exciting, the battles of life and death exhilarating, adding to the way it had felt to be with him. She wanted that back. She wanted him back.

Taig caught hold of her hand and pressed a kiss to the back of it. His lips never left her as he kissed up her bare arm, drawing her towards him at the same time. Strands of his hair tickled her skin, a precursor to each kiss. Her eyelids fell to half-mast when he reached her shoulder and then his mouth was on her neck, feeding the fantasy unravelling in her heart and mind. Her breath left her on a sigh and she leaned her cheek against his, lost in the feel of his cool mouth devouring her throat in the most sensual of caresses. He bit lightly. She moaned and then got the better of herself and shoved him away.

"Too high."

"You're hungry," Taig whispered with another smirk, a knowing look in his eyes. He dropped his gaze to his wrist and hers followed against her will. She swallowed when he idly ran his fingers over the scars on his arm. "Protection and a taste. That's my offer. What's yours?"

Damn him back to Hell.

Lealandra flicked her long hair back and glared at him. The bastard was leaving her little choice and it tore her up inside as her heart waged war against her mind.

It would be so easy for her to give in to her desire. The only thing stopping her was that she knew deep inside he was doing this, demanding this price, because he wanted to make her pay for leaving him, not because he really wanted her back. She had broken her heart once already. She couldn't survive breaking it again.

Her grey gaze met his black and she narrowed her eyes on him. Power rose and spiralled through her, filling every inch of her body, awakened by the thought of his blood. Damn him. There was only one way to get out of the corner he had backed her into and buy herself the time to convince him to accept her method of payment instead. She loathed herself for giving in to him even when it was only temporary and pushed the word out through clenched teeth.

"Fine."

CHAPTER 3

Taig grinned and leaned forwards, his hands coming up to claim his payment. Lealandra's single raised finger stopped him in his tracks.

"Protection first. You'll get your payment when you've done your job."

He glared and clenched his fists. Anger raced through his veins at her denial, burning deep and fast in his blood, and Lealandra seemed to respond to it. Crimson tinted her eyes. He could feel the magic rising inside her. Every time she looked at his arm or he mentioned blood, her power spiked. Charlie was lucky he was dead. If he had been alive, Taig would have been heading out to find him and bash some sense into his thick head. He was a bastard for the number he had done on Lealandra by denying her what she needed to keep control and keep strong, and a son of a bitch for taking her away from him in the first place.

Taig reeled in his fury and forced himself to relax.

"Deal," he said, too enticed by the thought of her being his again to care about the technicalities.

Lealandra had said it herself. It was a matter of days before she would go through the ascension. He had the scent of those demons now. He could kill them before she went through the change and see her safe. She had told him about the ascension several times, each time giving away a little more, until she had said enough for him to see that it frightened her. She feared dying during the ascension. Many paid with their life for their increase in power, even when their entire coven helped them. Her magic would become too strong for her to control. She needed her Counter-Balance, but someone had removed Charlie from the equation, plunging her into dangerous territory, making her desperate enough to turn to him for help.

Lealandra moved out of the booth, smoothing down the back of her long black skirt. The mark on her chest was no longer visible but he knew it wasn't gone. A witch's ascension mark was visible only to the carrier unless someone directly touched it. Fuck, it had felt good to lay his hands on her and he couldn't help thinking up excuses to touch her again.

"My place or yours?" he said with a sly grin, his hunger returning as he imagined laying her out on his bed naked and begging. He had always loved it when she had begged. The sight of her writhing on his dark covers, her slender legs rubbing together, fingers twirling the silken threads of her black hair around them as she waited for him was one of his favourite memories of her, seared on his mind for eternity.

"Yours." Her response caught him off guard and the smile dropped from his face. It had been a joke.

"Shouldn't you be heading to the coven?" Taig stood, a frown knitting his black eyebrows. It was strange for her to stay away from other witches. When her ascension hit, he wouldn't have a clue how to help her. She needed others like her around her. She needed to live.

Taig could deal with the demons and anyone else who wanted her dead, but he wasn't sure what he could do to help her survive her ascension. He glanced at his scarred wrists. Could his blood give her enough control over her power? How much would she need? He had given her blood in the past but usually he was out of his mind with lust and desire and he wasn't thinking straight. The thought of giving her blood turned his stomach. It was tainted. He didn't want that inside her. He didn't want it inside him.

"We are... but we're not staying. I just want to get my things and then go to your place."

Taig stared at her, studying the subtle changes in her expression and her body that gave away her fear. Why didn't she want to stay at the coven? She had been with them for six years and she needed her kin right now. His frown intensified. Unless she had a reason not to remain with her coven. She had come to him and now wanted to go and get her things. It was all backwards. Only it wasn't if she hadn't been staying at the coven since Charlie's death. That would make sense. She must have been staying somewhere else and, now that he had agreed to help her, she was going back to her apartment at the coven for her things. This was all messed up. Lealandra was powerful enough to handle herself and anyone at the coven. Why did she need him to go with her? A show of force to anyone who might be involved in this plot against her? Did she suspect the coven?

"You should stay with the coven." He tested his theory.

"No." Her flat tone made it clear that was the only answer he was going to get. She cast a quick glance around the dark bar. The few regulars that remained weren't likely to be out to get her. He knew them well and knew where they lived. They wouldn't dare hurt her. Her grey gaze skipped back to him. He didn't like the edge of fear that lingered in it. That wasn't his Lea. Someone had her running scared and he was going to beat the crap out of them for it. "Let's just get out of here."

Taig nodded and followed her towards the exit, his thoughts still lingering on the fact that she was keeping away from her kin. A niggling voice at the back of his mind said that she didn't trust them. Did she think they had something to do with the demons that were out to kill her? Surviving the ascension was rare but the increase in the power of the ascended placed them above others, making it often the subject of envy among witches. Envious enough to kill?

It troubled him.

If the local coven were responsible, then he was going to have to be on his guard. Demons he could handle, but witches had a tendency to fight dirty and nothing drained his strength like the right spell or five.

Lealandra led the way out of the backstreet bar. The flickering blue neon sign reflected in the lingering puddles in the cracked asphalt. The city still smelt like rain from this morning's storm, laced with an underlying trace of blood. Taig's gaze shifted to Lealandra again. He had never tasted her but she had taken his blood enough times for him to know her on the inside. Demon blood ran in his veins, stained him. It filled his mind with lust for violence and his heart with darkness. His blood had mixed with Lealandra's each time she had taken it into her, mingling with her power for a short spell, giving him insight into her innermost thoughts and feelings. Connecting them. A witch and a demon.

Taig clenched his fists until his short nails bit into his palms. A demon? Not quite. The progeny of both his father and mother. An aberration. Not belonging to this world or the underworld. One foot in each but no place in either. And no chance of finding that place. He deserved to stand alone and live between worlds. He didn't deserve what Lealandra had given him all those years ago.

"Penny for your thoughts."

His gaze snapped to Lealandra.

Warmth touched her eyes and the smile curving her soft lips pierced his heart and took him back six years. She had always looked at him like that. Open and accepting. With love.

Taig turned away and stared ahead. "I'd like to check out your place while we're at the coven."

Lealandra could probably sense the lie in those words but he wasn't about to let his guard slip and let her know his true thoughts.

He took hold of her hand. It was warm in his and trembled enough that he felt it. His thumb closed over the backs of her fingers and he kept the pressure against them gentle enough that she would know he wasn't after something. This touch wasn't about him wanting her. This was about letting her know that whatever she was afraid of, she didn't have to fear it anymore. He wasn't about to let anything happen to her. He only wished that she had come to him sooner.

Surprisingly, she didn't take her hand away. She stared up into his eyes, their difference in height noticeable now that they were standing. He stood at least six inches taller even though she was wearing heeled boots and he liked it. Something flickered in her eyes and he felt it trip down her spine and through him. A memory that made her warm and stopped her shaking. Her eyes fell to his chest and she blinked languidly. Was she thinking the same thing as he was? He used to love the feel of her in his arms, her head resting lightly against his chest, her heat seeping into him and her heart fluttering against his ribs.

"Penny for your thoughts," he husked and her stormy gaze rose to meet his. A hint of colour touched her cheeks and then she looked down and stepped away, taking her hand with her.

"We should get moving." She turned her back on him and walked down the narrow alley between the bar and the rundown apartment block next door.

They were both shitty liars.

Taig followed, gaze raking down Lealandra's back, taking all of her in. He didn't like how thin she was now. She had always been slim enough. Now she looked fragile. Breakable. Or was it this new side to her that made her appear that way? He hadn't seen her frightened before, not to this extent, and for some reason it rattled him.

And it made him want to protect her.

She was his after all.

He hadn't let her go forever.

He had only given Charlie temporary custody. He had expected Lealandra to buckle years ago and had been waiting for her return. Only, he hadn't realised that until tonight. Seeing her again had brought his feelings back along with that night. He never should have let her go. They belonged together.

An urge to stalk up behind her, pull her into his arms and kiss her so hard that she knew that tore through him. He tamped it down, telling himself that this wasn't the time to let his possessive streak take hold, no matter how alluring the thought of kissing her again was. The slide of her tongue against his, the feel of their lips barely touching, made him burn with need so fierce that it was difficult to control himself. It had been hard enough back in the bar. Out here, there was nothing stopping him from backing her up against the alley wall and showing her just what she did to him, and just what he wanted to do to her.

Lealandra turned and looked at him, a small frown creasing her brow. He was lagging behind but that wasn't the only reason she was giving him dirty looks. She had long been able to sense when someone was watching her, and when they were watching as closely as he was, she could probably feel every intent that was crossing their mind.

She reached the end of the alley and stepped up to a plain black sedan. It was nothing fancy but it was clearly standard coven issue. It didn't fit either. If Lealandra had left the coven and had waited to get him on her side before returning for her things, why did she still have the car? It was probably fitted with a tracking device. The coven would know exactly where she was at all times.

Lealandra paused, one hand on the car's roof and the other holding the driver's door open. She leaned against the roof and smiled at him, a warm one that burned itself on his cold heart. He hated those smiles. They made him want to be human so he could believe the feelings behind them were real. But he wasn't, and they weren't.

"I'm not stupid enough to let anyone track me... if that's what you're really thinking in there." She tapped the roof and her smile widened. "I had a guy I know take out the tracker and I haven't parked it anywhere near where I'm staying in case there's another less obvious one onboard."

Taig didn't pay attention to anything she said after mentioning another man. She could have come to him to have him check her car over but she had gone to see this guy instead. His jaw ticked and he ground his teeth. Had he been her last resort? That cut him deeper than he cared to admit.

"What?" Lealandra stepped back from the car, as though she was going to round it to him.

He yanked the passenger side door open so hard that the hinges creaked. She gave him a black look. She was lucky he hadn't torn the fucking thing off. Clenching his fists, he reined in his anger and glared at her, returning her dark look one hundred times over. Her eyes lightened and searched his. She could look all she wanted but he wasn't letting her in.

They stood there for long minutes, neither willing to back down, eyes locked in silent combat. He refused to give an inch. Always did in this kind of situation. Lealandra had tried countless times to get a grip on his feelings like this and every time she failed. Tonight would be no different.

With an exasperated sigh, she slammed the driver's door.

"What is it?" she snapped and then her tone softened. "Seriously."

How many others had she gone to before trying him? Had she tried every hunter in the city? She probably had countless reasons to be pissed off at him but it still annoyed the hell out of him that she wouldn't come to him when she was in danger. Whatever had happened in their past, he would always be there for her when she needed him, and right now she needed him, not anyone else.

"Taig." She reached across the car's roof to him. Her arm brushed away the fine layer of summer dust to reveal a streak of glossy black paint. She flexed her fingers, a silent order for him to take her hand.

As if he was dumb enough to do that. If he did that, she had more chance of reading his feelings.

Her hand shifted again, a soft rolling motion of her fingertips.

Against his better judgement, he placed his hand into hers and felt her power flow to meet his, felt the warmth of it as it crept up his arm. She wasn't the only one who liked how it felt when they touched.

"How long ago did Charlie die?"

Her fingers tensed against his. She hadn't expected that question. Did she think he was going to open up to her over the roof of her sedan in the grotty underworld of this heartless city? Not a chance in Hell. Who knew what people were listening in?

He had a reputation to maintain as the best hunter out there and she had a lesson to learn.

He wasn't the sharing kind.

Even if he had been, she had lost that privilege a long time ago.

She took her hand back and dusted her arm down, taking her time over it.

"Three weeks." Without another look at him, she got into the car.

Taig slid into the passenger seat and stared at the black plastic dashboard. Three weeks. Enough time for her to see most of the hunters in the city. None of them would take on a job this risky though. Only he was stupid enough to go up against the kind of power that could be after her.

And only because it was after her.

If it had been anyone else, he would have told them to skip town, hide and pray to whatever they believed in that they survived. Not Lealandra though. He wouldn't do that to her. Couldn't.

"You left the coven right away?" he said.

Lealandra put the car into drive and pulled out onto the quiet road, shaking her head. "No. I stayed there the first week and then I started to get the feeling that I wasn't safe. Things happened."

"Things?" Taig turned and studied her profile as she drove. Her fine dark eyebrows met briefly and then she relaxed back into the seat. Except she didn't feel relaxed. She felt more on edge now than she had done back in the bar and the alley.

Was the prospect of returning to the coven the sole reason she was suddenly so tense, or did the fact she was alone in a car with him have anything to do with it?

Waves of emotion flowed from her, tension mixing with fear, anxiety, hope and despair. He wanted to know the source of those feelings. Was any of it about him?

"Gregori and the two supreme mages wanted me to remain at the coven while they investigated what had happened. I wanted to get away. Shortly after I mentioned that I wanted to leave, someone broke into my apartment and painted... something... on the wall above my bed." Her pause told him what she couldn't. Whatever they had scrawled across her wall, it had been a threat and it had upset her enough that she had fled.

"Were you out?"

A small shake of her head.

"Fuck." He slammed his fist against the dashboard, leaving a crater in the black plastic. The car screeched to a halt and they both lurched forwards and then slammed back into their seats.

"Jesus, Taig! Are you trying to give me a heart attack on top of everything else?"

Taig grinned his apology but it faded when he saw her. She sat with her hands wrapped so tightly around the steering wheel that her knuckles were white and her eyes were so wide that he could see all of her irises. Thin dark red ribbons of magic wound around her hands and the steering wheel, joining them. He reached over and the magic shifted course, mirroring his actions and reaching for him. He brought his hand to hers and the red ribbons flowed around his fingers, tickling his skin with their warmth and then seeping into him.

"Sorry," he muttered and looked at her. She stared at their hands.

A horn blared behind them.

Lealandra jumped and the magic sparked in response, sending a strong jolt up his arm that left it tingling. He took his hand back and rubbed his arm, hating how weak it suddenly felt. A potent reminder not to mess with her power. She could drain him and leave him feeling as weak as a kitten if she felt like it. His strength returned to his arm as Lealandra started to drive again, muttering dark things under her breath.

He shouldn't have frightened her like that. She was already on edge without him helping but the thought that someone had broken into her apartment and written on the wall above her bed while she had been sleeping in it and vulnerable twisted his gut with anger. He felt Lealandra look at him.

"There's no need to look like that. I'm still alive. It was just a warning."

To look like what? As though he wanted to kill someone? As though he was planning their slow painful death right that minute? How else was he supposed to look when someone had threatened her?

Taig flipped the visor in front of him down and stared at his reflection in the small rectangular mirror. Red eyes glared back at him, bright and flickering like flames in the darkness of the night.

Yeah, he wanted to kill them. He wanted to rip them to shreds for frightening her. And for threatening her? Well, he hadn't come up with a punishment severe enough just yet but he was working on it.

His eyes gradually melted back to black and he flipped the sun visor up. He listened to the sounds of her driving as he mulled over everything that she had told him. The steady tick of the indicators punctuated the constant drone of the engine. The sound of it was soothing, strange background music when combined with Lealandra's soft breathing and the quiet whoosh of cars as they passed by on the opposite side of the road.

Taig pressed his knuckles against his lips and frowned at the dent in the dashboard. Who in Hell was after her and why? There were too many possibilities at this stage and he couldn't discount the witches. There were bound to be people at the coven who were willing to climb the ranks by doing away with those above them. But just because the attacks had taken place at the coven, didn't mean it was an insider. He could easily slip in and out, quick enough to leave a message on her wall and disappear before someone noticed, even her. Things like that were simple for demons. But why the message? She had been asleep, giving them a golden opportunity to kill her.

Or was that too easy for whoever was behind this? There was no honour in killing someone while they slept. Whoever was after Lealandra had principles, rules they lived by, and that made him uneasy. The two thugs back at the bar hadn't looked like the type who would have qualms about killing a woman in her sleep.

Someone was using them to do their dirty work.

Lealandra moved out of the corner of his eye and his attention shifted to her. She pushed her long straight black hair behind her ears and frowned at the road. Taig glanced there, checking their location in the city, and then back at her. They were getting close to the coven now. It was on the other side of the river in Queens. The area was nicer than the one they had just left but both neighbourhoods were dangerous, especially at night. Humans thought that they were safe but they didn't know any better. They didn't live in the real world where demon wars raged and witches struggled to rule.

Witches like Lealandra.

Her eyes briefly met his and then she stared ahead again. Her legs shifted as she slowed down at traffic lights and his gaze fell there. The thin black skirt did nothing to hide the slender shape of her thighs or the apex of them. The material moulded to their lithe shape, sparking his imagination into life. He remembered her body intimately, could feel the ghost of her legs around his waist as he lost himself in the memory of their six months together.

Her corset skimmed her stomach just above her navel, leaving it on display. The memories became clearer, until he could almost taste her. She had sweet skin, warm and like honey. He loved the smell of her and the way she would react when he ran his tongue around her navel, occasionally dipping the tip of it in to tease her. He loved the way she would arch into him when he travelled lower and the way her hands would come down to guide him, to push him onwards and tangle in his hair, as though he needed any encouragement. He never did.

Taig tried to move into a more comfortable position without her noticing as his body reacted but she turned and looked at him, her grey gaze penetrating his.

He raised his eyebrows and slumped into the seat, bringing his leg up with some effort and resting a heavy boot against her newly dented dashboard.

"Are we there yet?" He smirked, gunning for his usual self and all the while struggling to hold back the grimace as his black jeans bit into his groin.

Lealandra rolled her eyes and then pointed a little off to the right. A tall glass and metal building stood there. Not quite a skyscraper but it dwarfed the surrounding older buildings. He had never been to this city's coven but he knew it had a vast number of members. There were at least twenty storeys on the building and it was wide. He figured it housed around seven hundred witches.

That was six hundred and ninety nine more than he was comfortable with.

The human in him didn't give a damn about witches. The demon in him said to get out of the car now, while it was still in motion, and get the hell away from such a place. He was tempted to do just that but Lealandra's hand softly came to rest on his knee. The warmth of her seeped through his jeans. His gaze tracked up her pale arm to her face.

"I won't let them near you," she said in a mocking tone, as though he was a small child frightened of a fairytale big bad wolf.

Taig pushed her hand away and pressed the sole of his boot against her dashboard, glaring at the building. He cursed her for being able to catch enough of his emotions to know that he didn't want to go into the coven and damned her for daring to make him sound as though he needed her protection. She knew him better than that.

He wasn't the child.

He was the wolf.

Dropping his foot to the floor of the car, he leaned over and pressed a kiss to her shoulder. His lips lingered against her warm skin, barely touching her, and he breathed her in as he spoke.

"Don't fret, sweet cheeks, I can handle myself." He grinned and swept a lone finger across her lower lip. They parted for him, a sigh escaping her as her eyelids dropped. "Just like I can handle you... I knew you'd come back to me."

She slapped his hand away and her eyes snapped open.

"I'm not back, Taig." Her tone was blacker than his heart. "Remember that."

Taig grinned at her and pressed one more kiss to her shoulder before leaning back in the seat and resting his hands behind his head.

"I'll remember it... and I'll remind you of it when you're crying out my name and begging me to never let you go."

CHAPTER 4

Lealandra yanked the steering wheel hard to the right and slammed her foot down on the brake pedal. The car jerked to a halt. She shot Taig a glare that she hoped contained every ounce of irritation and anger that was pounding through her just in case he couldn't already sense it. She really needed to find a way to get him to take the money because he seemed dead set on getting his price for his services rather than hers, and, now that she had a little more control over herself, she didn't want to go there.

Taig raked his fingers through his hair, tousling the messy black threads, and smirked.

Not that he wasn't attractive or she didn't want him.

But she wasn't about to pay for his help with her body. If he wanted her back, then he could work for it. It wasn't as though he had put up much of a fight when she had left him. He had to prove that he still wanted her. Not just this casual flirting. Really prove it.

The corners of his lips lifted, narrowing his fathomless black eyes and turning his expression warm. She cursed him. He knew what he was up to, knew the right faces to pull to make him look his best, knew the right smile to use on her—the one that made her weak at the knees and made her want to kiss him.

Damn him back to Hell.

He really was the Devil.

"Lead me not into temptation," Lealandra muttered beneath her breath and put the car into park. She gave him a hard look. He wasn't going to affect her with just a smile. Not this time. She had grown up in their time apart and wasn't about to fall at his feet as she had then. There were more important things than sex right now.

Although sex did sound good.

Taig's smile widened a little more, heading for full meltdown mode. She yanked the keys out of the ignition and shoved the door open. The bastard was trying to get her flustered. It was bad enough that she had to come back to this place and back to that apartment. She couldn't walk in there reeking of desire, not bare weeks after Charlie's death. Isabelle would never forgive her.

"We can walk from here." Lealandra needed the time to get herself together again. Just one smile from Taig had undone all the hard work she had put in during the drive. She'd had her desire back under control. Now her heart was fluttering and her body was calling out for his touch. Damn him. She slid out of the car and slammed the door.

Her fingers shook as she smoothed her skirt down, cursing Taig all the while. Perhaps she had made a mistake in asking him for help. She had laid low for as long as she could but the ascension was getting closer and she needed to end this before it hit her. She needed someone to help her through it. Taig was the only person who could do both of those things and she knew he wouldn't let her down. For all his bravado, he had a good heart and he cared about her.

And regardless of what he thought, she cared about him.

She only wished that he had been willing to see that all those years ago.

Stubborn bastard.

The sound of the car door shutting jerked her out of her thoughts and she found that she was smiling. It seemed like forever since she had smiled. She looked across the roof of the car at Taig, knowing he was the reason behind it. He always had been stubborn. It was one of the things that she loved about him.

His black eyes held hers, sparkling in the strange mixture of streetlight and moonlight. The intensity of his gaze sent a shiver of awareness through her followed by a glimmer of his feelings, only she couldn't read them and she wished she could. It had never bothered her before that he was difficult to read. But then, she had never felt unsure of his feelings, or his motivations, not as she did now.

"I'll lead." Taig stomped off ahead and stopped a few metres along the pavement. The white streetlights barely lit the dank world but she could see him well enough. The look in his eyes had changed to one she could recognise and read. His patience was wearing thin and he wanted this over with.

Lealandra locked the car and followed him. She wanted it over with too.

The moment she reached him, he walked on, jamming his hands into his jeans pockets. He was an imposing figure at the best of times. At the worst of them, like right now, he screamed danger. He hunched up his broad shoulders and glared at the coven building ahead of them. Her magic responded to his surge in anger and tension, feeding off the increase in power it triggered within him. She took a small step closer to him, wanting her magic to absorb his power. It had always calmed hers. A Counter-Balance took a fraction of the stronger witch's power, lowering it and giving them more control. Taig's power did the opposite. It fed hers and soothed it. It was as though her magic knew he was stronger and obeyed his power because of it. Charlie's effect on her had never been as potent as Taig's was. Taig could make her feel human.

She only wished she could do the same for him.

Sometimes, when they had been together, she'd had the impression that being human was what he wanted most. She didn't understand why. He was powerful, handsome and intelligent—three things that meant he could do anything he wanted and be anything he wanted. Yet, he didn't seem to want anything other than being normal.

She had been normal once, before her magic had found her and she had become a witch like her parents. It wasn't anything to write home about. She was happier now than she ever had been then.

Taig glanced at her out of the corner of his eye, removed his hands from his pockets and rolled his shoulders. His aura spoke of irritation laced with anger and his gaze fixed on the coven building. Hers traced his profile, following the defined line of his square jaw over his kissable lips, up his straight nose to the black eyes that made her tremble whenever she looked into them. He was one hundred percent gorgeous.

She just wished he was one hundred percent hers.

In all their time together, she had been aware of his distance, of the fact that he was holding back for some reason. He had never given all of himself to her. It was only towards the end of their relationship that she had realised that underneath the layers of confidence and strength beat the heart of a human.

A human who had fears just like any other.

She should have told him everything that she had planned to that night. Maybe then they would have remained together and she wouldn't have drifted through the past six years of her life thinking about him but denying her feelings for him.

The coven building loomed ahead and the focus of her magic shifted to it. The gathering of witches in this city was strong. Their leader saw to that. Gregori was a force to be reckoned with and had been in charge of the coven for almost twenty years. For a witch his age, that was incredible. He had taken control of the coven at the tender age of twenty six, the same age she had been when she had left Taig to join the coven. She couldn't imagine being responsible for so many witches at that age. But then, Gregori had powerful allies in his supreme mages. Both men were older than he was and bore magic almost as strong as his. There wasn't another coven on the planet that commanded the power that hers did.

And that frightened her for some reason.

Lealandra had thought it would be a good place, one where she could learn and feed her magic, satisfying its needs and becoming one with it. Instead, she had found an archaic society in which they gave every member a position and made them work to achieve a better one. Many saw it as pitting one witch against the other, promoting the strongest and those most willing to do whatever it took to reach a higher rank.

Did that include killing other witches?

She didn't know the answer to that question and, deep in her heart, she didn't want to. She just wanted to get her things and get away. Her original vision of a harmonious society, a place much like her old coven out in the New York state countryside, had shattered barely weeks after accepting Charlie as her Counter-Balance. Charlie and Isabelle had made her stay. They, like many others, had been too afraid to leave. They followed Gregori without question and bought into everything he told them about how their coven was leading the world of witches into a new glorious age. Magic had been around for millennia, passing from one witch to another, evolving and growing, lending them strength. It wasn't their power to abuse and use for their own good. It was a symbiotic being that they should work in harmony with and not use to rule others. Her world and the demon one could co-exist.

Lealandra glanced at Taig. Most witches would have her head for thinking such a thing, but she believed in her heart that the long feud between their kind, the deep hatred and distrust, was responsible for poisoning their minds and that they could get along if they tried to see past the bloody history between them and look to the future instead.

"Where's your apartment?" Taig said, his gaze sliding to briefly touch hers.

Lealandra pointed. "Twelfth floor on the east side."

"Can we get there without causing trouble?"

Lealandra stopped and stared at her apartment window, aware of what he was really asking. Trouble for Taig was all out war. Taking a demon into a building full of witches was a risky move. She didn't want to see her friends at the coven hurt but she wouldn't go in without Taig. If anyone tried to intervene, she would handle it. If she couldn't, she would let Taig do things his way.

Not that she would be able to stop him anyway.

She started when his hand slipped into hers, their fingers interlocking briefly before his shifted again to a less intimate hold. His skin was cool against hers, barely warm. That had never frightened her, not even the first time they had kissed. Before then, she hadn't realised that demons didn't have body heat in the way a human did. She smiled. Taig had told her that night that his father had been a cold bastard. She didn't believe that for a second. Not the way that Taig had meant it. His skin might have been cold, but she was sure that he had loved his wife and his son.

Taig's black eyes met hers and he paused, his widening slightly as he studied hers.

Lealandra hesitated a moment and then stepped closer. She didn't know what to say to him. How could she make him understand everything she felt right now and back then? He needed to know, to hear it, but her tongue became tangled on the words and she couldn't get them out.

Before she could speak, Taig's hand snaked around the back of her neck, sending sparks of electricity leaping across her skin. He drew her closer. She could only stare into his eyes as he slanted his head and brought his mouth down to meet hers. His cool lips captured hers in a kiss that was nothing like she had expected. It was slow and soft, an almost tender exploration that warmed her from the depths of her heart out to the tips of her fingers. She leaned in for more, eager to take all she could of this elusive side of him. Taig didn't do gentle. He had never kissed her like this before.

As though he loved her.

Her eyes slipped shut and she pressed her hands against his broad chest, steadying herself as she tiptoed towards him and feeling his firm muscles beneath his black shirt. He slid his other arm around her waist and splayed his hand against her lower back. His lips caressed hers in mesmerising waves that washed away all reasonable thought. She pushed her hands upwards to his shoulders and tilted her head, beginning to kiss him with more heart, and more heat. The moment she did, he stepped back, breaking away from her.

She found him smiling at her when she opened her eyes.

She smiled back.

"One heck of a good luck kiss you have there," he said and her cheeks coloured. His smile became a smirk and his tone darkened. "Did you kiss Loverboy like that?"

Lealandra slapped his left cheek, hard enough that his head snapped to one side and his eyes closed. His jaw tensed, the muscle pronouncing itself as his nostrils flared, and he rolled his neck.

"You dare!" She shoved his shoulder and he placed one foot back, bracing himself, and glared at her. "You don't know anything, Taig. Don't act like you do."

With a huff, she stormed towards the coven building, leaving him behind. He would follow. He wouldn't let her walk away, not as he had done all those years ago. Her heart thumped in her throat. Damn him. Why did he have to spoil a perfectly nice kiss, one she had actually been enjoying?

He wasn't going to let things go and she wished that he would. Contrary to Taig's belief, Charlie had only been her Counter-Balance. She had never kissed him or intimately touched him the whole time that they had been partners. Her heart and body had pined for Taig all the time they had been apart. She had denied it, had blocked it out, but looking back now she could see it was the truth. She hadn't stopped thinking about him or wanting him.

Tonight had been divine. It had been wrong of her to kiss him but she wouldn't change what had happened for anything. The smooth but dominant glide of his lips over hers, the aggressive thrust of his tongue into her mouth, and the rough grip of his hands had been heaven, but it had come with a price. It had awoken her hunger for him and every minute she passed in his presence, it became harder to ignore her desires. Now he had upped the game. A single soft kiss had been enough to melt her reserve towards him, stripping away one of the barriers around her heart and leaving her open to him.

Vulnerable.

His words had hurt but not as much as the belief that she had felt in them. He really did think that she had been intimate with Charlie. She didn't know whether to laugh at him for that or slap him again. Her heart had been too full of him for her to care about anyone else. Her feelings for Taig hadn't changed in the slightest.

Taig fell into step beside her and she resisted the temptation to look at him. She didn't want to play his game. The rules were in his favour and his victory assured. That victory would only hurt her more than leaving him had and that pain had lingered the whole time she was away from him.

A ripple of awareness ran through her when she pushed open the glass double doors and walked into the brightly lit foyer of the coven building. It was Taig's power spiking, not hers. She could feel him more clearly when he was like this—alert, on edge, ready for a fight. Something about it had always triggered a reaction in her and made her conscious of his strength and his hidden power, of his demonic side.

That awareness stole her breath and brought her body alive with desire.

She had been with him when he was like this, had made out with him in not too savoury places because of the way it made her feel, and it had been nothing short of Heaven. The dominance and possession that laced his actions, the way that he held her as though he would never let her go, heightened everything and stripped her of her inhibitions.

But not tonight.

This was no place to let her feelings for Taig get the better of her. She buried them deep inside her so he wouldn't sense them and her need. So no one would sense them.

Lealandra walked further into the pale marble foyer, her footsteps loud on the grey tiles, and suppressed all of her feelings. The elevators were ahead to her left, opposite a large sheer marble wall that had water trickling down it into a clear pool at its base. Ferns and other greenery surrounded the water feature, instilling a soothing feeling into the lobby. The plants and water weren't only there to create a calm mood and make the building look like little more than a normal office. Witches drew power from the elements so they liked to surround themselves with as much nature as they could when enclosed in a concrete world. The building had several water features on the communal floors and plants spread throughout it, as well as using natural stone in the apartments and open areas. Every piece of nature they brought into the coven boosted the power of its inhabitants.

She nodded to the neatly attired short middle-aged witch that acted as the concierge of the building and went straight to the elevators. They could have easily teleported into her apartment but it was better to sneak in. There were barriers that acted like nets around the building and would sense such a spell as they passed through. She wanted to get in and out without trouble and that meant taking the risk of walking through the front door and someone seeing them.

Her finger found the call button once and then twice, and then she started pressing it repeatedly, mentally chanting for the elevator to come quickly and for it to be empty when it arrived. She could already feel the eyes of the concierge digging into the back of her head. The witch was on to them. She knew Taig was part demon.

Lealandra went to press the call button again.

Taig caught her wrist and held it. "We're good, sweet cheeks."

She wished he would stop calling her that. It made her blush and this wasn't exactly the best place for him to be showing such familiarity towards her.

At the same time as she heard a soft click behind her, the elevator doors opened. Lealandra stepped in and turned to find the concierge staring at her across the wide foyer, the phone receiver pressed against her ear. The doors closed and Lealandra pressed the button for the twelfth floor.

Definitely on to them.

By the time they reached her apartment, Gregori would know a demon was in the building and that she had returned. She should have teleported them in. It had been stupid of her to try to get in unnoticed. Gregori had probably given the receptionists orders to report in if they saw her.

The elevator doors pinged and opened and she went straight down the hall, hurrying towards her apartment. Gregori wouldn't dare confront her there. He would wait for her to surface again. If they could reach her apartment before he could reach her, they would be safe for a while at least. Her magic reached out and she sensed the barriers around the building. All lights were red. The spells had already changed so people couldn't teleport out. She would have to go back down and out through the foyer.

Lealandra fumbled with the key but managed to get it into the lock. It was difficult to twist it with Taig standing so close to her, his broad hard body brushing hers and towering over her, but she didn't want him to back off. She needed him close. He soothed both her heart and her power, making her feel safe even as everything in her screamed that she was in danger.

The door gave and she stumbled inside. The moment Taig was through, she slammed the door, turned the locks and slid the chains into place.

"They know," Taig said, an observation not a question. He would know if witches were coming for him. Demons had strong instincts and his half-blood status didn't change that.

He moved fluidly through her apartment, gaze darting over everything, taking it all in. She stood by the door with her heart in her mouth, struggling to steady her nerves. Her fingers brushed the mark on her chest. It sparkled and flared into life. Each symbol guided her on her path to ascension. She understood the main ones but didn't know what part they would play. She had never learned to read an ascension path because she had never thought it would happen to her. She stared at the one close to her left breast, opposite Taig's mark. Conflict. There was only one way she could interpret that.

They had made it into her apartment.

Now they just had to make it out.

That wasn't going to happen without a fight.

CHAPTER 5

Taig stood in the middle of Lealandra's small apartment. The living room and kitchen were open plan, combined in an L-shaped space no bigger than thirty foot by twenty, with the kitchen situated behind him to the left of the entrance. A door on the wall between the kitchen and entrance was open, revealing a bathroom. Two more doors punctuated the opposite cream wall. One of them was ajar. A bedroom. The other?

He looked at Lealandra. She stood by the entrance, her right hand nervously stroking her left forearm, long red nails grazing her skin. Her eyes bore into the couch, her expression distant and glassy. He had seen the dark brown stain that marred the beige covers and had noticed the bullet hole in the wall to his right and the patched up window to his left. He had taken everything in the moment he had stepped into the crime scene.

Everything including the leap in Lealandra's fear.

"Two bedrooms?" he said and her grey eyes came to rest on him. She frowned at the doors for a moment, as though struggling to remember, and then nodded.

Taig was tempted to ask why there were two bedrooms but held his tongue. Maybe he had been wrong about her and Charlie. He wasn't about to admit that though and even if she hadn't been with her Counter-Balance in that sense, his feelings about the man and her weren't going to change. She had gone with Charlie. Charlie had taken her from him. This coven had taken her from him. Nothing was going to change that or the anger he felt about it.

Small tables stood like bookends at either end of the beige couch. A lamp occupied one. An empty mug the other. He touched it. Lealandra. She must have left in a hurry when she eventually had. There were dirty pans in the kitchen too and the stale air held an undertone of rotting trash.

He glanced at the wall with the bullet hole and then went to the window. Someone had taped cardboard over the point where the bullet had entered. Jagged fault lines spread across the entire glass pane from beneath the torn cardboard. They caught the lights of the cars passing along the streets below, flaring up and then dying away. He looked at the building opposite. Disused and ready for demolition by the looks of things. This area was on the up. Chances were it was set to become an office building or fancy apartments. His gaze fixed on the window directly in line with him. It was open. Whoever had shot Charlie hadn't cared about giving away their position.

Taig turned around and looked at the bullet hole in the wall opposite. The plaster surrounding it was broken, some of it still covering the modest flat screen television below it. What had they been watching at the time, sitting together on the couch like lovers? Lealandra had never done that sort of thing with him. He glanced at her and then at the couch. She stood by the doorway and looked paler now, as though the room was sucking the life out of her.

He touched the bloodstain. Fury swept like wildfire through his veins at the thought they had made Lealandra stay in the apartment when it was such a mess. The least they could have done was clean it up and repair it for her. He crossed the room to the wall, bent over and peered into the bullet hole. Something glinted. The bullet was still in there. He held his hand over the crater to see what he could sense from it and his frown hardened.

He looked over at Lealandra. She stood there. Silent. Expression empty. Watching him.

"My brand of bullet." Taig straightened. "My kind of gun."

"I know." She stepped away from the door, towards him.

"We going to have a problem here?" He held his ground. He was sure that Lealandra wouldn't turn on him, but someone was pinning the murder of her Counter-Balance on him and he was in a building full of witches who probably knew what she did.

Lealandra shook her head. "I don't believe it was you… but somebody wants me to." She glanced at the door and then back at him. "I don't want to talk about it here."

His gaze shifted to the door for a brief moment and then to the bullet hole. He could understand her unease about discussing this here and now but he wanted to know what in Hell's good name was going on and why someone was out to frame him for a murder he would never have committed. He only took out marks. If someone had tried to hire him to kill Charlie, he would have told Lealandra to get the hell out of the city and to take her snivelling Counter-Balance with her.

When Taig stepped towards her, she stepped backwards, her gaze darting to the door again. No one was there. He checked the ceilings for signs of a camera but found none and then reminded himself that witches had other methods of listening in on conversations. Lealandra had used such spells when they had hunted marks together.

"The message?" He pointed towards the bedroom with the open door and raised his dark eyebrows.

Lealandra nodded but didn't follow him when he went over to the room and pushed the door wide open. He flicked on the light and stared at the scrawl on the cream wall above the black wrought iron headboard of the double bed. The red of the message matched the bedclothes. He walked to the bed and placed his hand on the pillows. Lealandra. To think she had been sleeping there when someone had done this. A gnawing hunger for violence and vengeance blazed in his blood, hard to ignore when everything in him urged him to surrender to it. He would have but he didn't have a target for his fury. Not yet at least. When he knew who had done this, he was going to unleash everything on them. No one threatened his woman and lived.

His focus shifted to the message. It was rough, hand drawn by someone's fingertips. He didn't understand the symbols. A circle within a circle, much like Lealandra's ascension mark, but the glyphs within it were different and a line intersected the circle and the central symbol. He stared at the huge mark. It was at least two foot tall and just as wide. An intricate jagged pattern with sharp corners that reminded him of the tribal tattoos the young gang kids wore.

Taig reached out to touch the mark and stopped just short. He looked over his shoulder at doorway.

Lealandra stood in it, her arms wrapped around herself, fingertips pressing deep into her sides as though she was trying to hold herself together.

"This is..." he started and she nodded. "Whose?"

She swallowed and tears lined her eyes. "Charlie's."

Taig crossed the room in a heartbeat and gathered her into his arms. She didn't uncurl. Her arms remained wrapped around herself even as his encircled her too, holding her close. She trembled against him and he closed his eyes, his whole body tensing as he vowed to keep her safe. He wouldn't let the sick bastard who had done this near her again.

"They broke into the morgue in the basement. Took his blood." Her voice was tight, strained by emotions that he could feel rushing through her.

The urge to stroke her hair, to kiss the top of her head and whisper to her that it would be fine, that he would protect her, was overwhelming but he kept still and silent. She leaned her cheek against his chest and then her hands were on him, pressing into his pectorals and tugging his black shirt into her fists. She shook with each sob, the sound tearing at his heart. He never should have let her go. This never would have happened if he hadn't let her leave him. He would have been there to protect her. She would have been safe with him.

"What does it mean?" He pulled her closer, letting her feel the strength of his arms around her and his resolve to look after her. She had come to him and he would take care of her now, would ensure her safety and never let anything bad happen to her again.

"Death," Lealandra whispered and buried her face against his chest. Her hands moved to his back, fingertips digging into his shoulder blades as she clung to him.

Taig growled and his bones ached with the desire to shed his human skin and surrender to his dark hunger to hunt and destroy whoever had done this to Lealandra, whoever had turned his strong woman into this fragile girl quaking in his arms.

"The mark in the centre?" He lowered his head a fraction, enough that he could smell her hair and feel her warmth against his lips. Almost within kissing distance. It soothed the beast inside him enough that he retained human form.

Lealandra came out of his embrace, not moving far away enough that he had to let go of her, but placing herself beyond reach of his lips. Her eyes were bloodshot, lashes wet with tears. She took a deep shuddering breath.

"It's a mark that means ascension. The line breaks it and pierces symbols for death and Hell." She ran her fingers beneath her eyes, erasing her tears and the black marks left by her mascara, and then pointed a shaky finger at the symbols in question. "It's a warning that I'm going to Hell."

"It's nice this time of year." Taig flashed a soft smile but she didn't return it. He kept one arm around her while he gently wiped away the remaining trace of her tears with the pad of his thumb. His fingers paused against the delicate curve of her jaw, his thumb resting close to her lips. He held her gaze, making sure her grey eyes stayed locked with his as he spoke. "I won't let them hurt you, Lea. I won't let Hell have you. I'd go down there and bring you back."

She smiled at last. It was faint and only lasted a split second, but it was a smile nonetheless.

"I should freshen up and get my things." She pulled away and he frowned at his outstretched hand, missing the feel of her against it.

"I'll take a look around," he said for want of something better to say.

She crossed the apartment and disappeared into the bathroom.

Taig looked at the mark. Death and Hell. Someone was out to kill her. There was no doubt about that. He turned and stared at the bullet hole in the wall of the living room. Someone who wanted to separate Lealandra from those who could protect her. They were trying to isolate her. Charlie's death had taken away her Counter-Balance and weakened her. If she had believed that he had killed Charlie, it would have weakened her further and would have stripped her of a powerful ally. And the message that was designed to flush her out of the coven and force her into seclusion. They wanted Lealandra scared and alone during her ascension, a time when she would be both vulnerable and extremely powerful. They had managed to do one of those things but he wasn't about to let the other happen. Lealandra would never be alone. Not while he lived.

He was still staring at the bullet hole, trying to piece everything together, when Lealandra stepped out of the bathroom and crossed the living room to her bedroom. His gaze immediately moved to her. Her eyes were still red from her crying but that didn't change how beautiful she was and neither did the make-up she had reapplied. She was beautiful period, and looked her best first thing in the evening when he was waking up next to her. He smiled with the memory of all the early evenings they had shared. Nothing beat the feeling of waking slowly with her in his arms, their naked bodies entwined.

Lealandra stopped in the doorway of her bedroom, a large black holdall in her hand, and stared at him with wide grey eyes.

She looked her best when he kissed her so hard that her lips turned rosy and full and her pupils dilated to darken her eyes. When she wanted him, when he could read every thought crossing her mind and they were only about them, about him, then she was the most beautiful woman in the world.

When she looked at him as she was now.

Her painted red lips parted, showing a trace of white teeth. He remembered the feel of them against his flesh, the playful nips that she used to mark her path across his bare body, and the way she would kiss him better if he ever pretended that she had hurt him. Her pupils widened, hinting at her rising desire. His rose too, driven by the sight of her so full of hunger.

Driven by the sight of her.

Taig didn't make a move towards her. The slightest movement by him would shatter the spell, the trance they had fallen under, and remind her of their surroundings and the things that had happened between them. Six years ago, he would have had her in his arms by now and would be pinning her to the bed as he kissed her. But this wasn't then, and she wasn't his anymore. Not yet, anyway.

Protection and a taste.

Did he really want to do things this way? Was he that much of a mercenary or that desperate to have her in his arms again? She would hate him for it.

A tiny part of him said to take the money she had offered him. It wasn't much, but she wasn't lying when she said it was all she had. He was surprised she had even that much. The coven barely gave an allowance and they didn't pay people a salary. She must have come into the money some other way. He didn't want to think about the possibilities. He hoped it had been from her previous coven.

She blinked and walked on, disappearing behind the wall. He stared through the doorway at the bed, listening to her moving around the room, pulling drawers open and closing doors. A zipper sounded and then she reappeared. A long dark red coat clung to her figure, tight against her torso but flaring out from her hips downwards. It was undone, revealing that she still wore the same black skirt, corset and boots she had been earlier.

When her eyes rose to meet his, he looked past her at the bedroom. The mark bothered him. So did the gun. Whoever had left the message knew about magic, possibly could even use it.

"Did you tell anyone that you didn't think I was the killer?"

Her look turned thoughtful and she idly stroked her free hand down the length of her black hair. Taig's fingers itched with the desire to replace them, to feel the silken strands of her hair slipping through his rough hands and to raise them to his nose and breathe in her delicate fragrance.

"Yes. It came up and I denied that you would do such a thing." She placed her bag down at his feet, snapping him out of his reverie. "I said that even you wouldn't go that far, at least not this long after I had left you."

He winced internally at the reminder that she had been the one to leave him. It wasn't one that he needed. Life had been hell without her.

"Do they know about this?" Taig stroked his fingers over her chest. The ascension mark sparked into existence, shimmering bright red beneath his fingertips and casting an eerie light over his hand.

A nod was her reply. She didn't look happy about the fact that others knew of her impending ascension. His list of suspects was growing though. If she had told the coven that she didn't think he would kill Charlie and that she was approaching the ascension, then there was a chance that this was an inside job. It would explain the message but not the demons that had been at the bar tonight. If it was a witch after Lealandra, why go to the length of working with demons?

Unless the witch wasn't strong enough to face him themselves or they didn't want to get their hands dirty.

Taig rubbed his head. It hurt to think this much when all he wanted to do was find the son of a bitch responsible and teach them a lesson. He was sorely used to someone giving him a mark and then him taking care of them. No need to think. Contract. Kill. Paid. That was the sort of life that he preferred. Investigation wasn't in his repertoire.

Maybe he could start with the demons. They wouldn't be too difficult to track and he could kill them and quench his thirst for vengeance.

"Taig," Lealandra said, pulling him out of his pleasant thoughts. The wary look in her eyes spoke volumes. He reined in his anger so his demonic side receded and the red faded from his irises. She never had been comfortable with his true nature. He couldn't blame her. He wasn't comfortable with it himself. "We should go."

She went to pick up her bag but he beat her to it. She raised a fine black eyebrow.

He smiled at her and shrugged. "Consider chivalry part of the deal."

Her other eyebrow rose. "Chivalry? I didn't think you even knew the word existed, let alone what it meant."

He deserved that one. He never had done the gentleman thing with her—no opening doors or protecting her from cars by walking on the road side of the pavement. Unless you counted smashing doors in to get to their mark or shielding her body with his as a car crashed into them. He had done that before. He grinned and followed Lealandra to her door. It had been nice to have someone hunting with him.

And victory sex was fantastic.

His attention switched to their surroundings when Lealandra stepped out into the hall and his mind cleared. Reaching out with his senses, he did a sweep of the entire floor. The presence of several witches nearby sent him into high alert and his focus sharpened. He swapped the bag over to his left hand, leaving his right free for fighting if they ran into trouble.

Lealandra led the way down the pale neat corridor to the elevator, an invisible trail of nerves and fear in her wake. He moved closer to her, knowing that she would be able to feel his power and his intention to protect her, and that it would calm her.

They reached the elevator and she started her constant drumming of the call button. It wouldn't come any quicker just because she was doing that. He was tempted to catch her wrist again to stop the irritating fast clicking of the button but gritted his teeth instead. Tapping it seemed to alleviate her nerves a little. Anything that did that was fine with him, even when it was the most annoying sound on the planet.

The elevators doors opened and he almost thanked God when her finger left the button and she stepped inside. He pressed the button on the panel to take them down to the foyer and stood in front of it, blocking Lealandra so she couldn't start up her button pressing compulsion again.

The silence in the elevator was oppressive, making the space seem far smaller and more cramped than it was. Taig looked at the grid of lights above them for a short while and then at Lealandra. She was watching him, grey eyes narrowed slightly. Expectant. Was she waiting for him to say something?

"We never did it in an elevator." He flashed a sly grin. "I could stop it and we could give it a go."

She didn't frown or hit him this time. She merely rolled her eyes and folded her arms across her chest in a way that said it wasn't going to happen and she was going to pretend she hadn't heard him.

"You sure?" He tapped the metal door and then the wall. She finally frowned when he ran a hand along the brass rail that edged three sides of the elevator at hip height to him. "It would probably hold your weight."

"Not going to happen." She glared at him, eyes cold and empty.

"The price of this contract—"

"Doesn't get paid until it is fulfilled."

He smirked and leaned back against the door. His elbow knocked against the stop button and the lift juddered to a halt. "And then we get fulfilled."

She huffed and tried to reach around him. He moved to block her path to the buttons.

"You're incorrigible," she said on a sigh.

"You always said that was a good thing." He countered her when she made another reach for the button.

"Will you just get out of the way?" Lealandra shoved him in the ribs, sending him off balance and crashing into the side.

The steel box of the elevator wobbled and the metallic skittering twang of the cables above warned that the impact hadn't been welcome. Lealandra grabbed his arm, holding on for dear life until the elevator settled again.

"Christ, I thought you were suppose to stop me from being killed, not the reverse. That's twice now." She hit his arm and stepped away.

Taig righted himself. "I'm here aren't I? You think I enjoy being surrounded by witches liable to kill me on the spot for just being in their territory? I have plenty better things I could be doing. And that time wasn't my fault. You pushed me."

She tilted her nose up and pressed the button. "Just get me the hell out of here and we'll call it quits."

Ascension

Tension didn't suit her. Taig decided it as he stood beside her waiting to reach the ground floor. Some people could handle it, like himself, and others went crazy. She was definitely one of the crazy ones.

The elevator doors opened.

In the lobby stood a reminder of what had Lealandra so worked up.

Gregori.

CHAPTER 6

Half of the coven filled the vast bright lobby in front of Lealandra, a mixture of faces she was glad to see and ones that she knew were only there to either fight or see her fall. A thirty-foot strip of open grey marble floor separated her from them, forming a no man's land on which three others stood. Two supreme mages, neat elderly greying men who wore the traditional ankle-length silver-buttoned navy coats of their office, and a younger man.

Gregori.

Taig thankfully remained quiet and still. She never knew what to expect from him and had never brought him into a situation like this. He was right. She had no reason to doubt his desire to protect her when he had walked right into her world, into the coven's territory, placing himself in great danger.

Lealandra slowly stepped out of the elevator, her attention locked on Gregori.

He stood a few feet in front of the two supreme mages, closer to her. Rather than the normal garb of his rank, he wore black slacks and a dark blue shirt with a faint silver pinstripe that made him look more like a businessman than a powerful witch. His hazel eyes fixed on her, unwavering even though rogue strands of his jaw-length brown hair had fallen out of his ponytail and were in front of his eyes. His stern expression suited the harsh angled contours of his face, matching the pulses of disgust and anger emanating from him.

"Lealandra," he said in a mild voice, one so smooth that it set her nerves alight. The calmness of it masked the emotions she could sense in him. He was annoyed with her for leaving and furious with her for bringing Taig into the building.

Taig stepped out of the elevator and stopped a few feet behind her. It was unlike him to be this quiet and this sensible. His power spoke to hers and she understood it for once. He wanted to get out of the coven. Her stomach felt heavy, fear sitting in it and weighing her down. If Taig wanted to leave without a fight, they were in more danger than she had thought. Not wanting to fight definitely wasn't like him. He wasn't the type of man who did things the easy way or backed down.

"Gregori." Lealandra glanced at the double glass doors to her right and the darkness beyond. It was only a few metres. Could they make it there before someone tried to stop them? There was nothing in the barrier spells that would prevent her from walking out. She forced a casual smile. "I just came to get some things."

Gregori's hazel eyes slid to Taig and narrowed. "So I see."

Damn. She had forgotten who was holding the bag. The last thing she had wanted to do was draw more attention to Taig.

"I do wish you would reconsider," Gregori said and there was a murmur from the gathered crowd. It was hard to tell whether they were agreeing with Gregori or whether they wanted to see the back of her. "We are doing our best to find the person responsible for Charlie's death, although you seem to have brought one of the suspects with you."

Lealandra focused her power back on Taig, needing the reassurance that sensing him so nearby would give her. He was there if she needed him. A flicker of irritation crossed Gregori's face.

"I don't believe Taig is responsible for Charlie's death. I told you that at the time." Her heart trembled feebly her throat, threatening to die at any moment. She tilted her chin up, desperately holding herself together so Gregori would see that she wasn't about to be intimidated by him or the supreme mages. "I also told you that I had considered leaving."

"And then you disappeared in the dead of night without even a goodbye. We had thought you were kidnapped or worse. It is good to see that you are well and have returned." The emptiness of his tone frightened Lealandra. She had seen Gregori holding council and had witnessed him take out his anger on a lesser witch. That same anger was bubbling away within him right this minute, hidden by calm words and a clever façade.

"I haven't returned." She held her hand out when she sensed Taig's intent to move forwards to stand beside her. It was better that the gathered witches thought that Taig was acting as her servant, as an inferior. It was the way witches saw demons. If he stepped up beside her, he would be declaring himself an equal. Doing that openly in front of witches that were already on edge would only trigger a response from them. She didn't want a fight. She just wanted to leave, the same as he did. "I only came for some things. Now I'll be on my way."

"Can he help you when the ascension comes, Lealandra?"

She stopped mid-step and looked at Gregori. She honestly didn't have the answer to that question. Her gaze shifted to Taig. He was still standing by the elevators, staring at Gregori. The barest flicker of red rimmed his black irises.

"You would align yourself with a demon, one which cannot guide you through this most dangerous and important time, rather than remain here with your friends, with we who can see you through the ascension? You are vulnerable, Lealandra. You are leaving yourself open to attack by whatever dark force is after you."

She swallowed. Her stomach turned, churning away, increasing the unsettled feeling growing within her. Gregori was right. It was insane to leave with Taig when she needed the assistance of powerful witches to help her survive the ascension, but it was also insane to stay where she felt vulnerable and with people whom she could no longer bring herself to trust.

"Taig will protect me." She believed that. Taig would see her safe. He hadn't told her it, but actions spoke louder than words. Everything he had done tonight, when she filtered out the flirting and the things he did to cover his true feelings, told her that he would do all in his power to protect her, even if it meant sacrificing himself. He would ensure she survived this.

She believed in him.

She had to.

He was her only hope.

"It is your decision to make," Gregori said in that same calm tone that unnerved her. She swore she could detect a hint of malice in it, anger at her for daring to leave with a demon, "but I wish that you would reconsider. We are all so worried about you and the council believes that it is best for you to remain here. We will protect you, Lealandra. You are one of us."

He didn't mean that she was a part of the coven. He was making a distinction between her and Taig, between witch and demon. The crowd murmured in agreement this time, but she still wasn't sure what they were agreeing to—the fact she was a member of the coven or didn't belong with a demon.

Gregori stepped towards her. Taig walked behind her, keeping his distance, but she felt his power as he passed and it strengthened her own. She sensed him stop near the doors and look back at her.

A silent message that he was leaving with or without her.

"You need your Counter-Balance, Lealandra, something a demon cannot give you." Gregori's light eyes penetrated hers, holding her fast as though she were under a spell, only no magic passed between them. He knew better than to threaten her power right now. It was bordering on impossible to control. Back in the car when Taig had frightened her, she'd had no command over it. It had come out of its own free will in an attempt to protect her. She pressed a hand to her chest and felt the hum of magic in her veins increase as she touched the ascension mark. Gregori looked at her hand, as though he could still see what she had foolishly dared to show him. His hazel eyes narrowed and his lips compressed to form a thin menacing line. A flicker of magic, power stronger than hers, laced his aura. Her magic didn't respond. Didn't it believe that she was in danger? She felt as though she was.

"Taig will take care of me," she whispered, barely able to find her voice to deny what Gregori had said. She wasn't a fool. She needed a Counter-Balance more than ever and it was something that Taig couldn't give her. Gregori's power washed over her but quickly retreated, forced back by one it couldn't defeat. Taig's. His shielded her, caressed her skin and spoke to her own power, steadily bringing it under control and soothing her fears. Taig would take care of her.

"We are close to securing you another Counter-Balance, one from your old coven. I believe you know him... grew up with him. A man called Matthew."

Lealandra tensed and stared wide-eyed at Gregori. Matthew? They were trying to bring Matthew to her? She had to warn him to stay away. Bringing him here would only drag him into danger and she didn't want to see anything happen to him. He was the closest thing she had to a brother. She couldn't lose him.

Gregori held a hand out to her, palm upwards.

She instinctively stepped back.

Suddenly, everyone's focus shifted from her to Taig.

Bad move on her part. She should have been more aware of what she was doing. Moving towards Taig and away from Gregori was the worst thing she could have done.

The power of the gathered witches rippled through her, a warning that she was treading on thin ice now. She had openly chosen a demon over her coven.

Magic bled from her fingertips in thin red ribbons of smoke. They curled around her hands and she looked down at them, surprised by the sight of them when she hadn't called her power. It was taking control again. Her eyelids dropped when it rose in her blood, surging through her and leaving her dizzy from the rush. It whispered in her mind.

Protect Taig.

Her eyes snapped open and she frowned at Gregori.

It wasn't there for her sake. It didn't perceive the witches as a threat to her but rather a threat to Taig. Her magic had never chosen to protect another before. Taig's power rose and hazy bliss ran through her, melting her just enough that the tension drained from her body. Her power rushed to meet his and drew strength from him. It wanted blood and knew that Taig would give it to her. It hungered for him the same as she did. Only she felt there was something more to its desire to protect him than sustenance.

She took another step backwards and her magic began to abate, satiated by the feel of Taig's power.

Her grip on it slipped and before she could grasp its true intention it had faded from her mind.

She stared into Gregori's eyes a moment longer, wary of the darkness in them, and then stepped back so she was in line with Taig.

His fingers closed around her arm, his grip so tight that she felt his strength, and her knees trembled at the feel of his hand on her and the memories it stirred. Things between them had never been slow and gentle, and his rough hold on her arm brought everything flooding back.

"If you leave with him, you can never return."

Lealandra didn't hesitate.

She turned and walked out of the door.

It was difficult to cross the threshold and feel the tug of power as the protective charms allowed them through. She couldn't stay. The tiny part of her that said the coven was the safest place to be was wrong. That was just fear talking. Everything bad that had happened to her had happened there. She was safest away from it. She would find a way to deal with her ascension without them and her Counter-Balance.

Matthew.

Had Gregori really been in contact with her old coven? He must have. She had never told anyone at this coven about the people she had grown up with back at her old one. The thought of Matthew coming to New York City and finding himself pulled into the mess she had found herself in turned her stomach.

Taig looked at her.

"I have a phone at my place," he said, as though he had read her mind.

Lealandra nodded her thanks, too deep in thought to say the words. She needed to warn Matthew to stay away. Whoever was after her would kill him if he came to her. He was strong, powerful, and had always been able to handle himself, but she didn't think he could handle this and she didn't want to see him dead.

She had already lost one person, and that was one too many. She couldn't lose another.

Lealandra pulled the car keys from her coat pocket. Taig held his hand out and she didn't put up a fight. She dropped the keys into his palm and rounded the black sedan to the passenger side. She didn't know the way to his place from the coven and she wasn't in the mood for driving, not when she had a crowded mind and her feelings were weighing her down.

When he had unlocked the black sedan, she opened the passenger side door and dropped into the seat. She buckled her seatbelt on autopilot, staring at the coven building.

She hoped she had made the right decision in breaking company with them. When the peak of her ascension hit, she would be vulnerable without them to protect her and help her control her power. It was already too powerful to fully command. Tonight had made that clear. Magic was normally something that lived harmoniously in a witch's blood and worked with them. It chose them as its carrier. Different genes attracted different magic. Her family had always had strong old magic but hers had never reacted the way it had this evening. She was sure that it had wanted to protect Taig. She just wasn't sure why.

Her hand rose of its own volition and came to rest against her chest and the mark there. She couldn't read the path, could only understand the symbols and their individual meaning. Her magic knew the path though. Taig was important somehow. Perhaps more so than she had first thought.

Lealandra looked at him, taking the time to refresh her memory of his profile as he drove, his focus intent on the empty black road ahead. Lights created a rhythm to his backdrop, whizzing past, punctuating the darkness at intervals that got shorter and shorter as Taig accelerated. He never had cared if the police caught him and his senses and reactions were quick enough to help him avoid an accident.

"What happened the night that Charlie died?" he said, breaking the silence that she had been enjoying.

"I told you."

"Then tell me again."

Lealandra sighed. She didn't want to remember what had happened that night. She had tried hard to forget it all and she had managed to gain some distance from her feelings. If she talked about it now, everything would come flooding back again.

Taig needed to know though. Maybe he would see it differently to her or notice something that she hadn't.

"We were sitting together watching some stupid reality television show that he loved. Isabelle was supposed to be watching with us but she was running late. I was telling him about the ascension mark." She held her feelings inside, not letting them control her, not even when her throat began to tighten and her hands trembled in her lap. She played with the ties of her black skirt, jingling the bells to distract her so she could tell Taig everything without falling apart.

"Had he seen it?"

She nodded and then remembered that he was looking ahead of them, at the road. "Yes."

"Bet he was pissed off." Taig smiled, oddly proud looking.

Lealandra gave a short laugh when she realised why and remembered Charlie's reaction to seeing Taig's mark emblazoned on her chest.

"Yeah, he was. He said it was typical of you to stick your oar in without even being around." Her smile faded and she sighed again. "I think he was a little jealous."

She could understand why. All witches had a mark too, something specific to them. Charlie's mark hadn't been present. Taig's had taken a prominent place. It had probably hurt him to see that Taig would be involved in her ascension somehow, in an important enough way for his mark to appear in her path. Charlie had always loved her. And she felt terrible that she hadn't loved him.

"What happened after that?" Taig glanced at her.

"After that... I told you what happened." She couldn't bring herself to say it again. It all played out across her mind. One moment she was teasing Charlie about his jealousy, laughing with him about the stupid things that humans did for the sake of getting on television, and then there was blood all over her and he was dead. She hadn't even heard the gun fire. She blanched and swallowed. There had been so much blood, and Charlie had just been sitting there, stock still, head blown open.

She pressed her hand over her mouth.

Taig's hand came to rest on her shoulder, heavy and solid, a weight that comforted her. His cool skin soon warmed to match hers but she fancied it was a degree or two colder, enough that she noticed it when she focused on the spot where he touched her.

"Breathe, Lea. Let it go," he whispered and she closed her eyes. Before she could stop herself, she had turned her head to the side, brought her shoulder up, and was resting her cheek against his fingers. A tear slid down the side of her face and tickled her.

"It was a few days after that when they told me the type of bullet used and the sort of guns that fired it. I didn't believe them, Taig. Not for a second."

"And you told them."

She nodded against his hand.

"And then you told them about your ascension."

She nodded again.

"And then someone wrote that message on your wall."

Lealandra stiffened, the memory of waking to find that scrawled on her wall turning her blood to ice. She trembled and Taig's hand tightened against her shoulder.

"And then you left."

"Something like that," she whispered against his skin. It was so comforting to be close to him like this. Not just because she could feel his power, but because she could feel him and she needed that more than anything. She wanted him to stop the car and hold her, to tell her that he wouldn't let anything happen to her and that they would be safe. His hand was cool against her burning cheek. She turned her head a fraction, so her lips were close to his knuckles. If she kissed them like she wanted to, she would only be making a fool of herself and getting herself into trouble. Taig would respond, no doubt about that judging from his behaviour so far tonight, but she wouldn't know if it was real or just done to spite her. She wouldn't know if he would wait until she had opened up her heart to him again and then say something as cold as he had after their last kiss.

She couldn't bear that.

"You suspect the coven don't you?" he said and she sat up when he took his hand back and turned the car to the right.

She didn't recognise the area. It looked like the Upper East Side but he hadn't lived there six years ago. Perhaps they were just passing through, taking a different route up towards the bridge that would take them over into the Bronx. There were demon communities on that side of the river too.

"I suspect everyone." She felt his eyes come to rest on her.

"Even me?"

Silence.

Lealandra didn't want to answer that question.

CHAPTER 7

Taig pulled the car to a halt just down the road and turned off the engine. It was unmistakably the Upper East Side.

"We can walk from here." He exited the car.

Lealandra followed, confused as to why he had brought her to such an affluent neighbourhood. She had thought he was taking her to his place. They walked for a while, passing beautiful apartment buildings and high-end expensive stores. When he turned and walked into a tall building, she paused on the pavement. The old sandstone façade was as graceful and stunning as those they had passed, exuding class and a high rental price tag with its elegant canopied walkway that extended out to the road. She stared at the uniformed man stood holding the highly polished glass door open. Taig lived here now?

Taig came back out, her bag in his left hand. Her raised eyebrows didn't fall even when she looked at him. They stayed there in silent question.

He shrugged. "I fancied a change."

A change? She followed him in when he turned around and glanced at the doorman as she passed him. This was more than a change. Taig's old apartment had demons for neighbours and rats in the garbage, and the only doorman had been the superintendant, a demon who had over-indulged in food to the extent that he barely fit in his human skin and liked nothing more than sitting on the steps terrorizing the local women with failed amorous advances. This was a whole new world for Taig. She studied the bright cream corridors with their perfectly polished brass and mirrors, and the polite staff that stopped cleaning as she approached and smiled at her as she passed. This was a very human world.

The only demon in the vicinity was Taig.

Had things gotten that bad since she had left him? Her shoulders slumped. Was she the reason he had moved? She hadn't left him because he was a demon. Only afterwards had she considered what kind of effect her leaving might have had on him. She had convinced herself that it wouldn't have pushed the wrong buttons. Obviously it had and in a major way.

Taig looked back at her. A hint of nerves touched his eyes for some reason and she smiled, hoping to alleviate whatever was playing on his mind. When he turned away again, her smile faded. She stared at his broad shoulders and the back of his head. This wasn't his world. He didn't belong here. A couple exited an apartment ahead, waving farewell to someone standing in the door. Lealandra guessed from their outfits that the party they had attended well into the early hours of morning wasn't the sort that would wake the neighbours and have the police banging down the door. The man wore a fine suit and the woman carried off a sparkling plum-coloured cocktail dress to perfection.

Their laughter died when they spotted Taig and her. Lealandra's eyes met the woman's as they passed. Disgust shone in them.

This was their world, a human world of rules and societal structure, one in which Taig would never fit. He was the opposite of these people. Money and finery weren't things that he lived for. He was fooling himself by being here. Did he think that by standing in this world, surrounded by this kind of human, he would become one of them? They would never accept him.

Not if they knew the real him.

He stopped at a wide mahogany door, opened it and walked in, leaving it open for her. She peered in to see him slinging her black holdall onto an equally black couch in a large living room. He came back and turned into the room to her right.

Lealandra frowned when she stepped through the doorway and something tugged at her power. She turned and closed the door, and then froze when she saw the wooden doorframe.

Cuneiform-like symbols covered the wood, scratched deep into it. She couldn't understand them, just as Taig didn't understand the ancient language of witches, but they radiated power in waves so strong that she felt sick and her magic retreated. She looked at Taig where he stood in the brightly lit kitchen, rummaging through a massive dark red refrigerator.

"I take it you don't invite the neighbours in." Markings like the ones on his doorframe would make humans question his sanity.

He didn't answer her. He kept his head in the refrigerator.

When he straightened at last, he was holding two dark brown bottles of beer in his right hand, their necks wedged between his fingers.

"Drink?" He grinned and waggled the bottles.

He was ignoring her. She nodded and he opened the beers and handed one to her. She swigged it and walked further into the apartment.

It was sparsely furnished and the refrigerator provided the only colour. Everything else was either black or white. The pale walls caused the already huge apartment to appear massive. The kitchen cupboards were shiny and black, matching the polished granite work surfaces below them and on the long counter that separated the kitchen from the living room. A flat screen television that had to be over fifty inches took up a large portion of the wall to her right at the end of the living area, and a large black couch faced it, devoid of pillows and as lifeless as the empty black coffee table and the rest of the apartment.

She walked towards the couch, her footsteps loud on the wooden floor.

It looked like a showroom for expensive designer furniture and minimalist living. Not the Taig that she knew. It didn't suit him.

A closer look at the black door to the right of the television revealed that there were also markings on that doorframe. She turned to the two huge windows on her left, opposite the kitchen. The black blinds were up. Symbols covered the wooden window frames and sills.

Ascension

Taig might have moved into human territory to feel more like them but his protective instincts had gone haywire because of it. Surrounded by demons, he hadn't needed to defend himself to this extent. The other demons he had lived with would have alerted everyone if they had sensed something wrong. Out here, in this human world, Taig was alone.

And it showed.

Lealandra took another swig of the beer and stared out of the windows at the myriad of buildings that crowded the scenery. She couldn't see Central Park but it was there somewhere. They were facing west. Taig always liked his apartments to face west. It was a demon thing. He had never been able to explain it rationally but she suspected it had something to do with the setting sun and the onset of night.

Night was on its way out right now. The sky was slowly lightening. She looked around the apartment for a clock but found none. No pictures or anything personal adorned the walls and table in front of her. Nothing that made it feel lived in, like a home. She wrapped one arm about herself and frowned. The whole place felt cold and lifeless. Was that how he felt inside? Was this void a physical representation of what Taig held within him?

She didn't like it. It wasn't Taig, no matter how much he believed it was.

He moved out of the kitchen, leaned his broad frame against the counter next to the square white column at the corner nearest the front door, and swigged his beer. The messy black spikes of his hair threatened to cover his equally dark eyes. He had them glued on her and they sparkled under the white ceiling spotlights.

What had happened to the man she had fallen for all those years ago?

Lealandra took a step towards him but he walked away, disappearing into the room beside the television. She rocked back on her heels when she caught sight of something out of the corner of her eye. It was odd and as out of place as Taig was in this stark environment, but it gave her hope. She walked over to the long black side cupboard that lined the back wall of the apartment and stared at it.

A picture.

It sat alone on the expansive low cupboard, right in the middle of it, as though on display. The only sign of life. A glimmer of the Taig she used to know.

The picture was no bigger than six inches tall and framed with silver. She lowered her beer to her side and studied the photograph it contained.

A dark haired and dark eyed very handsome man was smiling up at her. In his arms, a lighter haired pretty woman stood with her back against his chest. He had his arms looped under hers and his fingers tangled with hers over her stomach. Her pregnant stomach. It was large and round, stretching the seams of the flowing white top the woman wore. She looked happy enough to burst. They both did. They radiated love so strongly that Lealandra felt a hint of envy. Her gaze fell to their hands, clasped together over their future baby.

Taig.

It was such a human picture and a very human thing for him to have. It sent a chill through her, made her smile but want to cry at the same time for the things he had lost. His parents. She was sure if they had still been alive, he would have grown up differently. He would have seen his demonic power as a gift rather than a curse.

She reached out to touch it.

"Don't!" Taig's voice made her jump, the harshness and volume of it startling in the quiet room.

Lealandra withdrew her hand and then held it out a little again, fingers hovering just above the intricate markings engraved on the silver picture frame. It exuded power more potent than that protecting the doors and the windows. She closed her eyes and tried to understand it, tried to decipher what it would do if she dared to touch it. It was marked so only he could take hold of it. Her eyes opened and she stared at the photograph of his parents as her power deciphered his. It would kill anyone other than him.

He was protecting the picture more than his apartment.

Lealandra looked over her shoulder at him. He stood halfway between the bedroom door and her, shirtless and perfect, as beautiful as she remembered him. Bronzed skin stretched taut over the powerful muscles of his torso, the sight of them rekindling the desire he had stirred with his kiss in the bar. Her gaze wandered upwards, over hard pectorals and strong collarbones to the tense corded muscles of his neck, and then to his face. All sense of desire fell away when she saw his lost look and the way he was staring at the picture.

Her heart went out to him.

Taig turned away and pulled a black t-shirt on over his head, and her eyes betrayed her. They dropped to his back, watching the delightful way his muscles shifted with his movements. The mark on his left shoulder blade was barely visible, a shade or two darker than his skin. His lineage. A symbol so intricate and beautiful that it outshone any witch's mark. She had traced it with her fingers in the past, following the swirling lines and trying to distinguish their path. The whole symbol looked almost like a heart. Taig didn't see it, but then he never had liked to talk about his mark.

He never liked to talk about himself at all. He hadn't told her much about his parents, only that his mother was human and his father was a powerful demon, and that they had disappeared when he was thirteen and he believed they were dead.

She couldn't imagine how hard it had been for him to lose his parents when he was only a teenager, how hard it must have been for him to live not knowing what had happened to them, and how difficult growing up alone had been. He had gone from a world full of love to one completely devoid of it.

Taig walked away, back into the bedroom, and reappeared a few moments later with a pillow and a blanket.

"You take the room. I'll sleep out here." He flung the pillow down at one end of the black couch.

His prickly demeanour was a warning not to argue and that he wanted to be alone. Lealandra took another look at the photograph, at the happy family, and then grabbed her bag off the couch and went into his bedroom. It was as void of life as his living room and kitchen, with a solitary large double bed standing against a black wall, and two small side cupboards. The wardrobes were built-in, white to match the rest of the walls, and the black blinds on the two windows were down, blocking out the morning light. She opened them and idly traced her fingers over the markings on the frames as she stared out at the dawn.

She took a deep breath and sighed.

This room smelt like Taig.

It smelt of spices and warmth.

It comforted her.

Lealandra set the beer bottle down on the side cupboard and sat on the bed. Her dark red coat blended into his bedcovers. She ran her hands outwards, feeling the lingering presence of him in the room and on the bedclothes. At least she would feel safe while she slept, imagining him wrapped around her, holding her close. She shut her eyes and fell back onto the bed. She wanted to ask him to hold her but that would only lead to trouble and she still wasn't sure what Taig wanted from her or if he still had feelings for her.

Her focus shifted to him.

Was he lying in the living room wondering what she was thinking, just as she wanted to know what was going on in his mind?

Rolling away so her back was to him, she frowned when she noticed the slim black phone beside his bed.

Matthew.

She picked up the phone and dialled his number. It was early enough in the morning that he might already be awake. If he wasn't, then she hoped it waked him. She had to speak to him. The call connected and she listened to it ringing at the other end.

"Hello." The sound of Matthew's sleepy voice swept her back to her old life and a time when magic had been all about having fun.

Now it was anything but that. It was dangerous and she was forever on the verge of losing control to it. She longed to go back to those happier times and then her senses shifted to Taig and she didn't want to go back after all. Even though her magic was more powerful now and life was difficult, no longer carefree and full of laughter, she wouldn't sacrifice it and her tentative relationship with Taig in order to return to her old life.

"It's Lea." She swallowed and didn't give him a chance to say anything. "I know my coven have contacted you. Don't come to New York, Matthew. It's too dangerous and I... I don't want to see you hurt too."

He yawned and she heard material rustling as he moved.

"Lea, what's wrong? This Gregori calls me out of the blue and says that you're in trouble and need a new Counter-Balance, and now you're calling me to tell me to keep away? I'm coming to see you. Just tell me where you are."

"No." Her heart beat faster at the thought of him trying to find her. She didn't want him anywhere near the city. "I mean it, Matthew, stay away. I'll be fine. I have all the protection I need, but I might lose that if you come here. I can't guarantee your safety. Once I've made it through this, I'll come to see you and everyone, I promise."

"Does your protection have a name?" There was a smile in Matthew's voice. She smiled too. When she had left Taig, she had spent a few days with her old coven before leaving for her new one. Matthew had been her shoulder to cry on. He had held her together, spending almost a day listening to her and letting her cry all she wanted and not saying a word out of place. Without him, she would have fallen apart completely.

"I think you know his name."

"I also know that I'm not needed then. I won't come... but if you do need me, you only have to call, okay?"

"Okay." She nodded and held the phone for a moment. "Don't tell Gregori. Just... go abroad for a while or something."

"You're that worried? You don't need to answer that. I can almost see your frown from here." He laughed and then sighed. "I've always wanted to visit Europe. Maybe our coven will go out of town for a while. How does a month sound?"

"Perfect... thank you."

"No, thank you. I might have walked into a war and the last person I want to fight with is you. Call me if you need me and I'll be right there. Stay safe, yes?" The concern in his tone touched her and she held the phone tighter, wishing she could see Matthew and hug him instead. He would be a powerful ally in her time of need, and could help her survive her ascension, but she couldn't risk him. It was better that he stayed away until everything blew over.

"You too." She ended the call before she faltered and asked him to come to her, and her attention moved back to Taig.

The impulse to go to him was strong and almost impossible to resist. She wanted to talk to him, to unlock his secrets and ease his pain. It laced his aura, a physical thing that she could sense as if it were her own.

Her brow furrowed and she stared at the wall, not seeing it. Just feeling him.

Lealandra knew that he didn't like himself and that his part-demon part-human status left him feeling as though he had nowhere to belong. If she could find her voice, she would tell him that he did belong somewhere—he belonged here on Earth, with her.

But she couldn't.

Countless times, she had planned to tell him that and every time she had failed. No matter how often she had practiced it in mirrors or recited it to herself while she showered, whenever it came time to say it to his face, the words fled her lips and her voice died.

She lay on the bed, not brave or strong enough to face him and make him believe her.

He would argue against it and she would crumble.

She had to find the right moment, the precise point when Taig would actually believe her, and then she would try to tell him. All she could do right now was let him know that he wasn't alone in the world and that her feelings for him hadn't changed. If he wanted her, all he had to do was come and claim her, to make her see that he still felt something for her too and the games he was playing were only because he had been hurt.

Lealandra stood and removed her coat, folding it neatly and placing it on one of the side tables. She pulled her boots off and then began to unlace her corset but stopped. It had to be now. This was the perfect moment for giving him at least a sign that she still loved him.

Her footsteps were silent on the beech wood floorboards. She crossed the room to the door and hesitated on the threshold.

Taig lay on his back on the couch, bare chest exposed and one arm under his head and the pillow. His other hand rested on his stomach. The slow rise and fall of it said that he was asleep. Well, at least one of them was relaxed enough to sleep. Clearly, thoughts of her hadn't been playing on his mind and keeping him awake after all. She crept into the room. The light was low with the black blinds down and she knocked the coffee table. Taig's empty beer bottle wobbled at the corner nearest him, threatening to fall and spoil the moment, and then stilled again. She edged around the table and eased to her knees at his head.

Her fingers trembled as she brought her hand up and swept the long strands of black hair from his face, clearing his eyes. He really was beautiful when he wasn't shooting his mouth off or trying to make her angry. She ran her fingers over his brow, following the line of his dark eyebrows, and then trailed them slowly down over the contours of his cheekbones and jaw.

He frowned and turned his face towards her before opening his eyes. Their black depths met hers and she smiled.

Confusion filled his eyes.

Lealandra leaned towards him, closed her eyes, and brushed her lips against his. It took him a moment to respond and butterflies danced in her stomach and chest when he kept the kiss light. His tongue traced her lips and hers came to meet it, softly tangling with his and luring it into her mouth. He tasted of beer but she didn't mind. She was sure that she did too. She dropped her hand to his neck and leaned in closer, wanting more, and then reminded herself that this wasn't supposed to go anywhere, not tonight, and if she kept going, it would do just that.

After one final brush of her lips over his, she pulled back.

Taig stared at her, eyes wide and lips parted.

"That's how I kiss goodnight," she whispered and rose to her feet.

His gaze tracked her across the room. She trembled inside, wondering if her goodnight kiss had been a wise idea and whether Taig would come to her.

She fell flat on her front on the bed and sighed.

It had been a stupid idea.

She touched her lips.

It had been nice though.

She focused on Taig and realised that he was doing the same, using his power to sense her.

The ball was in his court now.

CHAPTER 8

Taig stalked around his apartment, still amazed that he had managed to resist going to Lealandra last night and still cursing himself for it at the same time. She had kissed him, and she had given him those come to bed eyes that she had used on him so many times in the past.

And he had been sorely tempted.

But something had stopped him. Some ridiculous sense of chivalry had kept him pinned to his uncomfortable makeshift bed. By the time he had convinced himself that maybe she wanted him to go to her, maybe she wanted to try again and this wasn't just fear controlling her actions and making her seek comfort from him, she had fallen asleep. He had sensed her soft rhythmic breathing and heard the steady beat of her heart in the silence of his apartment.

Now he was in a foul mood, but that wasn't a bad thing. He had business to attend to tonight and normally things went quicker when he was pissed off.

Lealandra stood in the kitchen, doing something to the stove that had seen little action since he had moved in.

Which was more action than he had seen in six years.

Taig walked past Lealandra and stared at her, his gaze raking down the length of her shiny black hair to her creamy shoulders and the tight deep purple strapless corset she wore. He diverted course, heading for her rather than the en-suite bathroom in his bedroom. His hands came up as he neared her, ready to claim her waist and pull her against him. He needed to kiss her again. He needed to taste her and be inside her.

She turned to face him.

One hand immediately dropped to his side while his other ran through his hair, nonchalantly pushing the black mess out of his face. He smiled his best smile, the one that always got her hot and bothered.

Her cheeks burned and then she turned away and attacked something with a spatula.

"What's for breakfast, honey?" Taig said and, when she didn't answer, moved around her and leaned against the black counter-top. He folded his arms across his bare chest so his biceps bulged and his pectorals tensed, and peered down at the pan she had on the stove.

Her gaze darted to his chest and then back to the pan.

"Eggs," she mumbled and stabbed at them with the spatula.

Taig sidestepped, distancing himself in case she started hitting him with it next. Whatever the poor eggs had done to her, it had been bad. Still, at least he wasn't the only one grouchy this evening. Abstinence made the heart grow darker.

His was about as black as they came.

Lealandra moved towards him and he sidestepped again, and then again when she picked up a knife and started dicing the hell out of some perfectly innocent potatoes.

"Damn it," she muttered and sucked her left index finger.

He frowned and caught her wrist, pulling her finger from her mouth. "Let me see."

She tried to tug her arm free but he tightened his grip. She huffed and rolled her eyes while he inspected the cut on her fingertip. A tiny bead of blood blossomed to the surface when he squeezed it. The way she had been cutting the potatoes, he wasn't surprised that she had cut herself too.

"Go a little easier on them," Taig whispered and then impulsively pressed a kiss to her cut. Her blood coated his lower lip and he licked it clean. His power surged and his eyes popped wide. Claws shredded his fingertips, dark brown scaly points breaking through the skin. He quickly backed away from Lealandra and rubbed his mouth, trying to get her blood out. His hands shook as he struggled to control his demon side. He didn't want Lealandra to see it. He spat in the stainless steel sink and then grabbed a glass from the rack on the drainer.

The skin on his fingers tore apart when he turned on the tap and filled the glass. He took a great gulp of the water and choked, coughing it back up into the sink. The glass in his hand smashed, cutting his palm to ribbons, and blood dripped down into the sink, mixing with the water and turning the pieces of glass into islands on a swirling red sea.

"Calm down." Lealandra's tone was soft and soothing, a melody he wanted to listen to above all else, but he couldn't focus on her, couldn't stop the hunger to change and shed his human mask. Her hand came to rest against his bare back, sliding over his skin in a way that stirred his blood. He felt her power seep into him, straining to reach his, and he let go a fraction, enough that they would meet. He needed the connection, needed to feel that she was here with him and that this wasn't frightening her. "Taig."

His demon side pushed again, threatening to expose his true form to her, and panic joined the emotions rushing in his blood. He couldn't let her see it. If she saw it, she would never love him. She could never love a monster.

He pulled out of her grasp and walked away. Blood ran down his arm when he raised his hand.

"Taig?"

Without looking at her, he stalked to the bedroom door.

"Eat without me." He slammed the door, headed into the bathroom and threw that door closed too before locking it.

Red eyes stared back at him from the mirror. He spat into the sink again, convinced that her blood was still controlling him to a degree. It wasn't, but it had been, and it had been frightening to feel as though he wasn't in control of himself. Was that how Lealandra felt when the power demanded things of her, when it grew too strong for her to contain? He shuddered and rinsed the blood off his hand. The wound was already healing but it was going to make his work more difficult tonight. He picked a few splinters of glass out of his palm and dropped them into the sink.

A sense of balance returned inside him.

His claws receded, the skin repairing itself until his hands looked human again.

Just how he liked them.

Taig cast a glance towards his right, to where the kitchen stood on the other side of the wall. To Lealandra.

Had he frightened her? She hadn't felt afraid when she had touched him. He laughed at himself for thinking that. Of course he had scared her. He was a demon and had been on the brink of showing her just what lurked beneath the human skin she liked so much. No sane person wouldn't be frightened.

And no one as beautiful as her could truly love a monster like him.

"Taig?" Her voice was loud through the bathroom door. "Come and eat with me."

There wasn't even the slightest tremble in her voice and she didn't feel scared. Only her usual calm acceptance came through on his senses. If she was afraid, she was hiding it well.

"In a minute," he said in a gruff voice, needing more time to gather himself and regain total control.

His eyes altered back, the red dying away and leaving them black.

"Come out," she whispered. "You don't scare me."

He wished he could bring himself to believe that.

"Taig." There was a note of impatience in her voice now.

He unlocked the door. If she wanted to see him that badly, she could let herself in. The door opened and Lealandra stood on the threshold, her wide grey eyes meeting his in the mirror. He turned to face her, keeping his hands behind his back.

"Let me see." She tried to peer around him.

Taig considered not doing as she had asked and then slowly brought his hands out from behind him. He watched her closely, gauging her reaction. She frowned at his hands and he turned them over, showing her, letting her see that there was nothing to be frightened of now.

"There, all man again, no mon—"

"You're always a man, Taig," she cut him off and reached out for his hands.

He lowered them before she couldn't touch them. She had told him the same thing before and he hadn't believed her back then either. She didn't know the real him and couldn't judge whether he was man or monster until she did, and that was something that was never going to happen. His demonic side was dangerous. When he surrendered to it, his impulse to kill was too strong to fully control. His father had told him to change often during his youth, to learn to control himself, but then he had left him alone in the world. His demon side had despaired.

His human side had blamed his demonic one.

If his father hadn't been a demon, his mother would have still been alive. He was sure that his mother had died at the hands of a demon because of his father. His demonic blood was responsible for their deaths. Blood that ran in Taig's veins now.

Taig clenched his fists when the urge to change struck him again, his demon side pushing for freedom and snarling within him, outraged by his thoughts. He moved away from Lealandra, as far as he could in the confines of the pale bathroom, backing towards the shower cubicle.

"I'll skip breakfast." He grimaced when his demon side pushed again, threatening to tear the skin from his fingers with his claws.

It subsided and settled when he caught Lealandra's steady gaze. Not a hint of fear touched it and her heartbeat was stable. How could she stand there so calmly when she knew what dark desires were surging through him? How could she look at him without fear or disgust?

She took a step towards him.

He didn't move.

Her reaction fascinated both sides of him—the demon and the man.

"I need a shower." His quickly spoken words stopped her in her tracks and she glanced at the large shower cubicle at his back, and then her gaze returned to him. He raised his eyebrows and smiled. "You could always skip breakfast too and join me."

Lealandra frowned, her expression dark and unimpressed.

"I think I'll skip the shower and have breakfast." She stepped over to the door and hovered on the threshold. She looked back at him, opened her mouth as though she was going to say something, and then left.

Taig stood there a moment, trying to make sense of things. His head was full of enough complicated things without adding in trying to understand Lealandra. He pushed her reactions to him out of his mind and told himself to forget about them. She was just being herself. She had always managed to tie him in knots and confuse the hell out of him. He had never understood why she had wanted to be with him for all that time but he had been thankful. For a few months of his life, he had felt human, even when his demon had prowled just below the surface.

He turned on the shower, stripped off, and stepped in. The water was a degree too hot but he didn't care. It was good to feel warm once in a while. When he was done, he turned off the shower and then dried himself, all the while thinking about the demons that were after Lealandra and wondering who else was involved. Definitely a witch or at least someone who knew magic. There were plenty of people out there that couldn't use magic but knew enough about it to have written the message on Lealandra's wall.

A quick check with his senses placed Lealandra in the kitchen. Taig walked out of the bathroom, naked and unbothered by the possibility of Lealandra seeing him. If he was being honest with himself, he wanted her to see. He wanted her to take a good look and remember everything they had done together so she would want him again, so she would realise that she had been missing out because of her decision to go with Charlie.

Taig growled at himself for being idiotic enough to let her go with the bloody bastard. He should have known that her coven wouldn't know how to look after her, that Charlie wouldn't know. Taig traced the thin white lines on the inside of his forearm with his fingertips. They were a record of their time together than was inerasable. Marks for her, to feed her power and soothe it. It needed blood. Her genes were suitable for old magic, the kind that had been around long enough, passed from generation to generation, that it had cravings and desires, and if it didn't get what it wanted, it was likely to go nuclear and take over its host and force them to do its bidding.

Lealandra needed blood.

He had caught her looking at the scars, each time with hunger shining in her eyes. Six years without blood would have left her magic desperate. She hadn't flipped yet but she had almost lost it twice last night. He had never seen her magic respond like it had in the car and in the coven, and her reactions told him that she hadn't either.

He turned his left hand over and looked at the cuts on his palm, jagged dark red lines from the broken glass. He could give her what she needed. Dressing quickly in black jeans and a tight black t-shirt, he mulled over the idea of offering Lealandra his blood. He didn't want to taint her with it but she needed his blood. It would ease her magic and give her more control. No matter what he felt about it, he had offered her a taste as part of the deal. He curled his fingers into a fist and stared at it, making his decision.

Taig walked out into the living room to find her sitting on the couch. When he sat down next to her and held his hand out, palm up and open, her grey eyes fixed on it and her pupils dilated. Her soft pink tongue swept over her lips, dampening them and making him want to kiss her again.

"Take it." He offered his hand to her.

Lealandra hesitated barely a moment before she grabbed his hand with both of hers and yanked it towards her. The feel of her mouth on his palm was divine, her tongue sliding sensually over his flesh, tickling and teasing him. Her warm breath stirred his blood almost as much as her steady gentle suckling. She moaned softly on an exhale and her grip loosened, her fingers stroking his wrist and thumb, tangling with his fingers in movements of sheer desperation. He tilted his hand towards her, giving her better access, and inhaled slowly, trying to control himself. She needed blood and he had promised it to her.

Blood and nothing else.

No matter how much he wanted it. When she was like this, the magic making her hungry, it wasn't her in control. It wasn't her who reacted to him in lustful ways. It was her magic. It wanted more than just blood. It wanted his power. It wanted his body.

Lealandra suddenly pulled back, releasing him and gasping at air. Her chest heaved with it, bosoms pressing against her rich purple corset top and threatening to spill over. He stared at them, watching the rough rise and fall, tempted to reach out and touch, to take this to the next level regardless of his knowledge that she was barely in control. Until the power in his blood was absorbed into hers, the magic held the reins.

She knocked the air out of his lungs when she slammed into him, her hands on his shoulders, gripping tight. Her mouth was on his before he could stop her, the taste of his own blood stirring his demon until it verged on taking control. He grabbed her arms and shoved her away.

Red eyes glared at him with pure anger.

"Lealandra," he whispered and touched her cheek. The colour instantly drained from her eyes and they widened in shock. She sat back, fidgeting with her long black skirt, her focus intent on it.

Taig sat up and then stood, needing distance to stop himself from kissing her. It would take a few more minutes for his power to temper hers. He went over to the long black side cupboard that lined the back wall of his living room and opened the doors below the picture of his parents. He didn't look at it. His gaze tripped over it straight to the guns in the cupboard. Sleek, black pistols greeted him. He took out his black shoulder holster and slipped his arms through it, and then grabbed his two favourite guns and slid them into the holster, one either side of his ribs. The weight of them felt good. He grabbed a couple of spare clips, in case tonight's mark was less cooperative than he expected.

Lealandra was watching him when he turned around. The colour and life had returned to her face. His blood had calmed her magic for now but he wasn't sure how long the effect would last. With the peak of her ascension approaching, it was only going to get more difficult for her to maintain command of her power. If she needed more of his blood, could he let her take it? He wasn't sure. The thought of her taking his tainted blood into her body repulsed him.

"Where are you going?" She leaned one arm against the back of his black couch.

Trying to look casual. That amused him in a small way but he didn't let it show. How many times were they going to do this merry dance before they finally gave up the fight against their desire? They both wanted it, wanted each other. He was normally a reach out and take kind of man when he wanted something, but this time he couldn't bring himself to do it. Lealandra had to take the first step. She had to be the one who risked the fall because she had been the one to separate them.

"I have a job." He walked past her to his bedroom, took his beaten up leather jacket from the wardrobe and put the clips in the inside pockets. Lealandra was still watching him when he came back out. "You'll be safe here."

He went to put his jacket on.

"No."

He quirked an eyebrow. "No?"

She shook her head. This wasn't the time for her to start with her stubborn streak.

"You need reminding that you're high on someone's hit list?" He finished putting his jacket on, tugging it around until it sat snugly over his chest. "You're staying here where it's safe."

"No." Lealandra stood, a scowl on her face that she didn't wear well. He preferred her smiles to her anger. She hesitated and then cleared her long black hair out of her face, defiantly flicking it over her bare shoulders. Those shoulders shifted back and she raised her chin. Standing tall. A defensive posture if ever he saw one. "I'll be safest with you."

Taig waved a hand around his apartment, drawing her attention to the protective marks that covered the points of entry. "Here is where you'll be safest. No one can get in easily. The moment I leave this apartment, all routes are closed. You're staying here and I'm not hearing another damn word about it."

"No!"

He sighed when she went and got her long dark red coat from the bedroom. She put it on, her steely look telling him that she wasn't going to back down. He flexed his fingers to loosen up and realised that there was only one way of making her stay.

"I don't want you to come. The last thing I need is your help." He regretted it the moment he said it. Hurt filled her grey eyes and her shoulders sagged. He clenched his fists to rein in his feelings and then dragged a hand through his hair, tousling the wet black strands. "I'll be distracted if you come."

Lealandra huffed. "Worried. The word is worried, Taig, not distracted. I'm going regardless."

Taig stepped up to her, using his full height to intimidate her and standing so close that she had to tilt her head back to meet his eyes.

"No!" He growled the word.

"God, Taig! Stop being so thick-headed about this. I'm going with you!"

He snarled now. "God has nothing to do with me, so don't bother calling his fucking name."

Rage pounding through him, Taig turned on his heel, grabbed his keys from the kitchen counter, and stalked out of the apartment.

Lealandra followed.

It was pointless telling her to go back so he didn't bother. If she really felt safest with him when he was on the hunt, then she could tag along. After all, she was paying for his services as a bodyguard.

Not that she needed to.

He would do anything for her.

He would protect her with his life.

CHAPTER 9

Taig's breath left him in a sharp burst when he hit the side of the crypt. He growled, pushed himself back onto his feet and ran through the darkness towards the lit path and the man responsible. The slim man grinned at him and then turned towards Lealandra. Bloody immortals. Taig growled again and threw himself at the man, tackling him to the ground and trying to pin him there. The man hit him solidly across the jaw. The taste of blood filled his mouth but Taig didn't back down. He closed his hands around the man's throat, throttling him. It wouldn't kill him, but it satisfied the deep craving for revenge crawling around Taig's insides.

The man choked and Taig tightened his grip, grinning down at him. He hated immortals. They were a bitch to kill and this one had taken a fancy to Lealandra. A distraction. He had told her that was what she would be if she came with him and she was. He wasn't worried about her. She could handle herself. But he wouldn't let the immortal near enough to her in order for that to happen.

Taig frowned when the man rolled him over, landing on top, and pushed his hands down on Taig's arms. He struggled to keep hold of the man's throat and got a knee in the ribs for his effort. His hands slipped from the man's neck and he was gone. A moment later, pain exploded in Taig's right side. The heavy black boot swung towards him again and Taig caught it, pushed it up, and sent the man crashing to the ground.

Before Taig could jump him, Lealandra had shot a dazzling red bolt of power towards him, sending the man hurtling into the same crypt that had given Taig a headache. The stone shattered into a heap under the impact, burying the man. Taig dragged himself to his feet and breathed hard. It hadn't been an easy fight so far but he was getting into now, and could sense that Lealandra was too. Her power flowed through him in tangible waves, ones that he could feel the strength in. She was far more powerful than she had been six years ago. Something told him that her impending ascension wasn't the only reason behind it. Her magic had been growing in their time apart.

Grey rubble tumbled down the pile in front of them and the man crawled out of it. He stood, a scowl darkening his pale eyes, and calmly dusted down his black coat.

Taig readied himself.

The sharp rise in Lealandra's power told him she had too.

The man carefully neatened up his brown hair and then ran at Taig.

Taig drew both guns, firing one round after another, each one hitting its target. The man kept running, blood streaming down his coat, drenching his pale shirt. Taig shot him in the head. The man hit the dirt.

Silence reigned as Taig waited, knowing that the man would get up again. Bullets would only slow him down. Taig needed to find a way to put the man out of action permanently.

Lealandra's power rose another notch. Red ribbons spiralled around her hands and forearms. She was gearing up for a fight. The sight of her so focused on their mark, her eyebrows drawn tight and her lips compressed into a dark line, made him think of all the times he had hunted with her.

And all of their victories.

Arousal tightened his gut, heating him from the inside out as his body responded to the memories of making out with Lealandra.

He told himself that it wasn't going to happen this time. Things were different now.

Or were they?

Lealandra's gaze crept slowly over to him. Red ringed her grey irises. Her pupils widened into dark chasms of hunger that told him he wasn't the only one thinking about victory sex.

Taig took a step towards her.

The immortal did one better. He shot to his feet and ran at Lealandra. She was too slow to turn. Unprepared. Distracted by him. Taig sprinted across the open ground to her, caught her around her waist and pulled her close to his chest. The immortal didn't slow his approach. He threw a punch at Taig. Taig ducked backwards to avoid it, let his claws burst through the skin on his fingers and grabbed the immortal's shoulder. His claws sunk deep into his enemy and he twisted with him, still holding Lealandra close, using the combination of the immortal's momentum and his own strength to slam the man into the grassy earth. Lealandra gasped and Taig looked across to see her staring at his hand on her waist.

That was the trouble with needing his claws. He never had mastered the ability to change only one of his hands. The one holding her waist was now dark brown and scaly, his fingers transformed by thick armour and claw-like tips.

Taig released her, hauled the immortal off the floor and growled as he slashed his claws across the man's throat and then snapped his neck with such force that his head came off. The immortal's body dropped to the ground. Come back from that one.

Taig casually dropped the head, chest heaving as he struggled to catch his breath. His hands shook, the skin on his wrists starting to tear and reveal more of his true appearance. Panic threatened to overwhelm him but he tamped it down and slowed his breathing in an attempt to settle his heart and stop the emergence of his demon side. The skin on his wrists slowly repaired itself, meshing together with a new layer that appeared over the back of his hands.

Lealandra touched his shoulder from behind.

Taig turned towards her, raising his human hands at the same time. "All man again—"

He didn't have a chance to finish his sentence. Lealandra's mouth captured his and the force of her kiss stole his voice. Her tongue thrust between his lips and her fingers raked through his hair, mussing it and making him groan. Taig wrapped his arm around her waist and dragged her flush against him, holding her so tightly that he was sure he would hurt her. He couldn't help himself. She ran her long nails over his scalp and down his throat, and then looped her arms around his neck.

Her body pressed against his, rubbing in a way that had him aching in his jeans, hard and ready for her. He shifted, thrusting his hips into hers and she moaned into his mouth. Such a sweet sound. He ground again, eliciting another low sigh from her, and lowered his hands to her backside. Heat spread through him as he cupped her bottom, idly reacquainting himself with it while she kissed the breath from him. This felt too good.

He frowned and closed his eyes when her mouth left his and she pressed wet kisses along his jaw, her breathing rough and laboured, and her movements jerky and frantic. The desire to claim her as his again, to dominate her and make her surrender to him was too strong to ignore. He held her closer, pulling her possessively against him and letting her feel his strength. She moaned again and arched into him, tiptoed so the apex of her thighs was against his. Too good.

Her red nails scored his leather jacket's sleeves and he growled. It seemed his little witch still liked it rough sometimes. He pressed his body hard against hers, grasping her backside so she couldn't move. He could do it rough. He could do it any way she liked as long as he was back inside her.

As long as they were one again.

The tempo of her kisses changed when she reached his neck. They turned slower, deeper, showing all of her hunger for him. She devoured his throat with blunt teeth and groaned. Her warm breath tickled his skin, stirred the fire within him that burned with a desire to respond, to give her just what she wanted.

Blood.

His mouth had other ideas.

"It'll cost you extra this time."

Taig closed his eyes the moment she pulled away, not wanting to see the hurt he could feel in her, and cursed himself for being stupid enough to say such a thing. The expected slap didn't come. When he opened his eyes, she had her back to him, her arms wrapped tightly around herself. He didn't know what was worse—her hitting him for saying something cruel or the silent treatment.

Lealandra hunched up and lowered her head.

The silent treatment won.

He reached out to touch her shoulder and then thought better of it. She had a right to be pissed off and he was being a complete bastard to her by treating her so poorly. All he wanted to do was welcome her back with open arms, to drag her back into his life and never let her go, but whenever he got close, he remembered the night she had left him and the man she had left him for, and he couldn't stop himself from snapping.

Withdrawing his hand, Taig sighed and then turned his attention back to tonight's mark. The body was decomposing. Time loved to play catch up with immortals and the longer they had lived, the quicker it happened. Judging by the man's rate of decomposition, he had been alive for centuries. Taig stooped and took the signet ring from the man's finger as it crumbled. It would have to suffice as proof that he had done the job.

He stood again and looked at Lealandra. She still had her back to him. He walked over to her, hesitated a moment, and then wrapped his arm around her chest, drawing her towards him so her back was pressed against his front.

She sighed.

Was sorry a strong enough word to erase everything he had ever done to her? If it was, he would say it a thousand times over so she knew just how sorry he was, and then he would say it a million times more. He didn't mean to push her away but years of resentment lingered inside him and it had turned him bitter, and now he didn't know what he was supposed to do.

Except love her.

And believe that she loved him.

One he could easily do, the other seemed so impossible.

Lealandra kissed the hand he held her shoulder with and then ran her fingers over it.

"I'm sorry," she whispered and leaned back into him.

He sighed this time. How was it she could find the strength to apologise and he couldn't? His heart said it was her humanity. A demon like him didn't know how to behave in such a way.

Lealandra turned in his arms and looked up at him. He ran the backs of his fingers down her cheek. The moon made her pale and beautiful. Her eyes were so wide and open, so full of calm acceptance. A part of him said that he could apologise, that a demon knew how to behave just as a human did. It was the man in him who couldn't bring himself to admit that he had been wrong.

It was his human side, not his demon one.

His demon side had only one thing it wanted to say to her and it was something neither man nor monster had ever told her.

He loved her.

CHAPTER 10

The bar was dark and empty. The long batwing-tipped hands on the ridiculously oversized and cliché gothic clock on the deep red wall above the bar announced that it was gone four in the morning. The sun would be rising soon. Most of the patrons of the club seemed to have known that and had disappeared a few minutes after Lealandra and Taig had arrived. They sat in a booth near a fire-exit to the left of a stage. The thin black and red hangings obscured Lealandra's view of the rest of the club. It was nothing short of a Goth's wet dream. Red velvet covered everything. Gilt candle sconces adorned the black walls, their fake-candle bulbs flickering away. The tables in the bigger booths were mahogany coffins on legs.

And the thin dark haired man opposite her was a vampire.

Taig was talking calmly to him. Lealandra didn't bother to listen, knowing that it was all business. He held the ring out and the vampire raised one fine plucked black eyebrow at it. His black-ringed pale irises moved to her and then back to Taig. He didn't seem to like the fact that Taig had brought company. She had offered to wait outside but Taig had been insistent and it was impossible to change his mind when he thought she was in danger.

She didn't think that hanging around outside this club would prove that dangerous for her. Most demons wouldn't be seen dead somewhere that catered so openly to human fantasies of what life as a vampire was, rather than the slightly more grim reality of having to live on blood and being unable to go out in the sun.

Blood.

Her power whispered to her, speaking of Taig's blood and her need for it. She was still hungry. The small amount Taig had given to her had only soothed her power a fraction. She needed more to get it back under total control but she had the feeling he was being serious when he said it would cost her, and she knew the price he had in mind.

Her heart.

Lealandra had come to realise that he wasn't really after her body. He wanted her heart, wanted her to be his and only his, for the rest of his life.

She wondered if he knew that was what he wanted and whether he would accept it if she dared to offer.

"Seems genuine enough," the vampire drawled and then thoughtfully ran his thumb across his lower lip as he examined the ring. "It is a shame you couldn't bring the body back."

Lealandra frowned. The vampire had wanted the immortal's blood. She had heard that immortal blood had potent aphrodisiac qualities. Was the vampire after a strong fix or the bloody form of Viagra?

The vampire tossed a thick manila envelope onto the shiny black table. It landed in a wet ring left by the glass now held in Taig's hand. Taig necked the whisky and then casually took up the envelope. Lealandra hid her surprise when Taig opened it and thumbed the wedge of cash tucked inside.

That was a lot of money.

"It's all there." The vampire leaned back into the red velvet bench. Lealandra shifted uncomfortably on her chair. She was getting tired and restless. The hunt had taken most of the night and she just wanted to get back to Taig's place and sleep since he had spoiled her fun in the graveyard. The vampire glanced at her again and then back at Taig. "I have another contract you might be interested in. Fifty large."

Lealandra's eyes almost popped out of her head. She blinked at the vampire and then at Taig. He didn't seem at all fazed by the amount of money the vampire had offered him to do a job.

"I have another contract already," Taig said and the vampire raised an eyebrow before shrugging.

"If you change your mind, you know where to find me."

The sum of money the vampire had paid Taig for the job tonight and what he had offered for another, made it clear that Taig wasn't helping her for the cash. She had offered him such a tiny amount in comparison and he was making a fortune by hunting. Things hadn't paid this well back when she had hunted with him. He must have worked hard over the past six years to build a reputation worthy of that kind of payment.

The vampire's icy gaze fell on her again, sending a shiver of awareness through her that reached right down into her bones and froze them. His eyes lightened when hers met them, almost glowing in the low light of the club. A strange calm broke over her. Warmth chased the chill away and she relaxed in the seat, feeling oddly at peace.

Taig slammed his fist against the table, cracking it straight down the middle and making her jump. The chill returned when she looked at his hand where it pressed into the shiny black surface and the calm lifted, leaving her feeling as tense and tired as she had been before she had looked into the vampire's eyes. Taig's glass rolled off the table and smashed on the floor.

"You dare look at her again." Taig stood, leaning over the table and glaring at the vampire.

The shine left the vampire's eyes and he stared up at Taig, somehow managing to keep the fear she could sense in him out of his expression. Taig's power rose and swept through her. Her magic reached for it, hungry for the connection, and abated the moment they met, subdued by the strength of his and satiated.

Lealandra touched Taig's hand, sliding her fingers over his palm and pressing her thumb against his knuckles. He needed to know that she was here and she was fine. His fingers closed around hers, tightly holding her hand.

"Dare," he sneered and the vampire turned away, "and I will personally see to it you're the first vampire to die in this city this century."

Her heart missed a beat and intense heat suffused every inch of her. She loved Taig's possessive streak. He had always been like it, refusing to let her out of arm's reach in the company of other men, staking his territory by kissing her breathless, but he had never threatened a man for merely looking at her.

It was one hell of a turn on.

But one she wasn't about to reveal to him.

Lealandra stood and sensed the vampire's intent to look at her. He would be double dead meat if he did. Taig wasn't the kind of man who joked about killing and he was perfectly capable of taking out the vampire.

Not wanting to witness the kind of brutal violence that would happen if the vampire did dare to look at her, she lured Taig from the booth, away from the vampire, and headed for the door with him. His hand remained locked around hers, holding it so tightly that she almost smiled.

"Now that the mark is out of the way we can focus on those demons," Taig said as they broke out into the fading night.

Lealandra yawned and nodded. Trying to keep her enthusiasm rolling was impossible when she was tired. She knew that she should be more concerned about the demons who were after her but she felt so safe with Taig at her side that it was falling to the back of her mind. She didn't feel as though she was in danger. Everything felt as it had done six years ago, before she had left him. She was even beginning to forget that her ascension was imminent and she didn't have a clue how to survive it without the coven and her Counter-Balance.

Her fingers idly traced her chest.

"Thinking about the ascension?" There was a grin in Taig's voice. "Or how quick your little heart was pitter-pattering back there when I read the riot act to the vamp?"

She rolled her eyes. "You scared the crap out of me. What else was my heart supposed to do when you go breaking things like a caveman?"

He grinned ear to ear. She tried to contain her smile but couldn't.

"What did he do to me?" she said.

Taig's face fell and the air around him turned cold. "I don't follow."

"In the club, when he looked in my eyes, I felt... strange."

Taig's irises burned red and he turned around, heading back towards the club. He growled. "I'm going to kill the bastard."

Lealandra bolted after him and grabbed his arm, pulling back on it in an attempt to stop him. She had thought that was the reason Taig had stepped in. He hadn't known that the vampire had been trying something on her, something that had made her feel incredibly compliant.

"Whoa!" She yanked on Taig's arm and he spun on his heel to face her. The darkness in his eyes and the power she could feel running through him warned her to back off for her own sake. She held her ground, refusing to let him intimidate her, and stroked his arm. "Let it go... you stopped him. If he was trying to control me, it failed... I'm not his."

Taig stepped into her, so his hips grazed hers. She swallowed and stared deep into his eyes as he towered over her, dominant and emitting an aura of danger that lured her to him. Her lips parted and her heart pounded at the feel of him, at the outcomes her mind raced to imagine. She tried to keep her gaze steady but it flickered between his eyes and his lips, betraying her desire to kiss him.

He lowered his mouth to hers and whispered against her lips, "Just whose are you?"

Lealandra swallowed again, trembling on the brink of admitting that she was his if he would only come and claim her. Her breath bounced back at her from his lips. So temptingly close. She would only have to move a fraction and they would be kissing. Just a fraction.

It was so easy and so hard at the same time.

She couldn't bring herself to go through with it, to give him such a clear sign that she was his.

"No one's." She turned and walked away, heading down the dark empty street towards the car. Her heart leapt into her mouth and her voice trembled when she added loud enough for him to hear, "yet."

CHAPTER 11

The couch felt too wide with Taig sat at one end and her at the other. The television seemed too loud in the silence between them. Lealandra toyed with the ties of her black skirt, jingling the little bells that hung from their ends. Taig stared at the television.

They sighed at the same time.

She wasn't sure how to act around him now. When they had been together, a quiet time like this wouldn't have happened. They would have been all over each other the minute they had made it through the apartment door, if not a little before. A part of her wanted that time back, wanted to fall into a relationship with him again, but another part of her was wary, worried about the possibilities of him leaving her or hurting her.

So they both sat there, hands in laps, unsure of what to do and what to say.

She knew Taig was in the same boat as her. He kept looking at her out of the corner of his eye and when she had found her voice to ask him what the television programme was about, he hadn't known. He was thinking too.

She had to say something.

He had asked her about her mark when they had left the vampire's club. She touched it again, sending it shimmering.

"Is it bothering you?" Taig whispered.

Lealandra kept her eyes fixed on the ascension mark on her chest and shook her head, and then said, "A little."

"Do you know what it means?"

He didn't resist her when she took hold of his hand, brushed his fingers against her chest so he could see the ascension mark and then folded them over, keeping his index one extended. She pressed it to his symbol.

"This is you."

Taig smiled. His eyes shone with warmth and amusement. He was so handsome when he smiled that way, and so much more like the man she used to know and wanted to know again. "I know that."

She touched the mark opposite his near her left breast. "This one is conflict. I thought it meant we were going to have to fight our way out of the coven but I was wrong."

"What's this one?" Taig touched the mark to the left of conflict.

"Danger." She touched it and then the one to the right of conflict, nearer to Taig's mark. "Blood." She pressed his finger against the one between that and his mark. "Betrayal."

"Anything nice in there besides me?" He grinned again and she could see he was trying to cheer her up. When her ascension mark had first appeared, she had recognised most of the symbols. It had frightened her to see that so many negative things would happen in her path to ascension, but there were positive things too, like Taig's mark.

She brought his hand down, to the mark at the bottom of the circle and looked into his eyes. "Love."

Long silence stretched between them. Taig's finger remained against the symbol, his gaze fixed there. The red light from her ascension mark lit his face and reflected in his eyes, so he appeared as though his demon side was on the brink of making an appearance. She wished he would say something. His finger pressed harder against her chest and then his hand came to rest on her breast. She swallowed and stiffened, waiting. The weight of his hand on her breast was divine but something told her that he wasn't going to do anything. He was thinking and whatever left his mouth was bound to be nasty. If he mentioned Charlie, she was going to kill him. There was only one man in the world that she loved, and she had loved him for over six years.

His eyes finally rose, slowly coursing over her body until they reached hers. He stared deep into them and she lost herself in the endless depths of his black irises, mesmerised and entranced by the hint of warmth that flickered in them. It felt as though she could see right down into his soul. The soul he claimed he didn't have. Just as quickly as he had let her in, he shut her out, the barriers rising and his eyes losing the spark of affection.

"I know this one." His fingertip caressed the symbol beside the one for love. It sat between it and Taig's mark. She knew that one too. The room suddenly felt cold. "Death."

"Taig, I..." She wasn't sure what she had wanted to say. That she thought the symbol for love was about him. That she was sorry she had left him all those years ago. That she often wondered how she had messed things up and why he had let her go. That she needed to know if he loved her and if he would believe that she loved him, all of him, if she said the words. In the end, she said none of the things that she wanted to. She left Taig hanging a moment longer and then said, "I know someone who can help me decipher the mark."

His hand fell away from her, back into his lap, and a hint of disappointment touched his eyes before he nodded.

"We have to go in daylight though," Lealandra said, trying to fill the silence and desperate to leave his place. They didn't have to go in daylight at all. The person she was going to speak with would see her any time of day or night. She just needed some air and some time away from his apartment so she could get her head straight. When they were here, she wanted to kiss him, she wanted to make love with him and forget all the terrible things that were happening. She wanted to bury her head in the sand and lose herself in him.

"Fine by me," Taig said, a sharp edge to his words. He turned off the television, stood, grabbed his leather jacket off the back of the couch and stalked into his bedroom.

Lealandra sat on the couch, staring at the open door. Had she done the right thing? She should have been braver and told Taig everything that she wanted to because he wasn't going to make a move. She looked around his apartment. Stark. Lifeless. Defended. He had moved into this building and surrounded himself with humans, but hadn't allowed any of them into his home. Her heart went out to him again and she looked over her shoulder at the picture of his parents. He was right. She had to be the one to make a move on him, to show him that he was worthy of love and that his demon was an intrinsic part of him. It wasn't something to hide or be ashamed of, and it didn't mean that he didn't belong in this world. He did belong here. He belonged here with her because she loved him—all of him. Without his demon side, he wouldn't be the Taig that she had fallen in love with.

"Let's go." The sudden sound of his voice startled her.

She turned and looked at him as he walked to the door. His jacket and t-shirt were gone, replaced by a smart black shirt similar to the one he had worn the other night. He didn't like daylight. No demon did. While it wouldn't affect him physically, he always liked to cover up and spend as much time as possible in the shadows. She had never grasped why, and neither had he. When she had asked him about it, he had thought long and hard and then said it was just something he had always done.

Lealandra suspected that it had come from his father. A purebred demon would have felt a distinct reaction to the sunshine. Nothing like a vampire experienced, but enough discomfort to make them avoid it. Lesser demons weren't affected. Mixed-species like Taig had a fifty-fifty chance of inheriting the reaction. Taig hadn't.

She smiled.

He frowned. "What's that smile for? This person we're going to see another one of your blokes?"

She frowned too now. She didn't remember Taig being this jealous. In a way, she liked it because it made his desire for her blatantly obvious, but it was getting damn annoying at the same time.

"Actually." She stood and walked over to him, leaving her dark red coat on the back of the black couch. It would be hot today with the sun out. "I was thinking about you."

He paused and his frown lifted. "Do tell."

Her smile widened when she remembered more.

"I was thinking about old times." She went to the door and opened it. Taig followed her out into the hall and locked the door behind them. They walked down the bright cream corridor together while she thought about him and the things they had done. "I was thinking about when we used to sunbathe on the roof of your old building."

His eyes brightened, red seeping in around the edges of his irises. His eyebrows rose. "Oh."

That was about the reaction she had expected. She could still picture Taig's body, bronzed by the sun, muscles taut and exuding power. He had looked incredible in the small black denim shorts he had chosen to wear the few times they had tried to sunbathe. Too incredible. The body of a god, broad and strong, sculpted to perfection, mixed with the face of a devil, handsome and seductive. The combination was too good to resist. Normally they only managed thirty minutes of sunbathing and then things had turned heated. And normally she had been the one to make a move on him.

Taig stopped. Lealandra turned to look at him. All of the black in his irises was gone. He flexed his fingers and moved over to her. Her heart started at a pace, gaining speed with each inch closer he got.

His pupils widened and his gaze fell to her lips. Clearly, she wasn't the only one remembering sunbathing now. She had always worn a black bikini and he had always ripped it off her.

She gasped when he grabbed her arm and pulled her to him, roughly enough that she slammed into him. Desire shone in his eyes. His chest pressed against hers with each deep breath he took and she leaned into him, loving the feel of his strong grip and the hot hard steel of his body. It stirred passion within her. The fire he had started inside her six years ago had remained as embers, waiting for his touch to stoke it back into life, and it burned now, threatening to consume her, an inferno only he could tame.

His arm snaked around her back, fingers caressing the bare patch of skin between her dark purple corset and her black skirt. She trembled from the light touch and stared into his eyes, lost and waiting, silently pleading him to kiss her and put her out of her misery. She needed him more than air, needed him to breathe life into her again. Needed him.

She shivered when he brushed his thumb across her lower lip, his fingers caressing her jaw and neck, and closed her eyes. Her power rose at the smell of his blood and she sighed.

"You're still hungry," he husked and she murmured her agreement. Her power sought his, desiring the strength it held, and she reached for it too, wanting the soothing effect and the control it gave her. His fingers skimmed down over her throat. Her nipples tightened when he rested his palm on her left breast and then moved it over her heart. "Not just the magic... he did a real number on you."

Lealandra opened her eyes and stared into Taig's. She couldn't form a denial. Charlie had failed to give her what she needed, but it wasn't just his fault that she was hungry. She was responsible too. After all, she had chosen to leave Taig, even though she had known deep inside that she would be alone even with Charlie around.

She would always want Taig, and would never stop loving him.

Understanding dawned in Taig's eyes but uncertainty laced it. He drew her closer.

"You said you didn't belong to anyone." His soft voice sent shivers through her and she melted into him, relaxing in his strong embrace. His right arm tightened around her, holding her up and bringing her flush against him. "You meant that you haven't belonged to anyone in a long time."

She managed a nod. Now he was getting it. She hoped his bitter games would stop now. They cut her deep and she couldn't bear the pain. She never had been able to when it came to Taig. She was defenceless against him, her heart always partly open and always vulnerable.

"Charlie was only your Counter-Balance, wasn't he? You were forbidden to take blood, and yet you didn't give your power the other thing it would crave in the absence of blood... sex. Why?" His red eyes searched hers and she fully opened her heart to him, letting him all the way in. He needed to see why, even when she couldn't bring herself to say it. She loved him. She didn't want anyone else. "Did you even kiss him?"

Lealandra shook her head and her cheeks coloured when he brushed the backs of his fingers across them and smiled at her. A genuine smile. Her silent confession had made him happy.

The colour drained from his eyes and he frowned for a moment before relaxing again.

"Did you ever belong to me?" Those whispered words were laden with danger and emotion. She didn't want to hurt him. It would leave her even more open to him hurting her, but she would confess this one thing, and hope that he wouldn't throw it back in her face or use it against her.

She nodded.

She had back then.

And she still did now.

Her heart had belonged to him all this time and it would be his until the end of eternity.

Lealandra closed her eyes when he leaned in and rested his forehead against hers. His breath was cool against her face, soft and comforting. She raised her hands and cupped both of his cheeks, holding him in place so he couldn't shatter this moment of calm and peace between them. She needed it to go on a little longer, had to absorb how it felt.

He pressed a kiss to her forehead and his hand left her back. He took hold of one of hers and brought it away from his face, but didn't relinquish it.

"We're causing a scene," he whispered and her power spiked when she grew aware of the people in the hall with them.

She smiled and drew away from him. "Didn't we always?"

Taig grinned and tucked her hair behind her ear. She smelt the blood on his palm and her magic reached for him again. The tiny amount he had given her wasn't enough. It had only reawakened the craving for his blood. Just as his touch had reawakened her craving for him.

The couple in the hall were the same people who had given her disgusted looks the other night. She stared at the woman, tempted to unleash her power a fraction so her eyes changed to red and scare the living daylights out of her. Who was she to look at Taig and her like that? Taig had every right to live in this building. He earned his money by risking his life. This couple looked as though they had been born into theirs.

Lealandra didn't break her staring competition with the woman until she had looked away and turned towards her partner. The man looked at her when the woman whispered something. Lealandra stared at him and then relaxed when Taig slung his arm around her shoulders. He pulled her close, making her stumble into him, and squeezed her shoulder. She looked up at him and he smirked at her.

Not a cocky smirk this time.

Or amused.

In fact, it was more of a smile, but she had never really seen him smile so broadly without it either being cocky or amused. Was this the happy side of Taig?

"So you were saving yourself for me then?" His smile turned into a devious grin.

She sighed. Perhaps it was more pride than happiness.

Smug bastard.

Lealandra smiled right back at him and put her arm around his waist, playing along. Let him think that she had been saving herself for him. It was easier than having to admit the truth of it.

She had been.

They took the elevator down and walked to her car. She drove this time, leaving Taig to constantly flick through the rock stations on the radio and drum along to the songs he liked. She had missed him. Being back with him made her realise just how much and just how different her life had been. The coven had felt stifling and uncomfortable at times. This felt normal. This was where she belonged.

She drove deep into the north of the city, past areas that were undergoing heavy redevelopment and neighbourhoods that catered to demons. Taig looked at her when they passed the area in which he used to live and then leaned one arm on the door and stared out of the window at the buildings. She had liked it here with him.

It hadn't felt dangerous, not with Taig around to protect her. She kept going, through to the next neighbourhood and then the one beyond that. It was as rough as the one where Taig had used to live, but this time it was humans who caused the trouble, and that frightened Lealandra, but not for her sake. She didn't like the fact that the people they were going to see had chosen to live in this area. She wished they lived somewhere better and she had been saving money in order to make that happen. That money was now Taig's, if he would take it as payment for protecting her. She hoped that he would. It felt as though they had made enough progress that he would change his mind and accept her offer of payment rather than insisting on his.

Taig looked at her again when she parked the car in a quiet street. She put some money in the meter, enough to last the whole day, and then started walking. Taig followed. A wave of power swept through her and she knew that he was checking out their surroundings with his senses, ensuring her safety. He moved up to walk beside her and she smiled at him. It was a long walk to her contact. She had parked the car around a mile away so the coven couldn't track her. She didn't want them finding the woman she was going to meet.

She glanced at Taig.

How was he going to react to the person she was bringing him to see?

CHAPTER 12

Lealandra tensed the moment they reached the quiet familiar street and the old brick building came into view. Wedged between stores that had seen better days, the shop front looked exactly as it had done when she had last visited two years ago. Nothing had changed, not even in any of the grocery, pharmacy or local stores around it. The old couple running the grocery store still stood on the street surrounded by the boxes of their brightly coloured wares and trying to sell them to disinterested people as they passed. She crossed the road and smiled at the old man as he spotted her and nodded, and then looked past them to the store next door.

The round purple sign that stuck out into the street caught her eye, the crescent moon and stars on it glittering in the sunlight. Surrounding the stars was the name of the shop and then symbols that only a true witch would understand. It offered supplies, books, and other necessities. Things that would turn a human's stomach and things they didn't know existed.

Taig stepped closer to her and then past her. He pushed the brightly painted purple door open and held it. She walked inside, her footsteps loud on the old dark wooden floor. The smell of herbs filled her senses and she smiled. It always smelt the same. Sandalwood, rosemary, lavender and spices, all things that humans thought went into love spells and magic. Lealandra walked forwards, past the rows of candles and pentagrams. The circular racks of gothic clothing in the middle of the room were new. They were branching out.

"Hocus pocus," Taig muttered and Lealandra bit her tongue to stop her from agreeing. She didn't want the woman hearing her saying such things. It would only upset her and she was impossible to deal with when upset.

"Welcome, welcome!" A woman's voice reached out from behind a set of black velvet curtains. Some of the silver stars stitched onto the material had seen better days and were beginning to come undone, their points flapping down.

The curtains parted and the woman stepped out, wearing a black corseted dress and with her equally dark hair pulled up into a bun. Her grey eyes widened, smoothing the lines that edged them, and her lips drew wide into a smile.

Her arms instantly opened and she bustled towards them.

"Lea!" the woman said, her voice full of happiness that Lealandra could feel in her. Her power reached out to the woman's and a wave of comfort swept through her as they connected, chasing away all of her doubts and fears.

Lealandra closed her eyes and embraced her. "Mother."

Taig noticeably tensed. The change in his power marked it. It went from a calm ebbing and flowing within her to a raging storm.

"Mother?" he said and she heard him step back.

"By the gods, you've brought a man home! I have to tell your father," her mother said and Lealandra grabbed her to stop her from going and doing just that. She held her tight, not letting her escape, and wondered if she was going to have to do the same to Taig too. He took another step back towards the door.

"Don't make a scene." Her grip on her mother's arm tightened in a silent threat.

Her mother smiled and then her gaze drifted to Taig. "And who do we have here and why is he calling me mother?"

Lealandra looked at Taig. He frowned at her mother.

"It was a question, not a statement." Taig's power rose another notch.

Her mother froze. Her eyes slid to Lealandra. "A demon?"

Taig went to leave.

"Damn it, mother," Lealandra muttered and went after him. She caught him at the door and stopped him by slipping her fingers into his and pressing their palms together. Her power latched on to his. It was strong and steady, ready for a fight. She didn't want him to leave. She needed him here with her to help her through this. Taig looked over his shoulder at her and she whispered, "Stay."

For a moment, he looked as though he was going to leave, but then he turned to face her. He placed his other hand against their joined ones. Sensing her power? He was reading her. She opened herself and her magic to him, letting him in so he would see that she needed him because she was frightened of what her ascension path might say.

"A little touchy for a demon," her mother said.

Lealandra cringed. "Stay out of this, mother."

She held Taig's gaze, hoping her mother would keep quiet. Normally her mother was more relaxed about demons. Maybe it was seeing her daughter with one that had her reacting.

"Stay," Lealandra said again. "It won't take long."

Taig nodded, barely moving his head. His reluctance to stay wasn't just about the fact that her mother had mentioned his demonic status. It was because it was her mother. Maybe she should have warned him about who they were going to see. It wasn't as though she had brought him here to meet her parents. This wasn't anything like that.

"A demon!"

Lealandra grimaced at the sound of her father's voice. He sounded decidedly excited about it and that meant trouble. Her father wouldn't realise that he was doing anything wrong but he was bound to ask too many questions and stick his nose in Taig's business too much. She didn't want Taig to blow a fuse and she didn't want him to feel persecuted by her family.

"Lea has brought a man home, or a demon. I'm not sure which he is. Seems fairly human but there's a definite undercurrent of demon power in him." Her mother turned to face her father as he came forwards from the back of the store, the tails of his black frock coat flapping as he walked. Lealandra didn't like it. It always made her father look like a beanpole but he insisted on wearing it while at work.

When had her parents lives become nothing but theatrics? They had been two of the most powerful witches once and now they ran a store. They should have been teaching other young witches how to use their powers, not pandering to humans and their hungers for love spells and phoney magic. She supposed they were at least supplying the witch community with everything they needed for their day-to-day lives, but it still didn't feel right to Lealandra. She had wanted more for her parents. Things had never been the same since her mother had ascended. Lealandra hoped her life wouldn't turn out like this. She didn't want to hide away if she survived the ascension, fearful of what might happen if she used her magic. She wanted to make use of her power and do some good with it.

Taig's power jumped up another notch and his fingers twitched against hers. He was gearing up for a fight.

"Perhaps a mixed breed? I haven't met a mixed breed before. I wonder if he would tell us about himself... do you think he would, Lea?"

Lealandra tensed. Her temper reached boiling point and she turned on her parents.

"Stop talking about Taig as though he's an animal or a science project!"

Both of her parents' eyebrows shot up. Her father was the first to change. His expression became stern, his dark eyes penetrating hers. She stood her ground. She wasn't a child anymore. He couldn't tell her off for talking back when he was the one being rude about their guest.

"Taig?" he said instead, surprising her.

Her mother stepped forwards, scrutinising Taig, taking all of him in as though committing him to memory or looking for a weak spot. Her father stroked the greying goatee that Lealandra knew he only had so he looked the part in their occultist shop. It didn't suit him. She had laughed her backside off when she had first seen it two years ago. It was greyer now, marking the passing years and reminding her that none of them were getting any younger.

"*The* Taig?" her mother said.

Lealandra swallowed and then found the courage to nod.

"*The* Taig!" Her father grinned, causing deep wrinkles beside his eyes. "The first man you bring home is the man who broke your heart... I say, Lea, sometimes you are a muddled little thing. Come on through for tea... do demons drink tea? She never mentioned you were a demon, you know... half demon... it is half demon, isn't it?"

Taig nodded dumbly. He looked as shocked as she felt. Why did her father have to be at the shop today? Most days he lectured small classes on occult history over at the university. Everything would have gone a lot smoother without his presence. There was no way she could stop the combined power of both her parents. They were going to question Taig whether she liked it or not. She only hoped that he would play nice and humour them rather than losing his temper.

When her parents had gone into the back, she let go of Taig's hand and went to follow. Taig's fingers closed around her wrist and she looked back at him. He still looked lost. She often felt that way around her parents.

"Broke your heart?" Taig searched her eyes and Lealandra hesitated under his dark gaze. It wasn't her parents' insane rambling that had him confused.

She bit her lip and looked away. It was the truth, almost. Taig hadn't broken her heart. She had broken it.

"I may have mentioned you when I visited them before joining the coven."

"And every time after that!" her mother hollered from the back.

Lealandra curled her fingers into fists that shook and sent a warning wave of power her mother's way. The last thing she needed when she was still trying to figure it all out with Taig was her parents storming in and mixing everything up.

"You never told them I was a demon." Those words fell heavily in the quiet room. She had known the moment her father had said it that Taig would take it to heart.

"Only because I've never seen it as a problem, or anything that they needed to know, Taig. I don't see you as a demon, or a monster, or whatever you think people see you as... whatever you see yourself as." She caught his cheek with her other hand when he went to turn away and stopped him. His gaze fell to her shoulder. She sighed and stroked his face, keeping her voice low so their conversation would remain private. "You're a man, Taig, whether you believe it or not, and both sides of you make you who you are."

"A son of a bastard who broke your heart?" He closed his eyes and drew a long breath.

"I know it's not right... and it wasn't what I told them back then... and it was my fault... but it did hurt me. It hurt me a lot. It really did, Taig." She met his gaze when he opened his eyes.

Her mother called to them again, ordering her to bring Taig through. He didn't move and neither did she. She stood there, waiting to see if he was going to say anything or just leave her hanging.

"You and me both, sweet cheeks," he whispered, his eyes full of a strange fire, a combination of affection and pain. Both emotions laced his power, leeching into her through the hold he had on her wrist. It drew a response from her magic. It absorbed the strength from his power and rose within her, hungry for more. Taig released her and looked at his hand. The wound on his palm had healed. Had her magic done it? Normally it didn't affect anyone else without a command from her. She reached out and stroked her fingers over his palm. Why?

Her eyes widened when she remembered the night that Charlie had died. Her magic had done something similar then. It had tried to make her heal him, even when she had known that she couldn't save him. The magic had taken control of her in the lobby of the coven too and she had felt a strong need to protect Taig. At the time, she had thought it was her need that had driven it to react but now she wasn't so sure. Did her magic want to protect him?

"You do that?" Taig said and she shook her head.

"It's getting stronger." She touched the mark on her chest and frowned down at it. "The magic is getting beyond my control again. I can feel it pushing."

"Let's see what dear old mum has to say about it then and get you somewhere you can have some blood."

Blood. Just the word made her shiver in anticipation and roused her magic. She could feel how eager it was. It wanted to become stronger. Taig's blood would give it the strength it desired but would also subdue it enough for her to control it. She nodded, glad that he hadn't mentioned a price this time.

They walked side by side into the area behind the black velvet curtain. Her father looked up from his position at the back of the room in a small galley kitchen and paused with the stainless steel kettle held in one hand and a white china dragon-shaped teapot in the other. His eyebrows rose in silent question. She smiled her response. Tea would be nice, although she didn't think Taig would drink it out of anything other than politeness.

Her mother sat at a round blue table, leafing through an inventory. She smiled at them both, a perfect reflection of what Lealandra would look like in thirty years' time. Lealandra took the seat opposite her.

"So what brings you and Taig here? I have to admit, I'm more than a little surprised to see you with a demon—"

"Half-demon," Taig said, cutting her mother off. Her mother quirked an eyebrow at the interruption and then continued.

"A half-demon considering that the coven would frown upon such a thing."

"I've broken with them," Lealandra blurted out and then before her mother could ask why, added, "Things have happened. A lot of things. The safest place for me right now is with Taig."

"Is someone after you? Why would they be after you?" Her father placed the wooden tray of tea things down on the table. The china cups rattled against each other.

Both her mother and father looked at Taig. His right eyebrow rose. Lealandra sighed.

"Taig has nothing to do with it. Someone has it in for me and I think it has something to do with this." She took her mother's hand and brushed her fingers over the ascension mark. Her mother gasped, grabbed her father's hand, and shoved it against Lealandra's chest. His eyes shot wide. "They… they killed Charlie… and broke into my place at the coven. Taig is going to track them for me. I'll be safe with him."

"Track them?" Her father cast a curious look Taig's way.

"It's a doddle." Taig lifted his shoulders in an easy shrug. "I have their scent now. They'll be dead in no time."

"Dead?" Her father frowned. Lealandra wished she could use telepathy on demons. She had never been any good at it and demons were immune. She had tried to use it once on Taig to see if it worked on half-breeds but it had failed. At least, he'd said that he hadn't heard her. He might have just been ignoring her. She wanted to tell him that talking about killing, even if it was demons and he was in the company of witches, wasn't the way into her father's good book. Her parents didn't condone violence. "What is it you do for a living? You have a few scars there that say it's dangerous."

Lealandra's stomach flipped when she realised that Taig had rolled his black shirtsleeves up and her father meant the marks on his forearms. Gods, she didn't even want to go there with her parents and she hoped Taig didn't. If they discovered the sorts of things she had gotten up to with Taig, she would die of embarrassment.

Taig rolled his sleeves down.

He leaned back in his chair, so casual that he looked as though he owned the place, and raked his thick black hair back. Lealandra saw straight through him. Her father's question had made him uncomfortable. There was a lot of stigma attached to demons hunting demons and Taig had lost a lot of friends over his decision to go into that field. But then, he was fine with that. He had seen it as one step closer to drawing a line between the man he thought he was and his demonic side. She had tried to tell him that it wasn't possible, that man and demon were one and the same, but he hadn't listened to her. He never did when it came to his demonic side. He could pretend it didn't exist all he wanted, could kill all the demons in the world, and it still wouldn't change the fact that his father had been a demon and that blood ran in his veins.

Lealandra took the cup of tea that her mother offered Taig and placed it down in front of him.

"Taig is a hunter." She took her own cup of tea and ran her finger around the delicate rim of the bone china cup, using it to distract her so she didn't have to look her parents in the eye when she said this. "He hunts marks."

"Demons," Taig said with a sneer.

Both of her parents looked shocked. She had been too at first but then she had realised the reason why he hunted demons—he wanted to kill that side of himself, but he couldn't, so he eradicated the demons that he could. She wasn't sure whether he really wanted to kill his own demon side, or whether maybe he wanted to kill his father. She didn't understand why he would want to do either, unless he blamed his father for his mother's death. She could sympathise with him in a way. Sometimes, she felt as though the magic was a monster lurking inside her rather than a part of her.

It responded violently to that, pushing through her, filling her mind with dark thoughts. She grabbed Taig's hand. The moment he looked at her, he wrapped his other hand around hers, holding it tight. His power flowed into her, abating her own and calming it. The dark haze in her mind lifted but whispered words lingered, demands for blood and power.

Taig's power rose a fraction and the words disappeared, leaving her mind empty again.

"Better?" His voice was smooth and comforting, full of concern and reassurance.

Lealandra nodded, thankful for the power he had given her and the fact he could control how much he released. She had needed that little bit more. His normal level of power, the level which he unconsciously emitted, wasn't enough anymore.

"His power can control yours." Her father came to stand over Taig, studying him with an excited twinkle in his eyes. "Fascinating."

Her mother murmured an agreement. Taig's hand didn't leave hers. She was thankful for it. Holding his hand felt nice and not only because it tempered her magic. The feel of his large hands engulfing hers reassured her, telling her without words that he wasn't going to leave her and that there was still a part of him that loved her.

"I need to know what my ascension mark means." Lealandra touched her chest again. "I don't have long."

Her mother nodded and then waved towards Taig and her father. "Off you go. Show the boy around the store and make yourselves useful."

Lealandra looked at Taig. She didn't want him to feel as though he had to go and, in her heart, she wanted him to refuse and remain with her. She needed his support now more than ever. He squeezed her hand and his look softened enough for her to know what he was trying to tell her. He wouldn't go far. He would stay close enough that she would still be able to reach him with her magic if she needed him. She brushed her thumb over his as her silent reply. She was glad that he was doing this for her and she would be fine now that she knew he would remain nearby.

He smiled, his ebony eyes bright with it, and then it turned mischievous. She was about to ask him what he was up to when he raised her hand and pressed a long kiss to the back of it.

"Later, sweet cheeks."

She cursed and glared at him as he rose from the seat. He picked up the delicate teacup, his little finger sticking out demurely, and sipped it very politely before winking at her and following her father. Her anger melted away into a smile at his stupid behaviour and then widened into a grin when she thought about what he had said. He was trying to get her into trouble with her mother but she wasn't the only one who would get the third degree about his term of endearment. He would too. Her father was bound to mention it and start probing.

"He seems like a nice boy," her mother said and Lealandra looked away from the curtain and back to her. She nodded. Her mother leaned forwards and glanced at the curtain before whispering, "Have you two ever... you know... when he's in his de—"

Lealandra gasped. "Mother!"

Her cheeks blazed. She couldn't believe her own mother had asked such a thing.

"No!" Lealandra hissed, shock making her abrupt, and then calmed down and said, "I've never seen him in demon form. He... it's a long story and not why I'm here."

Her mother didn't look as though she was going to let it go now that Lealandra had made it sound interesting. She took hold of her mother's hand and touched the mark on her chest again, trying to get her to focus.

"This is why I'm here. I need to know what it means and fast. The ascension is coming and someone is after my life. I have to know what's going to happen to me, even in the vaguest sense."

A thoughtful expression settled on her mother's face and she took a pair of half-moon glasses out of a sparkly red case. Lealandra rolled her eyes at the theatrical things her mother had surrounded herself with since leaving her coven and setting up shop in the real world. That had been shortly after her mother had lost control of her power during her ascension and had come close to killing everyone, including her and her father. She had been a child at the time but she remembered the incredible fear and remembered seeing her father face death in order to save her mother's life.

Had Taig's father done such a thing? The photograph of his parents had such an aura of love about it that Lealandra felt certain that his father would have fought to protect his mother.

Taig didn't know how his parents had died. He only felt as though they had. If he had seen his father fight to save his mother, even if he hadn't been successful, she was sure that Taig would have turned out differently. He wouldn't hate his demon side. He would believe the things that she had told him and the things she couldn't voice.

She wanted that so much for him. When they had been together, she had asked the neighbourhood demons about his parents. She had learned from some of the older generation that Taig had moved there alone as a young man. They had never met his parents, but they knew his mark, and knew the demon lineage. They had seemed afraid of telling her much more than that, and the few times she had tried to talk to Taig about it, he had cut her off.

Lealandra waited while her mother inspected each symbol in the ascension mark, her thoughts with Taig. She couldn't hear her father or him in the other room. Either they weren't talking to each other or they were talking quietly. She unleashed her power a little, releasing the tight bonds she held it inside with so she could sense Taig. He wasn't nearby. She stretched her magic out to cover a larger area and found him out the back.

There was a small dusty courtyard there. Potted plants crowded the bright sunny space, throwing up their aromas as the warm light caressed them. She had always enjoyed sitting there amongst the herbs and breathing in the quiet as she studied. She pictured Taig leaning against the red brick wall, talking to her father, probably cracking jokes about her and hearing all the stupid tales of things she had gotten up to as a child. She was never going to live this down.

Her father would give Taig ammunition that would keep him amused for decades. He would store the information about her away for use at extremely inappropriate times. She smiled. That was Taig.

"Thinking about him?" her mother said and Lealandra tried to look innocent. Her mother gave her a sly smile. "I can feel you reaching for him. Can he feel it too?"

Lealandra nodded and then admitted, "He's reaching back. He likes to know I'm safe."

The sparkle in her mother's eyes brought a blush to Lealandra's cheeks, burning them up. Perhaps she should have asked Taig to wait outside rather than submitting them both to her parents. She hadn't realised that they would make such a fuss and find her bringing a man home so amusing.

"I don't recognise this one." Her mother drew her attention to the mark. The connection between Lealandra and Taig shattered the moment her eyes fell on it.

Her heart missed a beat and she touched the symbol.

"Taig's mark. It's on the back of his left shoulder."

"Well, he's involved then."

Lealandra rolled her eyes again. "Tell me something I don't know."

Her mother peered closer, pressing each mark. "Betrayal, blood, conflict, danger, love and death. That's quite a cocktail you have there. The order is significant."

"It is?" Lealandra hadn't realised that. "Where does it start?"

Her mother pointed to the symbol for death. "You said that someone killed Charlie. Was that the first thing to happen after the mark appeared?"

She nodded. "Charlie died and then someone wrote a message on my apartment wall, saying I was going to die and go to Hell. I left the coven, hid out and then went to Taig for help. When I went back to the coven, I thought that meant I was going to encounter conflict. Gregori tried to stop me from leaving, but nothing happened other than that."

"Did you take Taig with you? No, don't answer that. Of course you took Taig with you. You would have been a fool not to. Betrayal."

"Whose?" Lealandra didn't like the sound of that. "The coven?"

"It could be, or it could be your betrayal by bringing Taig to the coven and parting ways with them. Some would see a witch choosing a demon over other witches as betrayal."

Lealandra had feared as much but she was still uncertain about the symbol. Could it mean the coven? The person who had written the mark on her wall knew what they were doing. There had been intent behind it. A demon couldn't lace such a mark with such power. They could only draw the mark as though it was a picture. It had to have been a witch. She shook her head. She was being paranoid now. There was no reason for her to suspect anyone at the coven. But her blood was powerful right now. The magic in it would feed the magic of another, making it stronger. She shook her head again, trying to rid it of such dark thoughts and focused back on her mother.

"Blood." Her mother looked up at her. "We have always carried powerful magic in this family, old magic that makes demands of us. Your father may have overlooked the marks on that young demon's wrists, but I didn't. Tell me, Lea, have you shared blood with him?"

"No, not shared." Her voice trembled and she couldn't look her mother in the eye. She sipped her cooling tea and then drummed her nails against the side of the cup. "I have taken his blood. He had a taste of mine by accident the other day and it sent him off the deep end. His blood doesn't do such things to me. It placates my magic."

"A more powerful force of nature. Magic as strong as ours would only bow to something it believed was superior. It craves his blood?" Her mother touched her hand and Lealandra nodded. "The blood is Taig then. You will need his power to contain yours. Don't be frightened of taking what you need. The magic will make demands of you that you must fulfil in order to survive the ascension. Now that your Counter-Balance is gone, you will have no way of controlling your power. Taig's blood may provide what you need in the absence of the coven. Your father and I are willing to help too."

Lealandra shook her head against the idea and then nodded when her mother's look hardened.

"I'll come to you if I can. If I have time before the final stage begins." Her insides flipped at the thought of going through the ascension. It would happen soon and she still wasn't sure how she was going to survive it. She had always been close to her magic, giving it what it wanted. All she could do now was continue to do that and hope that, when the time came, it would go easy on her and work with her rather than against. She would give it whatever it wanted, as much blood as she could stomach if it asked it of her, and was sure that Taig wouldn't refuse her. He would want her to survive.

"Conflict and danger." Her mother drank her tea and then refilled her cup, her expression pensive. "There will be a fight in your future. Whoever is after you, they are not going to give up. You will have to defeat them in order to survive and these two marks together means it will be the fight of your life. Whether it happens before or after the ascension is inconsequential. They are linked to your survival and that is why they are in your path. You must be careful, Lea. Don't leave his side and don't rush into things. Protect yourself first and foremost." She touched the final mark and her expression lost its serious edge, melting into a tender smile. "Love."

Lealandra blushed and her power automatically reached for Taig. When she had seen that mark, she had hoped it meant him.

"I don't think this one needs deciphering." Her mother smiled with warmth in her grey eyes. "I think the answer to that one is tall, dark and handsome standing outside humouring your father. He's a good catch, Lea, regardless of his demon blood. Perhaps the two families could meet up when this is over?"

"Taig said his parents disappeared... died when he was younger." Lealandra severed the connection between them so he didn't feel her change in emotions. If he sensed that she was sad or upset, he was bound to come barging in. "I never met them but I've seen a picture and they looked happy."

"And powerful."

Lealandra frowned. "Powerful?"

"I felt it when he took your hand. Have you never noticed that Taig has more power than most demons, and yet he's only a half-breed? Which parent was the demon... no, wait... the male... yes, the father, and he was incredibly powerful. If they are dead, it would have taken more than a natural phenomenon or an Earth-dwelling demon to kill them."

She had never thought about that. Taig had mentioned that his father was powerful but she hadn't considered that Taig would only have half of his father's strength because of his mixed blood. When she doubled Taig's power, she found herself wondering just who his father had been and why he had been on Earth. Demons with that kind of power never left the underworld. Their presence on Earth affected the delicate balance, tilting it and endangering everyone. Her mother was right. It would have taken another demon from the underworld to kill Taig's father and that kind of fight would have left a deep scar on the planet. Taig had said that they had left him one day and never returned. What if they weren't dead? What if they had returned to the underworld?

But why would they have left Taig?

Unless they hadn't had a choice in the matter. God and the Devil existed. Would both parties consider a demon as powerful as Taig's father living on Earth as an offence? Had Taig's parents been captured and were being held for that offence? Or had they been taken to the underworld and eliminated just as Taig believed?

The only way of knowing for sure was to go to the underworld. Lealandra reached out to Taig with her power, needing the connection and desiring to comfort him. She vowed that if she survived her ascension, she would risk everything and go down there to find out what had happened to his parents. She would do all in her power to help him discover their fate, and, if they were alive, to reunite them with their son.

"It's insane to think what you're thinking." The deep male voice sent shivers of pleasure down her spine. She turned to face Taig. He was leaning against the doorframe with his arms folded across his broad chest. A trace of red lined his irises, a sign of his anger. "I know what you're thinking and I've even thought it myself from time to time. My parents are dead, Lea. Whether they're down there, or really gone, they're dead to me."

Ascension

Lealandra reached out to him but he turned his back on her and walked away. The shop door slammed a moment later. She clenched her fists and cursed him. He could be stubborn all he wanted, but he wasn't going to stop her. When everything was over, she was going down there to see if they were alive. She was going to make him see that his parents had loved him and that he had no reason to hate himself.

Lealandra hastily kissed her mother and father, embracing them in turn, and then went after Taig.

He wasn't going to stop her.

She was going to help him accept himself whether he liked it or not.

She was going to because she couldn't stand by and watch the man she loved destroy himself.

She had to save him.

CHAPTER 13

Lealandra caught up with Taig in the alley opposite her parents' store. It was darker outside now, heavy black clouds blocking out the afternoon sun and threatening rain. Wind tousled her hair and blew her long black skirt against her legs, making it difficult to walk. Taig's gaze remained firmly fixed ahead as they walked. He radiated anger in waves so powerful that she wanted to reach out and hold his hand, to comfort him and tell him that there was no reason for him to hate himself because she loved him for who he was.

She took her car keys out of her small black bag instead and toyed with them. The silence was oppressive and only grew worse, making her feel heavy as they headed back towards the car, snaking through the narrow alleys and avoiding the main streets. She knew why they were taking the back route. Taig's eyes were as red as blood and his fists were tight balls of barely restrained fury. Whatever he was thinking, it was dark. The aura of danger around him prevented her magic from wanting to connect to him. It shrank back within her, fearful. Lealandra went to touch his hand and then thought the better of it. He never had welcomed comfort. It made him feel weak and he was likely to react in a bad way, and she didn't want to push him over the edge. He would only hate himself more if he hurt her by mistake.

The alley nearest the car was so dark that the dim streetlights on the walls had come on. They did nothing to alleviate the gloom. The low grey clouds overhead and scent of rain urged her to walk faster so she avoided the impending downpour. She tried to send her power outwards to detect whether they were alone, but Taig's power interfered with it and her magic refused to do as she asked.

She twirled the keys around her finger and then glanced over at Taig.

A loud crack echoed around the street and suddenly she was in Taig's arms. They closed around her, one hand pushing her head hard against his chest. It took her a moment to realise it wasn't thunder. She shut her eyes and hunched against him, making herself as small as possible in his embrace. Another crack sharply followed another and Taig jerked in time with each one. Her heart exploded into action, beating faster than it would've done if she had been doing a flat out run. After the fifth bang, the world fell eerily silent. The sound of her pounding heart and ragged breathing filled her ears. She trembled all over, unspent adrenaline making her legs so weak her knees threatened to give out.

"You can come out now. They're gone," Taig whispered close to her ear, his breath tickling it and making a wave of tingles dance across her skin. "Your friends are certainly persistent."

Lealandra opened her eyes and they widened the moment she realised that it wasn't only Taig's arms around her. Thick black leathery wings enfolded her, forming a shield against her attacker. Taig slumped forwards, his weight pressing down on her slim shoulders, and she pressed her hands to his chest to support him as his grip loosened.

"Taig!" Panicked, she pushed against him, desperate to see his face and see if he was alright. His heart beat against her palms, strong and steady, a reassurance she badly needed. A few bullets couldn't kill Taig. She repeated it as a mantra as tears rolled down her cheeks.

She pushed again, struggling to hold his weight, and managed to get him off her. He was looking at her when she finally put enough space between them. He smiled and swallowed, no trace of the tremendous pain she could feel in him visible in his dark red eyes.

Lealandra cupped his cheek and her brow furrowed. "Taig?"

He rolled his shoulders, grimacing at the same time as his eyes brightened, all the fires of Hell burning in them for a brief flash. His pain tore into her through where she touched him and then abated when he growled and straightened. His wings folded back and then disappeared, and he shifted out of her reach. With a frown, he looked over his shoulder at his back and pulled on his ruined black shirt.

"They're gonna pay now," he muttered casually but she could hear the agony in his voice. "This was my favourite shirt."

Humour in the face of danger. It was just like Taig and it brought a smile to her lips even though it didn't reach her heart. That was still pounding with fear, sending tremors along every nerve in her body. She shouldn't have got him involved. The thought of him being hurt ripped her apart inside and stripped her of her strength. She wouldn't be able to bear it if something happened to him. It would kill her.

Her eyes roamed his face, searching for a sign of his pain. It echoed within her, her power detecting what he was hiding so well. It was just like him to keep her on the periphery and pretend he was fine when he needed assistance. She wasn't going to allow it this time. She was going to help him.

Taig turned to face the direction the attack had come from and she gasped when she saw the ripped back of his shirt and the five long tracks of blood trailing down his skin from his shoulders.

Without hesitation, she stepped up to him and touched the red angry skin around each wound. Her eyes widened further. "We need to get these bullets out of you."

He looked over his shoulder at her.

Lealandra stared at the wound directly in front of her. The bullet had lodged into his left shoulder, a bloody welt in the middle of his mark. She raised her hand, brought it close to the wound and focused on it. Taig unleashed an ungodly roar as the bullet eased out of his skin, drawn by her magic. She held it in the air with her power, wondering how such a tiny piece of metal could do so much damage, and then released it and watched it fall and hit the floor with a light metallic ting.

"You might want to give me a bottle of whisky before you try that one again." Red eyes met hers, his voice dark and menacing.

Nerves fluttered in her stomach. He would never hurt her but when he looked like this, so close to releasing his demonic side, instinct took over and told her to run.

"Don't be such a baby," she said with false lightness.

His eyes narrowed but melted back to black. He scanned the alley in all directions and then held his hand out. "Keys. Let's get you the hell out of here."

Lealandra frowned at his outstretched hand. She wanted to remove the rest of the bullets but his tone and expression said not to even mention it and to do as he was saying. She would wait until they were back at his apartment and safe before she convinced him to let her take out the rest.

"I'm driving. You're in no condition to get behind the wheel." Lealandra kept the keys tucked tightly in her hand.

Darkness swept across his face but quickly dissipated. His broad shoulders rose in a shrug that didn't fool her and he held his arm out to one side. She walked past him, heading for her car at the other end of the alley. Her heart jump-started again when she stepped out into the wide street, her eyes darting about as her power reached out to check her surroundings for any demon signatures. The only one that came back was Taig.

The demon must have tracked her car and been waiting for them to return to it. If they hadn't been so distracted, one of them probably would have sensed the presence of the demon before it could open fire.

Her thoughts drifted to her parents and a flicker of fear for them beat in her heart. They would be safe. Such a weak demon wouldn't stand a chance against them but it didn't stop her from worrying.

Taig kept behind her, a second shadow that moved so closely that she could feel him brushing against her body. His hip grazed her backside when she reached the door of her car and a quiet thrill chased over her skin at the contact, followed by a flush of prickly heat. She swallowed and pressed the button on her fob to unlock the doors.

Taig moved back a few inches when she opened the door and slid behind the wheel. He closed the door for her and rounded the hood of the car. She stared at his exposed back. His shirt was in tatters but the gunfire hadn't torn it apart. It had been those wings. She had never realised that he had them. What would he look like if he shed his human visage?

He slid his bulky frame into the seat beside her and nodded towards the road, a silent command for her to drive. She did. It was difficult to stick within the speed limit when she could feel Taig's pain and wanted to get him home so she could tend to his wounds, and she didn't bother to park far away when they finally reached his neighbourhood. The garage beneath his building was open. She drove down into it and spotted the space that matched his apartment number. It was empty. She threw the car into it and switched off the engine.

Taig stepped out of the car first, coming around to open the door for her. His chivalry drew a smile and the way he stayed impossibly close to her during the quick walk through his building made searing hot memories of their time together leap to the forefront of her mind. He slipped his arm around her waist and held her close as he unlocked his front door, and she found herself willing him to slow down so she could savour the feel of him against her. He slid the key into the lock, turned it, and pushed the door open. She kept still when he motioned for her to remain where she was.

He walked into the apartment ahead of her, stalking through the darkness like a predator while she waited on the threshold. He really wasn't taking any chances. She warmed inside and then a sudden emptiness opened within her. Watching him now, she wished she had never left him. Charlie may have been her Counter-Balance but Taig was so much more than that. He was everything she had ever wanted and he understood her better than Charlie.

Better than anyone.

"It's clear," Taig said and then disappeared again.

Lealandra flicked on the entrance hall lights and closed the door, sliding every bolt into place and turning every lock. She tugged off her knee high boots and then walked into the lounge. The large white space still didn't suit Taig. She preferred his old apartment. That one had colour and life. That one had felt like a home.

The sound of the shower kicking in drew her attention to the bedroom. Her feet carried her there of their own volition and she moved as though in a dream, pulled to Taig and filled with a need to help him whether he liked it or not. His clothes were scattered across the bedroom floor and her eyes idly scanned over them before moving to the door of the bathroom. It was ajar.

Swallowing her nerves, she pushed it open. She shed her clothes and her inhibitions on her way to the shower cubicle and slid the door open. Taig had his back to her, the hot water bouncing off his shoulders and running through his black hair, plastering it to his head.

"Don't turn around," she warned and he dragged a hand over his hair, long fingers tangling in it. "I'm purely here to get these bullets out of you. That's all."

Lealandra stepped into the cubicle and slid the glass door closed. Even though the cubicle was big enough for two, Taig took up most of it. His broad tanned shoulders drew her gaze as he moved to accommodate her, shifting away from the spray of the shower. She stepped under the water and tilted her head back to wet her hair so it would stay out of her face while she worked. Taig sighed and every muscle on his back moved with it, dancing beneath his skin in a symphony that echoed on her heartstrings. Her gaze raked over him, refreshing her memory of his body. It lingered on the sculpted globes of his backside and the two dimples in his lower back above them. She had forgotten just how breathtaking his body was when he was naked. Six years without him suddenly felt as though it had been an eternity in Hell and she was itching to touch him, to trail her fingertips over every inch of his body and never stop.

He moved and she realised he was about to look over his shoulder at her. Coming to her senses, she reached up and pressed her hand to his cheek, pushing his head back so he couldn't see her.

"No peeking." Either her chastisement or the way her breasts squashed against his back elicited a long sigh from him. "Do you want a drink before I do this?"

A shake of his head was his answer. She set down on the heels of her bare feet and moved back a few inches so she could get a better look at the wounds. Rivulets of red mixed with the water running down his back. The wound she had removed the bullet from was already closing. She had forgotten he had preternatural healing speed. In a day or two, all evidence of tonight's attack would be gone from his body. He would be perfect again, save a few new scars to wax lyrical about in the future.

Lealandra held her hand an inch from the first wound and slowly drew it away, using her magic to pull the bullet free of his flesh. It clattered onto the floor of the shower and she moved onto the next, wanting to do it quickly so it would cause Taig less pain. The only sound Taig made as each bullet popped free of his skin was a low grunt but his arms were tense and trembling, his hands clenched into tight fists of restraint. His body could heal quickly but he still felt pain as keenly as a human did. The final bullet fell and she moved backwards, under the jet of water. Her hands shook when she placed them on his waist and brought him backwards with her until the water was running down his back. He hissed and went rigid.

Driven by a desire to take away some of the pain he was feeling, Lealandra ran her hands up his sides to his elbows and from there coursed them up over his strong arms to his shoulders. He relaxed a touch but there was still immense pain in him. It called to her power and made her want to heal him, sparking her curiosity again. When Charlie had died, she had understood why her magic had wanted to heal him. It had wanted to restore her Counter-Balance. Without it, she was in danger of slipping into the darkness that such potent power evoked within her. Was it possible that her magic saw Taig as a replacement Counter-Balance that needed restoration and protection, or was it her heart that dictated her actions? Confusion swam in her mind, filling her with conflicting thoughts. Taig couldn't be her Counter-Balance. He was half demon and bore no magic.

It had to be her heart that desired to heal him.

She stepped closer to him, pressed her hands against his back, and fixed her gaze on one of the wounds on his right shoulder. He took a deep breath, as though sensing what she was going to do. Her vision shifted out of focus, a hazy blur everywhere but the red hole. Her power rose, anticipating the taste of him. Closing her eyes the moment her lips touched his skin, she held the moan at bay and covered the wound with her mouth. She melted into him, her body flesh-to-flesh with his. The first touch of his blood on her tongue jolted her with the intensity of fifty thousand volts and she leaned into him, her reserve forgotten. She suckled slowly, savouring the taste of his blood and the way it went straight to her head and made her feel invincible. She had never tasted such sweet ambrosia but it came with a price. To heal the wounds, she needed to take a substantial amount of his blood. She would need Taig even more now. She didn't have the strength to go cold turkey again. This drug was too addictive. He was too addictive.

With a lap of her tongue, she sealed the first wound and moved on to the next. Her power flowed through her into the bullet holes while his blood flowed into her. A fair exchange in her eyes. For an infinitesimal moment, she wished he would get hurt more often so she could heal him again.

When she had sealed the final wound, she leaned her forehead against his back, drowsy with the power coursing through her, elevated by his blood. She held his shoulders, breathing deep and slow.

"Did it hurt?" she whispered, desire stealing her voice. She hoped it hadn't hurt too much.

"Like crazy," he said with a mirthless chuckle. The atmosphere in the room suddenly turned heavy, making it hard to breathe as she stood with her front pressed against his back and her arms draped around him. The shower cubicle felt tiny and confining. "But I swore to protect you."

Lealandra drew away from him and looked at his back. The red welts were already disappearing. It was the first time he had allowed her to use her power to heal him, at least consciously. She still couldn't understand why her power had healed Taig's hand and why it had been close to making her heal him against her will just now. It had to be her heart, not her magic doing it. She was just confusing them.

She touched the wound on his marked shoulder. "I didn't expect my payment to buy this level of protection."

"It didn't." He hung his head forwards and she looked up at him, wishing she could see his face and read his feelings in it. "The oath I made six years ago did."

A frown creased her brow. "Oath?"

She really wanted to see his face now.

"The night you left, I swore I would never let anything happen to you. Never. I mean to keep that oath, Lea. I don't need your money or anything to make me protect you."

Without a second thought, she moved around him and placed her hands on the hard muscles of his chest. She stared up at his face, feeling the full head's worth of difference in their height without her shoes. His wet hair clung in black spikes to his forehead, drawing her attention down to the endless ebony depths of his eyes. The tenderness in them, the affection that glittered there, stole her breath.

He had placed himself in the path of danger to protect her and she believed that he wanted nothing in return—at least nothing but her heart, and that she was willing to give to him now. Her hands rose to cup his cheeks, fingertips grazing the curve of his jaw and his ears. His words had moved her like none before them.

She lured his head down at the same time as she tiptoed and heat exploded inside her when their lips touched. The light, soft kiss carried every meaning she put into it. It was a thank you, a confession and an invitation.

He caught her waist in a firm grip, returning a message of his own. He wanted her too and he was going to have her. Both of them had been waiting for this moment these six long years.

His arms slid around her when he deepened the kiss, pulling her up against him, and her eyes opened wide when she felt his hardness against her belly. She rolled them closed again, aching with hunger and the desire to feel him inside her. She needed him inside.

He turned with her and she looped her arms around his neck when he raised her and settled her legs around his waist.

"Taig," she husked, breathless from the kiss and anticipation. He rocked his hips forwards, his hard length pressing against her mound, and she sunk her teeth hard into her lower lip and moaned as she stared into his eyes, lost in their black depths. Hunger threatened to take control but she fought it, wanting this moment to be more than just mindless sex.

Her fingers traced his wet cheek, her eyes still locked with his, reading every feeling surfacing in them. He had never been so open with her, not even at times like this. He had always kept her at arm's length, never lowering the barrier around his heart, but now she felt as though she was looking deep into it and she didn't want to tear her eyes away. She feared that he would close his heart to her again if she did.

"Lea," he whispered and inclined his head to capture her lips. The softness of his kiss surprised her and it was impossible to contain the feelings it stirred.

Her eyes closed and she sighed into his mouth, clinging to him and wondering how she had ever managed to live without him when she loved him so much it hurt.

Looking back, she realised that she and Taig weren't so different inside. She had closed off her own heart during their time apart, becoming cold and indifferent to others. Everything had become routine. Feelings she had shown towards others had been a reaction based solely on judgement of what the situation demanded and what she should feel, not what she had actually felt. She had been afraid of the intimacy of friendship and fearful of where it would lead her. She hadn't wanted to love anyone, and hadn't wanted anyone to love her. Her friendship with Charlie and Isabelle had been real but she hadn't given all of herself to them. She had kept them at arm's length too, just as Taig had with her, fearing that she would feel something real if they came too close or she let them into her heart.

Ascension

The only one she had wanted to love, and had wanted to feel that emotion towards her, was in her arms now, sweeping her away with his passion and need for her. She kissed Taig harder, desperate to feel more and feel this moment was real, that she was back in his strong embrace and that it was alright to open her heart again because he loved her and that was what she had wanted all this time. The world was right again. They were together and nothing would ever tear them apart.

Taig drew away from her briefly and then claimed her lips again, slowing her down so the pace of their kiss was unhurried, a sensual dance of his lips against hers, so feather-light that hers tingled. Her desperation passed and her heart warmed when she realised that he wanted this to be more than just a physical attraction too.

Strong arms slid around her, one claiming her backside and the other pressing between her shoulders, forcing her body against his. He was so warm now, his skin heated not only by the water but also by his desire. The tiles were cool against her back when he moved her to rest against them. She hooked her feet together around his waist and pushed her fingers through his thick black hair, tousling it into glossy spikes.

He trailed kisses down her neck and a moan escaped her. The feel of his tongue teasing the soft sensitive flesh of her throat sent tingles chasing through her, blistering heat in their wake. She leaned her head back into the tiles, overly aware of every drop of hot water bouncing off her left side and the way they trickled down her skin. Her power filled her, strengthened by Taig's blood but restrained by it at the same time. It heightened her senses until she was aware of everything. Shivers cascaded over her skin as Taig's body brushed hers. His warm breath against her throat and each kiss he placed there increased her desire and her body cried out for more. The beat of his heart mixed with hers, creating a sweet symphony in her ears.

"Damn I missed you," she whispered on a sigh when he moved to the other side of her throat, devouring it with gentle but hungry kisses that promised passion, the sort she had shared six years ago with him—consuming and wild.

"Me or my blood?" he laughed against her neck.

Lealandra slapped his back in reprimand for suggesting that what she was feeling was only because of his blood. She had never felt anything like what she felt for him and she wished with all of her heart that he would realise that, and would accept that her love was true. A low feral growl was his response. It vibrated through her, making her shudder with it and bite her lip.

"You..." She leaned her head forwards and kissed his shoulder, needing to taste him and feel he was in this moment with her. "All of you."

He stopped and leaned back until she couldn't reach his shoulder.

"All of me?" His expression was so deadly serious that her heart jumped and fluttered in her throat.

Their last conversation six years ago came back to her. She had confronted him about his hatred of his own kind and the fact he loathed his demon side.

He hadn't believed she could accept that part of him. He hadn't given her a chance to say that she could and she did. He had driven her away and she hadn't seen him since then. She had forgotten that they had parted on an argument. It was little wonder he had withdrawn from the demon world even more. She should have found the conviction and strength back then to tell him what he had needed to hear and what she had needed to say.

Taig's black eyes held hers, demanding an answer. She had one. The one she had wanted to give him six years ago.

Lealandra interlocked her fingers at the nape of his neck and slowly drew him back to her, making sure that their eyes remained locked and he couldn't escape her this time.

When he was close again, she stroked his cheek and smiled, warmth and lightness filling her as she looked at him, thinking about her feelings for him and how deeply they ran.

"Every last part of you," she whispered and his eyes lightened to the colour of blood, his pupils wide. She sighed and ran her fingers through the wet tendrils of his black hair, combing it back, and then over the shorter hair at the back of his head. "There isn't anything about you that I didn't miss."

A smile touched his lips briefly before he dipped his head and pressed them against hers. She closed her eyes and frowned when tears raced down her cheeks. It felt so good to be back in his arms. Everything she thought that she had lost forever was on the verge of being hers again and she couldn't contain her emotions. Taig understood her now. She had made both her feelings and her fears clear to him, and she knew that he wouldn't use them against her. He would no longer tease her about Charlie or be bitter because of what she had done. He would be as he had been six years ago—a man who loved her and would never hurt her.

His hands grasped her backside and he raised her up the wall. She kissed him slowly, hoping to encourage him into reclaiming her body as his and his alone. A contented moan rumbled in his throat as he eased his hard length into her and she couldn't help joining him with a sigh of her own. His movements inside her were unhurried, gentle and deep, adding to the strange sense of peace filling her. They had never taken things so slowly before. She felt connected to him, one body with two hearts that held the same feelings.

With each tangle of their tongues and thrust of his body into hers, all sense of danger drifted a little more into the distance. It was so easy to forget everything when she was with Taig, locked safely in his arms, the only place she wanted to be. No other man had ever made her feel the way that he did.

Lealandra moaned her loss when he broke their kiss and leaned back. The strength of his thrusts increased, his fingers digging into her backside, and she grasped his shoulders, staring into his eyes. They were black again but full of emotion. Her breath hitched in her throat and she forced herself to keep her eyes open, to watch him in this moment and realise that he returned her feelings. Whether he could put voice to them or not, she knew in her heart that he loved her too. He frowned and his body tautened as he groaned, his teeth sinking into his lower lip.

Fiery heat engulfed her belly, tightening it and bringing with it a sense of desperate need. She clenched him in her depths, moaning with each plunge of his length into her, drowning in his eyes. He groaned again and it turned into a harsh guttural growl when she climaxed, her body quivering around him as fire flashed through her. With another low growl, he pressed his body into hers and thrust deep inside her, throbbing with his own release.

She closed her eyes and leaned her head against his shoulder, a smile winding its way across her lips as she listened to his heart racing and felt his arms around her.

He was holding her tight and close, so possessively that she couldn't stop smiling. It told her something, and it was something she had been aching to know since walking back into his life.

Now that he had her again, he wasn't going to let her go.

CHAPTER 14

Taig held Lealandra close, trembling all over as he fought to regain composure. He pressed kisses to her wet dark hair, savouring the feel of her warm body against his, supple and small, curved perfectly into his. His woman was back where she belonged.

He sighed into her hair and closed his eyes. Her confession had floored him. Would she have told him that all those years ago if he had given her the chance? The thought that an angel like her could love a devil like him, all of him, felt like an impossible dream, something that could never happen to a demon. Perhaps his mother had truly loved his father after all, had known exactly what he was and had accepted him as a whole. His good mood began to fade as he thought about them and what Lealandra had considered earlier. He had overheard her conversation with her mother. The shift in Lealandra's power and the way she had felt had made it clear to him that she was going to attempt to find his parents. He didn't want that. He wanted to let them go.

A voice deep within him, in his heart, said that he did want to find them. He needed to see if they were alive and discover what had happened to them but was frightened to go to the underworld, to another place where he didn't quite belong. He scoffed at himself for being so weak and foolish. If she wanted to find his parents, if she believed that they were alive and that they had left him against their will, then he had no choice but to go with her. It wouldn't do him the good that she thought it would or change the way he felt about his demon side, but he couldn't let her go somewhere so dangerous alone. It didn't matter that she was destined to become more powerful than he was. He would keep his oath and protect her.

Taig pushed his thoughts away, to the back of his mind, aware that she would feel the darkness in him and his feelings when they were so close to each other. He didn't want to ruin the moment. Lealandra had missed him, all of him. The man and the demon. She thought she loved what lived beneath his human skin, beneath the façade. He believed in that and that was enough for him right now. When she saw the real him, if he ever allowed her to, then he would see if that love was real and if she could truly accept him for what he was.

Because he couldn't accept himself, no matter how much he tried. He wanted to belong in this world and to do that he had to be human, something someone could really love without fear and without regret. Lealandra could say that she loved him now but would she still love him if he ever revealed himself? He was talking about more than showing her claws and wings. He was talking about a full change, unleashing his true nature and shedding the human skin that bound him, releasing the violence that burned deep in his black heart.

"Taig?" Lealandra whispered. Her hands were warm points against his chest that kept him anchored in this world and with her. Whenever she touched him, he forgot everything. She filled his mind until he couldn't think. He could only act on impulse.

He looked at her, right into her eyes. Without realising it, he started searching them, trying to see if she had been telling the truth. Could she really love all of him? There was only one way of knowing. He had to show her what he really looked like, had to make her see that he really was a demon because he was sure that his human visage was deceiving her into thinking that she had feelings for him. When she saw his true face, she would leave.

Taig shook his head, trying to shake the thoughts away, and focused on her. Her breathing was steady, her body warm against his, deliciously close and soft. He could hear her heart beating and it went from a gentle patter to a canter when he smiled at her. Her power connected with his, curling itself around him, speaking to his own. It was hungry again. Lealandra was hungry again. Blood and sex. The most basic of needs when it came to old magic like Lealandra's. Only it was Lealandra who wanted the sex and her magic was content with his blood, for now. He was sure that would change soon enough though. If he gave her blood now, the magic would also want sex.

So he wouldn't give her blood. Not yet. He wanted this moment to be about her, them, and not her magic. He needed her to be in control and show him that she wanted him, that she did have feelings for him, not to screw him because the magic compelled her to.

He craved a stronger sign that she loved him.

He craved her.

Lealandra mumbled a protest when he lowered her to the ground and moved her under the shower. He ignored it and grabbed the shower gel. Squeezing some onto his hand, he lathered it up and then began washing her from head to toes. They had never showered together before. He liked how shy it made her. She tried to cover herself with her arms as though he had never seen her naked and this was their first time.

A quiet sigh escaped her parted lips when he soaped the top of her breasts and she opened up a little to him, lowering her arms so he could run his thumbs over her nipples and elicit a moan from her. Fascination claimed him when the ascension mark on her chest flashed into being and he stared at the symbol that matched the one on his back. He was destined to help her. His gaze moved to the one she had said meant love. Was she in love with him?

She took the shower gel and squeezed some onto his chest. His hands stopped their work when she ran hers over him, lathering the soap against his skin with a gentle touch.

Her caresses remained light as she cleaned him and turned tender when she reached his back and circled the closing bullet wounds with her fingertips. She kissed each one. It wasn't need for his blood that made her do it. There was affection in the soft kiss, a wish for each press of her lips to instantly heal him and take away his pain. He closed his eyes and hung his head forwards. He was an idiot for forcing her to leave him all those years ago, for not believing all the times she had shown him a glimmer of love.

Her hands pressed against his back, followed by her cheek. She sighed and he felt it against his skin.

"It's getting cold."

He turned to face her. He hadn't realised the water temperature had dropped. He wasn't as sensitive to changes in temperature as humans were. She gave him a small smile, reached around him, and turned the shower off. He slid the cubicle door open and then stepped back to let her pass.

His gaze fell to her backside as she walked across the bathroom and took the white towel robe down off the back of the door. He had forgotten just how beautiful her body was. He frowned when he dragged his gaze up and saw the long thin scars down her back. An image of them in the bedroom of his old apartment flashed across his eyes, writhing against each other, rough and passionate, both so hungry they were out of control. He walked over to her and she froze midway through putting the robe on when he touched her back. He placed each finger of his right hand against the start of each line and traced the marks downwards.

"I never realised I'd been that rough with you." His frown stayed in place as he stared at the scars. "I must've hurt you."

She looked over her shoulder, hugging the white robe to her chest. Her grey eyes smiled at him. "It didn't hurt. I don't think anything we did hurt at the time... or at least I didn't feel it."

He grinned.

"Besides," she shrugged, turned to face him and smiled shyly, "I remember getting my own back a few times."

Her fingers stroked the ragged scars on his broad chest and then she stepped up to him and ran her hands down his back. He growled when she cupped his backside and squeezed.

"Half of these scars are mine," she whispered and kissed the silvery lines that marked his chest, "and I don't even have claws."

He grinned again, remembering the way she would rake her nails down his chest, crying out his name as she rode him into oblivion. His cock twitched, growing hungry at the memories. He wanted her to do that again, to pin him to the bed and give it to him hard and rough.

Taig cleared his throat and reined in his desire. It wasn't going to happen. Not tonight anyway. Tonight was about her, about setting a different pace for their relationship and proving to her that he could do things slowly and with more feeling. He could be human for her if she needed him to be.

Lealandra's grey gaze roamed down over his torso and settled on his groin. Her tongue swept over her lips and he groaned. Of course, if she kept doing things like that, it was going to get difficult to control himself, and if she played rough, he might not be able to stop himself from doing the same.

She slid her hand into his and started walking backwards, leading him from the bathroom and into the bedroom. Taig's heart thundered, his blood rushing downwards. Her white robe fell open and hung on her breasts, revealing the curve of them, her navel and the neat triangle of dark curls at the apex of her thighs. He reached for her but she sidestepped. A mischievous smile settled on her face. If he didn't take control, she was going to have him clawing her back to shreds again. He could see it in her eyes. She wanted rough.

Not tonight.

Taig moved past her, leading her to the bed. She frowned when he removed her robe and wrapped his arms around her, gentle and slow, setting the pace. She tensed and tried to get her arms free and then contented herself with stroking the patch of his chest that she could reach. He waited a moment, until she was giving him a look that no longer spoke of a desire to be rough with him, and then lowered his mouth to hers. The kiss was soft, an outpouring of his feelings, all of them so strong that his breath trembled with each sweep of his lips over hers. He wasn't used to experiencing emotions as deeply as he was now. These past six years had been hollow without Lealandra, void of any positive emotions, even when he was thinking about her. His bitterness had tainted his memories. Only now could he remember their times together as they truly were—times that had made him happy, that had made him feel as though he belonged somewhere. With her.

He lay her down on the bed, covering her body with his, but keeping his kiss unhurried. The slow exploration of her lips and the gentle meeting of tongues stirred his blood but not in the usual way. He felt warm and calm, not mindless with passion and hunger. He wanted to be inside her but not because of a need to fulfil his desire. This time, it was born of a need to connect to her and be as one with her. He needed to make love with her.

Lealandra moaned and placed her hands against his back. Her fingers coursed over his muscles, tracing delightful patterns on them that increased the feelings inside him, fuelling the heat that filled his chest. He smiled against her mouth, worshipping her lips as he intended to worship the rest of her. Because he loved her.

She ran her hands up to his shoulders as he moved downwards, pressing light kisses to every part of her that he passed. Her throat. Her shoulder. Her chest. Her breasts. He swirled his tongue around her pert rosy nipples and then wrapped his lips around her left one and sucked. She groaned and arched against him, her hands gripping his shoulders. Drawing back, he blew on the sensitive peak to tease it so she moaned again, and then moved on downwards. Each kiss against her skin was a sign of his love, a declaration. She was everything to him. He had never needed anyone as he needed her.

He reached her hips and kissed a scar there. He remembered that one. He hadn't done it. It had happened when they had been hunting together. She had healed it and he had kissed it better afterwards. He kissed it again, reiterating his vow to himself. He would protect her. He would make sure that she survived her ascension and whatever dark force was after her. He would keep her safe for the rest of their lives. If she would have him.

Would she?

The thought that she wouldn't made him feel small and vulnerable, on the verge of breaking. He didn't like how exposed he felt, how easily his strength had disappeared. He needed Lealandra to stay with him. He couldn't lose her again. She was everything he needed, everything he wanted but never knew he did. She was his air and his reason for living.

He looked up the length of her, over the beautiful soft peaks and valleys of her torso to her face. Her hands left his shoulders and ran over her sides, caressing her body in a way that made him want to replace her hands with his. He stroked her thighs, running his fingers up them and dipping his thumbs in towards her crotch. She moaned and tilted her head back into the dark red duvet.

Taig inched her legs apart and lowered his hands, skimming the inside of her thighs. Lealandra arched and moaned again when his thumbs brushed the length of her groin. He moved back, so he was kneeling on the floor, and pulled her towards him. She gasped and tensed when his tongue delved into her plush petals and found her aroused clit. Her fingers instantly tangled in the longer strands of his hair, gripping tight, keeping him in a place where he didn't want to leave anyway, not until she was panting his name.

He teased her mercilessly, flicking his tongue against her one moment and dipping it down to her sweet opening the next. She tasted divine, heaven on his tongue. He greedily licked again, hungry for her, and then ran his tongue around her nub. Lealandra's fingers tensed in his hair, tugging. He smiled, hooked his hands over her thighs, pulled her right against his face and lapped at her, alternating between light strokes and hard presses of his tongue. She gasped again and writhed, her muscles tensing against him.

"Taig," she whispered and he grinned. That was a sound he loved to hear. The way she said his name when she was close to orgasm, when she was on the brink and needing that final push, was divine. He swirled his tongue again. "Taig!"

She stiffened a moment and then, after one more stroke of his tongue over her flesh, her thighs jerked and she thrust her hips up with a low moan. Her fingers loosened and her hand fell to his shoulder and then her thigh. She breathed hard, punctuating the beautiful sound with little moans. Taig stroked her inner thighs and she giggled, trying to writhe away so he couldn't tickle her in her afterglow.

Lealandra pulled on his shoulder. He obeyed the silent command and lowered her legs before coming to lie next to her on the bed. She moaned and rolled into him, pressing her warm body against his side, and he watched her face, refreshing his memory of how she looked when contented. He loved satisfying her.

Her hand roamed downwards, over his stomach. He tensed it for her and she groaned her approval. Her lips followed her hand and he closed his eyes, stretching his arms up and locking his hands behind his head. He willed her on. She stopped at his navel, her tongue tracing a circle around it, and, for a moment, he thought she wasn't going to go any further, but then she moved on, ever downwards. The anticipation of her touch coiled tight inside him, making his hard length jump eagerly when she reached it.

She pressed soft kisses along the length of his erection before wrapping her lips around the sensitive head. Taig growled and tensed his fingers against each other, gripping the back of his head. Lealandra moaned hungrily and sucked, her tongue torturing the head of his cock and driving him out of his mind. He held back his urge to pump into her mouth, to fill her with his aching erection. Her mouth left him, lips trailing down his length to his balls, and then her tongue caressed him as she licked back up to the head. He groaned and closed his eyes, frowning.

It was Hell. He wanted to thrust against her, to make her suck him hard and pump him with her hand. He bit his lower lip, sinking his teeth in. They threatened to extend when she put her mouth on him again, taking him all the way in this time and then running her tongue up him as she pulled back, sucking at the same time. He released his lip, afraid he would bite right through it if his demonic side did get the better of him. It was pushing for freedom, stirred by the feel of Lealandra and the things she was doing to him.

She took him into her mouth again, moaning, and moved so her legs were astride his. The heat of them against him intensified his frown and he groaned when she pressed her hands against his hips, holding him in place. Her damp hair tickled his stomach as she sucked his length, moaning with each plunge of his cock into her, as though she was enjoying it as much as he was. He growled when she sucked hard up his length and released him. He looked at her. She was smiling mischievously. His cock jumped again at the sight of her bending over him on all fours, her breasts swinging freely. Need rolled through him deeper than before, an urgent feeling that wouldn't pass. It only grew stronger. He wanted her.

Her tongue caressed her lips.

Damn he wanted her.

As if sensing his need, she crawled up the length of him. Her mouth fused with his in a kiss that seared him, making him eagerly rub his erection against her crotch. Needed her.

Taig was about to roll them over and bury himself in her warm depths when she pushed her hands against his shoulders and drew back. He stared wide-eyed into hers, seeing her intention written clearly in them. If she did that, he didn't have a hope in Hell of controlling himself.

"Lea, I—"

"Shh." She pressed her finger against his lips to silence him. "I got the memo. Slow and steady it is."

He groaned when she took hold of his cock and positioned it at the opening of her slick warm core. Their combined sighs filled the silence when she eased back onto him, sheathing him in her body, and he bit his lip again and grasped her thighs. She settled on him, a satisfied look on her face, and then took hold of his waist.

Taig could only stare into her eyes as she rode him, slow and steady, just as she had promised. The feel of her hot body around his, of being one with her in this moment, made his power reach for her. They connected and entangled, until they too became one and he could feel everything that she did. It was bliss. Their feelings mirrored each other perfectly but the strength of one feeling within her outshone his.

Love.

There was so much love in her and the way she was looking at him made him believe for the first time that it was real. Perhaps she didn't just have feelings for his human side.

Lealandra moaned and her eyelids dropped to half-mast. He couldn't tear his gaze away from her. He was lost in the emotions running through her and how it felt to be inside her. Her rise and fall was steady, tender, everything he had wanted it to be. She tensed around him, clenching him in her depths, and he groaned, his hands tightening against her thighs. She smiled and did it again, eliciting another moan from him that verged on a growl.

His demon rose to the surface, drawn by her power, and he was surprised by how calm it was. It didn't push for freedom or threaten to take control. It was merely there, one with him for a change, lost in this moment together. All of him loved Lealandra and both sides of him needed to know that she loved him too. He needed to see if she could love a demon, because he was beginning to believe that she could and he felt more vulnerable than ever. If he accepted that her love was real, then their time together became more real too, and the future began to matter.

He had always lived for the moment, uncaring of the danger he placed himself in, almost seeking out death. If Lealandra really loved him, he would need to be more careful, and not only with himself. Her happiness would be his responsibility and he would have to find a way to live with his demon lineage and protect her so it would never be responsible for her demise or pain. Was this how his father had felt, fearing his demon side because it could be a danger to his mother?

Anger burned deep in his heart, bitterness filling his mouth with an acrid tang, and Taig pushed his thoughts of his parents away, not wanting them to ruin this time with Lealandra. One day he might be able to accept himself but he doubted he could ever accept his father now, not after everything he had been through because of him.

Lealandra slowed her movements and he sensed the shift in her feelings. His distant silence was concerning her. He focused on her where she sat astride him, her warm body wrapped around his. She was beautiful. Her wet black hair streamed down over her breasts, hiding their dusky peaks, and her slender thighs pressed into his. She grazed her hands over his sides and her grey eyes met his. He groaned when she moved on him, his cock sliding deep inside her hot sheath, and bit his lower lip again, no longer caring if he drew blood.

Her lips parted and her breathing quickened to match his. He tilted his head back and frowned, his eyes remaining locked on her. She pressed her hands into his stomach, riding him harder, urging them both towards climax. Taig grasped her thighs and thrust into her, slow and deep, countering her movements so as she moved down, he moved up into her. She groaned and closed her eyes, a frown creasing her brow.

"Taig," she whispered and he growled in response.

Her movements became jerky and then she moaned and stiffened. He plunged into her and she gasped, her body convulsing around his, drawing him close to the edge. He continued thrusting as she stilled, captivated by her climax. He growled at the feel of her body milking his and her warmth covering his cock. She opened her eyes and looked deep into his. He tensed and then buried himself inside her and came with another long low growl.

Lealandra smiled and eased down to lay on his chest, her breathing rough and warm on his skin.

He wrapped his arms around her and sighed slowly to steady his thundering heart.

"Growly," she whispered and circled his right nipple with her fingertip.

Lealandra was right. He wasn't normally like that. His demon receded, peaceful and sated. Satisfied. He had never had such control over it and it had never played a part in his lovemaking with Lealandra. He frowned, trying to figure it out.

It hadn't been a threat and he hadn't been close to changing. It had been one with him, a part of him, just as his father had said it would be if he practiced controlling himself.

Perhaps Lealandra was right and all this time he had been wrong.

He was a man.

And his demon side was a part of that man, not a separate being to loathe or hide.

He closed his eyes and drew Lealandra closer to him. Her breathing became soft and shallow. Her heart drummed steadily against his chest.

Thoughts kept him awake. He couldn't shake them.

Could he really come to accept his demon side and his past?

He still wasn't sure if he was strong enough to do such a thing. He had never been any good at letting go of his anger, and his feelings about his parents' disappearance and his demon side had fuelled him for over twenty years. Could he let go of such pain and move on?

Even if Lealandra loved him, could accept both sides of him, could he accept himself?

His demon blood still felt like a curse more than anything, a barrier that stood between him and leading a normal life, and the very thought of his father made his blood boil with a desire to destroy. He didn't want to be like him. He wanted to be human, because then he would never be a threat to Lealandra. She would always be safe around him then. If he were human, he would be certain, would easily believe, that she really did love him with all of her heart.

But he wasn't human, and he never would be, no matter how hard he tried to be one. He couldn't erase his demon blood. It pounded in his veins, a dark force that pushed for control. He was a monster and Lealandra's love would never change that.

Could she really love someone who was both man and monster?

Because both man and monster loved her.

Taig stared at the ceiling, emptying his mind. He focused on the feel of Lealandra resting softly against him, warm in his arms where she belonged, her legs tangled with his, and held her close, savouring the calm, a feeling that he had longed for from the moment she had walked out of his life. The conflict he felt about himself slowly drifted to the back of his mind, drowned out by positive emotions, but he couldn't rid himself of it completely. It lingered in his heart.

He needed time to think, needed space to come to terms with everything and get his head straight, but that wasn't going to happen anytime soon, not with Lealandra's ascension coming and demons to hunt. For now, he would see where things took him, and hope that Lealandra didn't push him.

Because he was a bomb with a very short fuse and she loved playing with fire.

CHAPTER 15

Lealandra slowly traced the intricate dark swirls of Taig's mark on his shoulder blade, her grey gaze following her fingertips. His breathing was slow and deep in the quiet low-lit room, bringing a smile to her face. An hour ago, he had awoken her in the most delicious way just to tell her that she had fallen asleep, kissing her softly and kneading her bottom with one hand while he caressed her breast with the other. She was tempted to kiss him awake but resisted. He sighed, rolled onto his front, the red bed covers riding low on his hips, and turned his head to face her.

Her exploration shifted course, rounding the dark pink marks on his broad back, inspecting each one to make sure they had healed, and eventually creeping up his neck to his cheek. She caressed the line of his jaw, swept the rogue dark strands of hair from his forehead, and sighed with him.

How could a man with so much brash confidence be so vulnerable? He would hate for her saying it, would deny it completely, but she knew how he felt on the inside. Only she hadn't realised just how strong those feelings were until she had come here and seen the level of protection he had put on his apartment. He could pretend all he wanted that there wasn't a problem but she could see that there was, and that it affected him. He felt inadequate, unloved and unaccepted. She ached to take that pain away and make him see that his parents had been in love, that it was possible for a demon of his father's power to love a mortal, and that it was possible for her to love Taig just the same.

It wasn't just that though. She was sure that she could make him believe that one day. It was also making him believe that his parents had truly loved him and hadn't abandoned him for whatever reason he thought—not because he was mixed blood or an aberration. The love in his parents' eyes in the picture told her that they never would have left him of their own free will.

Lealandra stroked his cheek, her eyebrows furrowing as she thought about everything that Taig had been through and all the times she had tried to talk to him about his parents. She wanted to help him but it was impossible when he slammed the door in her face at every turn and wouldn't even entertain the thought of talking about it with her, let alone actually doing it.

His lashes fluttered and then his ebony eyes opened and fixed on her.

"You think too loud." He smiled sleepily. "Something on your mind, sweet cheeks?"

Could she tell him?

If she did, would he shove her aside again?

Was she moving too fast?

It tore at her, turning her stomach and making her hesitate. She didn't want him to push her away, not this time, not after everything they had been through. She wanted him to listen for once and to talk to her. He was terrible at sharing, at opening himself up to her, but she needed him to give it a shot. He needed it.

"Your father—"

Taig growled. "Not this again."

He rolled away, heading for the edge of the bed. Lealandra wasn't about to let him escape that easily. She threw herself on him, hindering his movements, and managed to get astride him. His bare body felt cool and tempting beneath her hips and hands but she ignored the desire that just the feel of him stirred within her.

"Your father loved your mother." She pressed her hands into his shoulders.

"I know." His ebony gaze held hers, no trace of anger in it.

Her fine eyebrows rose. She had thought he would deny that. It gave her a little courage but she still felt as though she was walking along an eggshell covered path that was leading straight for a high cliff. He might look calm, might sound calm, but she could feel the tension growing within him and it was a warning not to push him too far.

Well, for once she was going to ignore the blaring sirens and risk his anger.

"And I'm sure they loved you."

"Did they tell you that?" He smirked and his eyes narrowed, the edges of his irises and around his pupils burning red. "If you have a hotline to them, do tell them I'd like to know why the fuck they left me."

Lealandra trembled when a dark wave of power surged through her. Her magic shrank away, going deep as though it was afraid too. She had never felt Taig this angry but it wasn't going to deter her. Talking about his father was treading on ice so thin that she was walking on water but she had to try to get him to talk. If he did, he would feel better. It was just an automatic reaction for him to act like this whenever she mentioned his father. She was sure of it.

"What if they didn't have a choice, Taig? What if someone captured them?"

"It doesn't change a thing." He caught her wrists and pushed her back. Lealandra twisted free of his grasp and grabbed his wrists, turning the tables on him. Her gaze locked with his. He snarled. "Drop it."

"No."

"I'm not talking about this." There was an edge to his voice and his power that warned her that he wasn't joking.

She wasn't either. "Talk to me."

"No." He broke free of her grasp and lifted her off him. "Shut up and go to sleep."

Lealandra climbed back on him, her gaze steely, and pinned his shoulders. Her heart thundered, blood rushing and causing her magic to rise when Taig's abated. Taig glared at her.

"Just let me in this once, Taig. Please? I only want to help you."

"Why?"

Lealandra had to look away, was too afraid to let him see the reason in her eyes or say the words. She loved him so much. If she said it now, he wouldn't believe her, not even when she had shown it to him in so many different ways. He would still think that she was lying, or would find a way to fault her love for him and make out that it wasn't real when it was. She had loved him from the moment she had met him. His demon side didn't frighten her. It was a part of him. It made him Taig. The man she loved with all of her heart. The man who hated himself with all of his.

"I hate seeing you loathe yourself. I hate seeing you trying to be something that you aren't." Her gaze flickered to his.

Taig growled and tried to get away again. She frowned and her magic surged through her, reinforcing her strength and keeping him stuck to the bed. He bucked and snarled. Lealandra didn't let go. She wouldn't let him go. Never again.

"Just talk to me, God damn it. Let me in!" Her throat tightened, fear and hope constricting it, and she bit back the tears as her eyes searched his. Just this once she wanted him to let her past the barrier and into the fortress that protected his heart. She wanted to share his pain and help him heal.

He stilled beneath her, his red eyes penetrating hers, daring her to make a move.

Lealandra touched his face, a light trembling caress, and felt his pain. She felt so much for him. So sorry. He would hate her for pitying him, belittling his strength with her worry and fears, with her love. She wasn't doing this to make him hate her but she would take it all if it would lessen how much he hated himself and would give him a moment's respite from his endless hurt and despair. It all flowed into her, every ounce of his pain, all of it stemming from his mixed blood and his parents' disappearance. What could she do to make him change his mind about it all and make him see that she loved him for what he was—a demon and a man? She would do anything.

"Speak to me." She brushed her thumb across his lower lip. "I'm not asking you to open up and let me in, Taig. I'd settle for just talking about it."

The dark look in his eyes said that it wasn't going to happen. She was fighting a battle she would never win, at least not like this. Trying to make him talk about it had been a foolish idea. She should have bitten her tongue and let him be the one to tell her, no matter how long that took. But she was impatient. She couldn't wait forever for him to let her in. She wanted it to be now, was scared that she wouldn't make it through the ascension and would never know if he loved her, would never hear the words that she so desperately needed him to say to her. She sighed.

"I meant what I said today."

"You'd better not try to find them, Lea." The venom in his tone matched the spark of anger that bolted through him.

She smiled slowly to herself. He never had been any good at seeing the meaning in her words. She always had needed to spell things out for him.

"No. Not that. I meant what I said..." Lealandra looked deep into his eyes and opened herself to him, so he could sense things through where they touched and would know that she was telling the truth. "I missed you. I broke my heart that day and fractured yours in the process... and I'm sorry... I... if I'd known it would turn out this way, and that I'd really hurt you... I didn't want to push you like that and make you—"

Taig tried to shove her off him, discomfort and anger written all over his scowl. Lealandra pushed his shoulders back against the mattress, making him stay and listen. He needed to hear this. She didn't care if he hated her for saying it. Someone had to tell him and make him see.

"This place isn't you, Taig! You know that deep in your heart." She lightened the pressure on his shoulders when he stilled again and then stroked his chest, following the line of his pectorals to the point over his heart. She rested her hands there and looked at them, focusing on his feelings and the growing connection between their powers. "You don't belong here... thinking you're fitting in when you're all alone."

Taig scoffed. "Where do I belong then? Tell me that."

"You don't belong anywhere. Not back there and not here." Lealandra took hold of his hand and brought it to her chest, placing it over her heart. Her eyes met his. "You belong here."

Taig's eyes narrowed. "You said I didn't belong here."

"Not this apartment." Her ascension mark shone when his fingers grazed it, lighting the room in red. "Here with me. I never should have left you."

"It's nothing I'm not used to." He took his hand back and the mark dulled back to black.

Lealandra sighed, gently caught his hand again, and kissed it. "Don't hate him... don't hate yourself... your parents loved you."

Taig shoved her aside, so she hit the bed, and stormed towards the door, grabbing his clothes en route. He turned back and glared at her. "Stay the hell out of my business."

He disappeared before she could say anything. Lealandra stared at the empty living room of the apartment through the door and then huffed. Stay the hell out of his business? She was in love with him, and she was damn well sure that the feeling went both ways and he loved her. That made him her business as far as she was concerned.

She dressed and walked through the lifeless apartment to the photograph of his parents. They were in love and she was sure that they had loved Taig. What had happened all those years ago? Was it as her mother thought and they were in the underworld, trapped there, separated from their son and forced to watch him live alone and suffer?

Would Taig try to stop her if she went there to find them? She would do that for him. She would do anything to make him happy and make him accept both sides of himself.

Her gaze swept over the apartment. This place wasn't him. He had hated her for saying it, but it was the truth. This was hollow and void of feeling, something that she knew he wasn't. He didn't know how to be a human. Neither did she. Couldn't he see that? They were in this together, neither of them human, both of them unable to live a normal life.

But they had each other.

She had to find him.

Lealandra tried to teleport out but a barrier blocked her. Closing her eyes, she sensed it, feeling her way around it and familiarising herself with the way that Taig had constructed it. It was powerful, but she could slip through it. There was a back door, a path that Taig had taken, and she knew him well enough to be able to find it and follow it. Latching her magic onto the trace of his power, she followed it to the point where he had reappeared. It was the area where they had fought the immortal.

There was no sign of Taig in the dark graveyard. She could feel him but he had moved on, heading back into the city.

Was he going to the club?

Lealandra headed there, pulling her long red coat tightly around herself to keep the chill off. It wasn't far to the club and she wasn't pleased to be back. She smiled at the bouncer when he let her in ahead of the stream of wannabe vampires and women in far too little clothing, and then it fell off her face when she made it inside and caught a glimpse of Taig through the crowd.

He was at the busy curved black bar, sitting near the far corner.

Talking to a very pretty blonde woman.

The woman laughed, smiled, spoke to him with a glint in her eye that Lealandra was intimate with. She had given Taig that look plenty of times. An open invite to do what he pleased with her.

Lealandra held herself and watched him through the throng of people for a few seconds more, and then turned away when the hurt became too much. Her chest ached and she blinked away the tears, telling herself not to be so foolish and read into things. Taig loved her. She was just overreacting.

If he loved her, why was he smiling and laughing with another woman?

She went to leave but stopped when she saw the vampire standing at the door, his gaze on her. He smiled, no trace of fangs on show, and pointed towards a quiet area opposite the bar. Lealandra told herself not to but she went with him anyway, part of her hoping that Taig would see and would know how much it hurt to be jealous.

"I had not expected you to return." The vampire's pale eyes met hers and he slid into the red crescent-moon-shaped seat.

Lealandra sat opposite him, the round black table strategically placed between them so he couldn't easily reach her. She could probably defeat him if he tried something but she wasn't willing to take chances. All she wanted to do was make Taig jealous and then leave. She glanced past the vampire to Taig where he was still at the bar, necking whisky and grinning foolishly at the woman. A dark snake coiled inside her and her power rose, entwining with her emotions and demanding that Taig return to them where he belonged. Whether he knew it or not, he was hers now, always had been from the moment they had met, and no two-bit whore was going to change that.

They owned Taig.

She cleared her throat and locked down her power and her feelings, pulling on the reins to bring them under control. Her magic was angry, hungry, and most of all ready for a fight, and that wasn't a good thing. The effect of Taig's blood on her power was wearing off and her patience was wearing thin. The combination was deadly and it was a struggle to remain calm and in control when she was feeling such strong emotions. She had to though. The consequences of losing it in a public place were enough to keep her fighting her magic. She didn't want to kill everyone here. She didn't want to be responsible for their violent deaths.

"Hunters often gather here. If she is bothering you, I can have her dealt with."

Lealandra's gaze shot back to the vampire. His dark-ringed pale irises mesmerised her and she dropped her gaze to the table, unwilling to fall for that trick again.

"Who is she?" Her gaze traced the echoes of glasses that remained on the shiny black tabletop, ingrained into it now, an endless pattern of circles. She thought about the vampire's eyes and how she was going to have to avoid falling under his spell again. She wanted Taig jealous, not her neck cut and her power stolen. If the vampire took her blood, he would take a trace of her magic too. Vampires were strong enough without stealing the power of another, but they were the lowest form of leech, desperate at all times to feed, and with blood came the abilities of those who had once owned it. The vampire had wanted the immortal's blood and therefore his power, and she had no doubt that he wanted the same from her.

"She is often here. A hunter but nothing like the demon you stare at so adoringly."

Her gaze crept to Taig across the sea of people and then away to the vampire when her power rose at the sight of him with another woman. The vampire raised his fine black eyebrows and leaned casually into the chair, stretching his arms out across the red velvet back. He smiled at her, all straight white teeth, as though he wanted her to see that right now he wasn't a threat. The lack of fangs didn't satisfy her instincts. He was still dangerous and could extend his fangs at a moment's notice. She wasn't about to trust him.

Lealandra unleashed her power a fraction, just enough that the vampire stopped smiling at her as though he was her best friend, and started being more honest with her and to the point.

"And do they often talk like this?" She glanced at Taig and the woman.

"They have partnered a few times." The vampire looked away when she stared at him with red eyes, her magic surging through her veins and whispering to kill him for saying such a thing.

Taig belonged to them.

Lealandra tamped it down and brought it back under control, but it was harder this time. Her power was growing tired of this game and if she didn't get Taig jealous and back to her soon, it was going to let the entire club know of its disapproval and she didn't think that she was strong enough to stop it.

"Not like that. Strictly professional as far as I know. He normally works alone. Ah, speaking of jobs... would you be interested in making fifty large? I still have a contract that needs fulfilling and you would be perfect for the job."

His smile unnerved her. It thinly veiled the hatred she could feel in him, the dark urges that flowed across the table from him and into her. They spoke to her power, teasing it with an offer of release and destruction. Fifty thousand dollars. She could use that sort of money.

"How about we discuss it over a drink?" The vampire was gone before she could refuse the drink and the contract.

What in the gods names was she doing? She had never taken a contract by herself and now certainly wasn't the time to start. Her gaze scanned the club. It was bad enough that she had come out here without Taig's knowledge and was risking his wrath to make him jealous. What if the bastards who had shot him came to the club and found her before Taig noticed? She could fight them, but she wasn't sure how it would end. There was a high chance that she would take the entire club with them if she unleashed her magic and that might include Taig.

The vampire returned, lazily sliding into the seat opposite her, and placed a short glass of something down in front of her. It looked like whisky but was darker. She picked it up and sniffed it. It smelt like whisky and drowning her sorrows had a certain appeal to it right now.

The vampire raised his glass.

"To future relations." He grinned.

Lealandra raised hers, tipped her head back, and drained the glass. It burned a path down her throat and then she felt strangely hot and hazy. Her gaze met the vampire's and his eyes were bright again, shining in the darkness. She smiled, pressed her hand to her mouth when she hiccupped, and then fought to keep her eyes open. She felt so weird. Her body seemed separate to her mind, numb and beyond her control. Her power shrank back and then exploded forwards, rushing through her. She threw her head back and then moaned when something traced a line up her neck, softly caressing her skin and setting her aflame. It felt so good.

Firm hands clutched her upper arms, pinning her in place, and she didn't resist. She didn't want to.

A mighty roar shattered the noise of the club, bringing silence in its wake, and she trembled at the dark power that trickled through her, making her blood buzz with anticipation and hunger.

Taig.

Incredible strength surged in her veins and through her body, pulsing over her in seductive waves that pulled her under and carried her away. She closed her eyes and licked her lips, aching to feel something stronger, rougher, something that could break her if it wanted to and could command her.

The thing that had been caressing her throat disappeared in a collision of sounds, all of them indistinct. She fluttered her eyes open and stared blankly, not taking in what was happening, only catching snippets of it in her throbbing mind. The vampire was in trouble. She giggled and smiled, amused at the sight of him fighting for his life in the space that had opened up in front of the bar. People edged backwards, cramming the crowd into an even smaller space. Their emotions pounded in her skull, conveying their conflict. None of them could decide whether to keep well clear or stick around to watch the brawl.

She couldn't blame them.

Taig was a very jealous man.

His eyes glowed red, teeth sharp and showing a trace of his demon side. He ripped into the vampire, beating the hell out of him, and then flung him across the room. The club patrons scattered as he and the vampire wreaked havoc, destroying tables and smashing everything in sight. It was glorious.

Lealandra laughed.

Taig turned on her, his red eyes meeting hers. Before she could laugh again, he had her wrist and was yanking her towards the doors. She pouted and stumbled along behind him, scratching at his hand on her. She didn't want to leave yet. Her gaze flicked back to the vampire. He was still breathing. It wasn't right to leave when their quarry was still alive.

With a grin, she snapped her fingers and the vampire contorted, his bloodied limbs twisting into strange shapes. She laughed and darkness pounded through her, whispering to destroy.

"Stop that." Taig shook her and she tilted her head back and looked down her nose at him.

Who was he to order her around?

She was about to snatch her arm back and teach him a lesson when his fist came out of nowhere, colliding with her cheek, and the world wavered and grew dark.

When the light came back, Lealandra was cold and aching. Pain wracked her and her magic flared back into life, dulling her feelings but not getting rid of them completely. She squinted to focus and found Taig standing before her, a dirty alley as his backdrop. He bit his wrist, his red eyes fixed on hers, and then pressed it against her mouth.

"Drink."

Lealandra didn't. She stared into Taig's eyes, watching the flickering flames. It felt as though they were burning into her, setting her on fire. Her skin crawled with fear and heat, tingling with a need that she couldn't place.

"Drink deep." Taig pressed his wrist harder against her lips and she swept her tongue over the ragged marks. The first touch of blood on her tongue was bliss, tempering her power until it ebbed away. The heat began to abate, leaving her feeling more aware of her feelings and more in control. "I'll take care of you, sweet cheeks."

Taig brushed his other hand across her cheek. "I'm sorry I hit you but you didn't exactly leave me a choice."

She was aware of that and embarrassed by her behaviour. It wasn't like her to take pleasure from someone else's torment and pain.

He ran his hand into her long black hair, caressing it back behind her ear, and she closed her eyes, shakily raised her hands and clutched his wrist to her mouth. She kept drinking, unsure of what she was doing but following Taig's command because she was starting to feel more like her normal self.

"I'll take care of that bastard's blood. Clean it all up and make you better."

Her eyes opened and she stared into the bright red pools of Taig's, lost in them and the horror that crept over her. The vampire had given his blood to her. He had spiked her drink and drugged her to control her. She felt so stupid.

"There. All better." Taig took his wrist away and carefully swept his thumb over her lips to clear the blood away. He looked into her eyes for a few seconds more and then pulled her into his arms, wrapping her tight in his strong embrace. "I won't let anyone hurt you."

Her eyes slipped shut and she grabbed fistfuls of his shirt, feeling weak. She had been such an idiot. Gods knew what danger she had placed herself in just to make Taig jealous. If he hadn't noticed, she would've ended up giving the vampire exactly what he had wanted. Blood. He probably would've drained her dry.

A flash of the woman crossed her mind. A reminder of why she had been drinking with the vampire to start with.

Lealandra pressed her cheek against Taig's chest and listened to the hard beat of his heart. Provoking him while he was on edge and ready to fight would get her nowhere but she couldn't let it slide. She had to know. He had to know.

"I already am hurt," she whispered.

Taig pushed her off him and his gaze darted over her, taking her all in and lingering longest on her neck. His eyes brightened until the fires of Hell burned in them.

"Did he bite you? I should've come quicker. I knew that bastard was after something the moment he spoke to you."

Her blood froze. Taig had seen her with the vampire and hadn't come to her? She pulled free of his arms and glared at him, breaking inside at the thought he would do such a thing. He had left her vulnerable. He had stayed with that woman.

Lealandra turned away.

Taig brushed her coat collar and hair aside and touched her neck, and she ignored the shiver that swept over her at the light caress. "No marks."

Idiot.

She wrapped her arms around herself and kept her back to him.

"Who hurt you, Lea?" There was a command in his tone. She ignored that too. He didn't let her. He grabbed her shoulder and spun her to face him. His eyes burned brighter, flickering from red to orange. "Who hurt you?"

She cast her gaze downwards and sighed. "You."

"I didn't mean to shout at you back at my place and I said I was sorry that I hit you."

A mirthless laugh escaped her. Had he always been so blind? Was his denial of her feelings for him the reason he always got the wrong end of the stick at times like this?

She took a deep breath and met his gaze. "The hunter."

He frowned and then it slowly melted away and his eyebrows rose. A moment later, he was rolling his eyes and dragging her back into his arms.

"Is that what this is about?" he murmured against her hair, holding her close as he stroked it. "You put yourself at risk to repay me for talking to that woman? And I thought I was insane. I never had you pegged as someone stupid enough to do that. Lea, I haven't looked at another woman since first laying eyes on you. There's no one but you. No one."

Lealandra cursed the gods and him, and leaned against his chest, seeking the comfort of his embrace. Calm washed through her, brought about by his tender tone and what he had said, and she wanted to stay in this moment with him forever.

"Were you even a little jealous?" Hope beat in her chest.

"I kicked the shit out of him, didn't I?" Taig went quiet and then sighed. "I wanted to kill him the other night for just looking at you... now I want to kill him a thousand times over. No one but me gets to touch you like that. You're mine, Lea, and I'm not the sharing type."

Lealandra closed her eyes, relief blossoming sweet and warm deep in her heart. It wasn't the confession of love that she had been hoping to hear for the past six years, but it was a start. It was enough to reinforce her belief that he loved her.

Deep in his heart, he loved her.

Taig kissed her hair and sighed with her, his broad chest pressing against her cheek. He rubbed her arms.

"We should get you home."

Lealandra stilled at those words. Did he realise what he had said? He had called his place her home. A smile snuck onto her lips and she warmed at the thought. Her home was right here in his arms. She wasn't going to leave it again, not for anyone or anything. She wasn't quite ready to admit it to him and to see him gloat, but she was glad that she was back and they were together again, and nothing would part them this time.

Not even her ascension.

"I can teleport us back." She emerged from his arms and looked up at him.

Taig smiled, the sort of one that always made her heart flutter and made her feel like a giddy girl. She never had been able to resist him when he turned on the charm. She stepped into him and his eyes melted from red to black. His smile faded, replaced by a serious look, and he stared deep into her eyes.

"It's a nice night for flying."

Lealandra searched his eyes to see if he really was serious and not just pretending to be. There was an edge to his ebony gaze that said not to question him so she didn't. This was the first step towards him letting her in and talking to her, and accepting himself, and she wasn't about to ruin it.

Her eyes widened when he backed away from her and unbuttoned his black shirt before removing it to reveal the smooth bronzed planes of his torso. She told herself not to gawp but her heart overruled her mind and she raked her gaze over his muscles, from the compact lines of his abdomen to the strong bulge of his biceps. He radiated power and she couldn't resist.

"I've already ruined one of my favourite shirts today." He tied the black shirt around his waist, causing his muscles to ripple.

He stilled when she stepped forwards and ran her hands over his forearms, heading upwards across his biceps to his shoulders. His gaze followed her hands as she swept them over his broad chest, marvelling at his strength and beauty, and then met hers. He was gorgeous, his dark eyes holding hers, challenging her. She inclined her head, luring him in little by little, tempting him to kiss her.

He didn't.

He bent and scooped her up into his arms, holding her around her back and under her knees.

Lealandra gasped when huge black leathery wings erupted from his back, almost filling the small alley. His wingspan was impressive, each wing reaching over ten foot when stretched. Would it be enough to support them both though? It was one thing flying alone, a completely different one carrying a passenger. He wouldn't notice her weight, but his wings would.

"Don't fret, sweet cheeks. We're good." With that, he beat his wings and lifted into the air with her.

Lealandra curled up against him, threw her arms around his neck, and prayed to every god that she knew that they would make it back to his apartment in one piece and that he wouldn't drop her.

Because teleporting when rushing towards the ground from a dizzying height was something that she had never done before.

And she didn't want to see if she could perform magic under that sort of pressure.

CHAPTER 16

Once they were flying for a few minutes, Lealandra began to relax. It seemed Taig's wings could easily take the extra weight and he had whispered quiet reassurances to her the whole time they had been airborne. She uncurled slightly, keeping a tight grip on Taig's neck, and looked around at the darkness. The city was a rush of lights below her. Rivers of red and white marked the roads. Taig had flown high at the start but her nails digging in to the back of his neck seemed to have conveyed her fear enough for him to drop lower. It was warmer nearer the buildings and the view took her mind off the fact that she was still a few hundred feet above a very hard surface. If she fell, would her magic be calm enough to teleport her to safety? It had survival instincts too. Surely it would save her?

Or Taig would.

She smiled at that thought and pictured it happening. He would swoop like an eagle to save her, catching her in his arms and making everything better. Lealandra cleared her throat. She was being so girlish and silly since walking back into Taig's life. Had she felt like this around him before? Usually she was strong, but around him, she felt as though she didn't need to be. She could be the woman she was inside, without fear of him thinking that she was weak. He would protect her.

"Almost there." Taig's voice was distant to her ears, barely audible over the rush of wind and the beating of his wings. It was incredible to fly with him like this.

His gaze remained fixed straight ahead, his dark eyebrows drawn together in concentration. She could feel his discomfort and how hard he was thinking, and she didn't push him to talk to her. He needed space and she was going to let him have it. This was enough for her right now, a sign that he would let her in one day and talk to her.

"You're pretty good at this." Lealandra smiled again when he glanced at her out of the corner of his eye.

Silence.

The sense of turmoil inside him increased and she wondered if she had said something wrong. She had only wanted him to see that the wings didn't scare her and neither had the claws that she had seen. Nothing about Taig frightened her. She loved him so much that it didn't matter what he looked like as a demon. If he ever showed her, she was sure that she would love that side of him too. It was still him.

Still the man she had fallen for.

"My father taught me to fly."

Lealandra's eyes shot wide and she tried to keep from tensing. This was a step that she hadn't been expecting. She wasn't sure how to proceed now. His unease increased, flowing through her, and she ran her fingers into his black hair, wanting to soothe him and give him support.

"He had wings too?" She stroked his hair and kept her gaze on his profile, studying the minute changes in his expression and his feelings.

Taig nodded, distant and focused.

Silence.

Was that it? It was a start, she supposed, but now she wanted more. She wanted to talk about this and slowly work her way past his defences and into his heart.

A smile tugged at his lips. "My mother used to have kittens whenever we went out flying. I always came back hurt."

"Why?"

"It's not exactly easy to explain. I don't think you'd under—what am I saying? No. You of all people would understand." He glanced at her again. "I lacked harmony with my demon blood even back then. I've never found it. My father tried to teach me all sorts of things but I could never do them properly because I'd see something like a bunch of kids playing in the fields and I'd want to do that instead."

The sound of his wings beating filled the pause and Lealandra looked at them and then back at Taig. She hoped he wasn't lacking harmony tonight because from what she could tell, he was talking about dropping out of the sky the moment he lost the connection to his demon side.

Taig's voice lowered to a whisper. "I never understood why he wouldn't let me... why he'd make me stay in and try to teach me all that crap."

"He wanted to protect you." The answer was obvious to Lealandra. Taig's father had been trying to teach him everything he needed to survive in a human world, a place where he would be in constant danger.

Taig's gaze shifted to her, his expression soft and open. "I get that now... but the cold bastard never said it that way. I had to learn. I was different. I wasn't human."

Perhaps Taig hadn't done a number on himself all these years. Perhaps it all stemmed from his father and their time together when Taig was a child. If Taig's father had told him repeatedly that he wasn't human, had made him do things that he hadn't wanted to, then Taig had probably rebelled against it all the moment his parents had disappeared and he had seen that everything his father had taught him meant nothing. It hadn't saved his parents. How would it ever save him?

Lealandra's brow furrowed and she stroked Taig's dark hair, trying to keep the pity out of her touch and her heart so he wouldn't sense it.

"He only wanted to keep you safe, Taig, and teach you how to protect yourself."

Taig frowned. "Why couldn't the old man have just said that?"

"I don't know." She wished she did.

He turned and swooped lower, and she saw the apartment building in the distance. He definitely wasn't a stranger to flying. He had been heading for it from the start, was familiar enough with the city from the air to find his apartment with ease.

She knew one thing about his father. He had been trying to keep Taig safe and that meant he had thought his son was in danger. Why? Had someone been after them, someone powerful enough to hurt Taig and his father?

"Did he protect the house?" Lealandra wasn't sure where her questions were leading but she felt as though she was on the verge of uncovering something about his past, something they both might have overlooked.

Taig nodded. "He taught me the charms and said to always use them... that when I felt safe, I was probably in the most danger. And then he was gone, and so was my mother."

"Did you feel they were going to leave?"

"No... maybe. I had a feeling that we weren't safe. Things had been different. My father had been teaching me more and more, pushing me to learn and practice so I would harmonise with my demon blood and accept my powers. When my parents disappeared, I no longer wanted to do that. My father was the reason they died. He got my mother killed."

"What if they're not dead?"

Taig's jaw clenched, the muscle in it ticking. "They're dead to me."

Lealandra curled up again when his grip on her side and knees tightened and he shifted position behind her, so his feet were lower. She screwed her eyes shut when they came in to land on the roof and tensed. Instead of the impact she had expected, there was nothing. One minute Taig was flying with her, the next he was casually walking on the roof.

"Therapy session is over. Let it go now, Lea." He set her down.

The ice was back in his voice and she knew better than to push him when he was in a foul mood. There was one way that she could make it all better though. Her own form of therapy.

Lealandra stepped into him, so the full length of her body pressed against his, and looped her arms around his neck. Her hands brushed his wings where they joined his back and she touched them, running her fingers over their rough muscled form. Taig's gaze burned into her mouth, intent and focused, and she felt his desire rising, sensed the surge in his power as it laced together with her own, knitting tight. He placed his hands on her waist, gripped it hard, and then dipped his head and kissed her.

She didn't hold back. She opened to him, her tongue tangling with his, not fighting for dominance but pushing him into letting go and unleashing himself on her. She wouldn't deny him this time. She wanted him to devour her, to pour out his passion into this moment, and show her just how much he needed her. Because she needed him too and she was going to make that clear.

She was going to make it clear that she didn't have anything against his demon side and that she didn't fear it.

She was going to embrace it.

She was going to prove to him once and for all that she loved him as a whole and help him accept himself.

All so his heart would heal.

He deepened their kiss, stealing her breath away and pulling a moan from her. His fingertips dug into her sides and she didn't care if it hurt or even if his hands changed into claws. She wanted all of him for once, and she was going to have him.

Lealandra grasped his wings, pulling him hard against her, and he groaned and tugged her closer. The sheer act of dominance and possession thrilled her, heating her blood until she was kissing him roughly, her teeth clashing with his and her breath coming in sharp short bursts. She stroked and tugged his wings, torn between wanting to caress and claw. She wanted him to let go and she wanted to let go with him.

Taig cupped her backside and raised her feet off the floor, grinding his erection against her groin. He backed her into the small structure of the roof exit and pinned her there, his hips bucking against hers with each kiss. She groaned and wrapped her legs around his waist, her mouth working furiously against his. His wings curled around her and she ran her hands down them, her fingers tracing the rigid line of the bones, and then back across his shoulders again. He was so beautiful and strong, so alluring and devastating at the same time. She couldn't resist him. Hadn't been able to from the moment they had met. She held his cheeks in both hands and tackled his tongue with hers, caressing and teasing him. He groaned and bucked against her again.

His need flowed through her, stronger than her own. She could feel it in every touch, every sweep of his hands over her bottom and every meeting of their lips. He needed to lose himself in her, like this, half man and half demon. All Taig.

He growled when he tugged her long black skirt up, freeing her legs from it. A chill breeze chased over her skin, making her shiver, but she didn't care about the cold. All that mattered now was this moment with Taig. She needed him, and he needed her.

A groan left his lips when he dipped one hand between her legs and she gasped at the feel of his fingers on her groin. In her rush to find him, she hadn't bothered with underwear. She had thrown on her clothes with her power and knew that he had done the same. She caressed the line of his stomach and then cupped his crotch, stroking the hard outline of his erection. His mouth stilled against hers, his breathing rough and heavy, and she smiled when he moaned and shivered with each run of her hand up his hard-on. She teased him.

He dragged her hand away, unbuckled his belt and yanked his jeans open. His hard length sprang free, eager between them, and Lealandra smiled. She wasn't the only one who had forgone underwear.

With a deep commanding growl, Taig thrust into her, joining their bodies in the most delicious way. Lealandra clung to his neck and then grabbed one of his shoulders and one wing as he pressed her against the roof exit and took her. It was swift and hard, demanding and passionate. She moaned with each deep plunge of his cock, each long stroke and rough kiss. He growled again and her power shivered with her, bowing to his superior strength and the darkness she felt inside him.

His mouth left hers and he devoured her throat, nipping and kissing, sucking and licking it, driving her out of her mind. She tilted her head back and pressed it against the wall, her body alive under his ministrations, aching with the feel of him against her. He moved faster and his fingers dug into her backside, slamming her onto his length, tearing breathy moans from her throat. She could take it. He could use every ounce of his strength on her and she wouldn't break. She wanted to utter those words, to push him further and give him leave to unleash himself on her, but she couldn't speak, could only cling to him as he drove into her with wild fury, faster and harder, until it bordered on painful.

Taig grunted and rammed deep into her, his cock throbbing as he spilled himself, and bit her shoulder, hard enough that she cried out.

He stilled and she immediately regretted not keeping her pain inside. Quiet words murmured against her skin took the hurt away along with his soft kisses and tender licks. He hadn't drawn blood but there would be a bruise.

Lealandra breathed deep, her body still taut and hungry, aching to climax. Taig drew back and swept his thumb over her cheek, and she realised that his hands had changed. Thick rich brown scaly plates covered his pointed claw-like fingers. He frowned when he noticed and took his hand away, shaking it as though he could get rid of them that easily.

She took a deep breath for courage and then took hold of his hand, running her fingers over the ridges that formed the armour over the back of his fingers and then grazing her thumb along the length of one of his short claws. They were dull but something told her that he could change that if he wanted to. He was being gentle with her. Careful. Taig was perfectly still as she explored him, barely breathing as though he was afraid that even that would hurt her. He wouldn't harm her. She was sure of that.

Distant light caught on his brown scales and they shone, reflecting a myriad of colours. It reminded her of how a beetle could hold the entire spectrum on its back, fascinating her.

"Beautiful." She breathed the word without thinking and Taig snatched his hand back.

Lealandra took hold of it again, brought it to her and kissed it, and then lowered it down to between them. He frowned into her eyes when she shifted and pressed his finger to her aroused nub. He tried to take his hand back again but she didn't let him this time. She held it, moving it against her, teasing herself towards a climax. Her lips parted and she panted with hunger and the feel of his hand on her. She wanted to close her eyes but forced herself to keep looking into Taig's, to hold his attention and let him see that she wasn't afraid of his true appearance. In fact, she wanted to see it, and to feel him against her when he wasn't hiding behind his human mask.

His eyes burned red when she moaned and he moved his hand for her, circling her and edging her closer to orgasm. She jerked against him and groaned when it crashed over her, sending a shiver up her thighs, a warm haze in its wake. Taig moaned too as her body trembled around his softening length and took his hand away.

Lealandra drew him back to her and kissed his shoulder, neck and then his cheek. She caressed his wings, warm and sedated from her climax, and smiled when Taig wrapped his arms around her. She held him close, standing on the brink of telling him that she really did love him. She wanted to say the words but it would be too much for him too fast. It would push him away. Instead, she kissed him and hoped he knew now that he wasn't a monster to her and he wasn't a man either.

He was just Taig.

And she loved him.

CHAPTER 17

Taig snapped awake. A wave of anger prickled his skin and he shot up in bed in the dark room. Lealandra fell away from him, moaning at the disturbance and curling up for a moment, then woke too, sitting up and clutching the covers to her bare breasts. Taig dragged her to him when something somewhere thudded to the floor. He glared at the bedroom door, his senses heightening and his vision shifting. Everything changed to a strange mixture of heat signatures and swirling scents overlaid onto the real world. Lealandra pressed against him. The rushing beat of her heart filled his mind. Her fear spoke to him, urging him into protecting her.

He kissed her forehead and then released her. Not a sound stirred the silence as he crossed the room barefoot and naked. He stopped at the bedroom door. It was open a crack, allowing him to see into the rest of his apartment. Someone was there. He held his growl inside. Someone had a death wish. Breaking into his apartment had signed their execution order.

Two scents swirled around his living room, marking the path the intruders had taken. He couldn't see them now so he reached out with his senses, relying on them to locate the bastards. Kitchen. Whatever they were up to, they were being quiet. Had they realised that he had a barrier around his apartment? They didn't have to enter via a window or door to break seal he had on the place. Teleporting in would have had the same effect. Only now they couldn't teleport back out. The barrier would stop them.

Lealandra reached him and went to look through into the living room but he caught her shoulder to stop her.

"Stay here," he whispered down at her and pressed his finger to his lips and shook his head when she went to speak.

She gave a pointed glance at his groin. He had no qualms about facing intruders naked but if it kept her quiet, he would cover up. In the low light of the room, he spotted his boxer shorts on the floor near the bathroom. He slipped them on and then held his arms out and gave her a look that asked if she was satisfied.

When she nodded, he went to go to the door. He stopped when he reached it, turned around, dragged her into his arms and kissed her hard. There was nothing like a good luck kiss. These weren't humans he was up against. His senses reeked of demon and they smelt familiar.

With a long, deep breath, he opened the door and stalked out into the dark living room. His vision outlined all of the furniture and marked the demons' path through his apartment, showing him where they had entered and where they had been. He headed straight for them, confident that he would be the victor in any fight that might ensue. A couple of young demons didn't frighten him. He ate devils like that for breakfast.

They were in the kitchen, going through the cutlery draw and arming themselves. He leaned against the wall in the opening next to the counter, beside the light switch, folded his arms across his chest and grinned.

Taig flicked the lights on.

"Looking for something in particular?" he drawled, cocksure and coiled tight inside, ready to burst into action. His skin rippled with the shifting of his demon side. It spread through him, held just below the surface, waiting for the moment he initiated the change.

The two men turned to look at him and he quickly assessed them. They were both in their late twenties judging by the skin they wore and had slimmer builds than his. Their clothes were cheap jeans and zip-up hooded sweatshirts, both in black. They looked like thugs—their hair shorn to the skin and faces gnarled into malicious grins.

Clearly, they were about to do the same thing every demon did when they met him—underestimate him.

His human side was a perfect mask for the demon in him, hiding his true scent and nature.

One disappeared with a fast step to his left and the other lunged at him with a butcher's knife. Taig dodged both, the lunging man with a step backwards and the man who had come around behind him with a swift step to his right. He was across the room in the blink of an eye. He glanced at the bedroom door, willing Lealandra to remain there. He would draw the men away from her as much as possible and kill them when he had the chance.

They attacked in unison again, the man with the butcher's knife rushing him while the other drew a gun. Taig stepped into the man with the knife, forcing his attack to miss, and grabbed his arm. He snapped it around with a sickening crunch. The man howled in pain, dropped the blade, and disappeared from his grasp, reappearing near the kitchen.

The man with the gun fired at him, once, twice, and then a third time, each bullet embedding itself into the wall as Taig ran to dodge them.

The second attacked him again before he could react, slashing down his shoulder. Taig leapt backwards, clutching his arm, and growled. The knife on the floor was gone. The man must have grabbed it when Taig had been running from the bullets.

These demons were fast. Perhaps he had underestimated them too.

The one with the knife gestured towards the bedroom door. Taig's eyes widened when he saw Lealandra standing there, leaning against the doorframe for support. Her skin was as white as moonlight, almost matching the bathrobe she wore, and her eyes were dark and large. She clutched at her chest. Something was wrong.

The gunman grinned and nodded in response to his friend, stalking off towards her.

Taig roared, freezing both demons in their tracks.

There was no way he was going to let them touch Lealandra. He couldn't fight them like this, in human form. He needed more strength. He needed his power. Only the demon in him could do this. Only that side of him could protect her.

It was time he found out whether or not she really was alright with his demon side.

The skin covering his fingers shredded, falling away as his rich dark brown claws grew, the nails as sharp as razors now that he was in danger. He shed the skin on his hands, flexing his fingers and feeling strength surge through him. The pale covering of his arms fell away as his body followed his hands, switching into his demonic guise, and he growled when his black dragon-like wings unfurled and stretched out from his back. His eyes turned the colour of flames and his flesh melted into deep brown scaly skin as his face distorted, his jaw strengthening and lips curling back. His teeth elongated and sharpened at the same time as his legs lengthened and his muscles expanded, filling out his new flesh. With a shake of his head, he threw off his human skin and the boxer shorts and roared out his fury as twin curled horns sprouted from the back of his head.

The mark on his back burned.

An urge for violence and bloodshed claimed him.

The first man didn't even see what had hit him. Taig beat his wings, crossed the room, grabbed him around the throat, and slammed him into the wall between the two windows in the lounge. Taig snarled at him, claws ripping through the young demon's throat and spilling his blood in a waterfall down his chest.

He turned to face the other demon and grinned when he saw he had changed into a blue lizard-like monster. He was clearly faster than his friend and more experienced. Taig stepped to his left and towards Lealandra. Her condition was worsening. Whatever was wrong with her, it was serious. He needed to get rid of this demon so he could tend to her. He needed to protect her and keep her safe.

The blue demon grinned to reveal a set of razor sharp pointed teeth and flexed his fingers. They morphed into long silvery claws, elongating until they were several inches in length. Taig readied his own far shorter claws. He needed some information from this one but controlling himself was becoming difficult. The lust for violence was strong tonight. He glanced out of the corner of his eye at Lealandra. She was slowly getting closer to the floor, her legs obviously unable to support her. It was the thought of her being hurt that was driving him out of his mind with anger and a desire to kill.

His momentary distraction cost him. The blue demon flew at him, catching his injured arm and twisting it sharply behind his back. He arched forwards and beat his wings, hitting his assailant. The demon released him and attacked again, his claws leaving long gashes down his back. Taig roared and turned on him, lunging for him with his own claws and sneering when they buried deep into the demon's arm. He curled his fingers and pulled his hand back towards him, slicing through the demon's bicep.

He kept his back to Lealandra and spread his wings out, placing himself between her and the demon, defending her.

The blue demon launched at him. Taig pushed off and slammed into him, tackling him to the floor. They rolled and hit the wall near the entrance, the impact making it shudder and crack, the blue demon landing on top. Taig swiftly moved his head to one side, narrowly dodging the silver streak of claws. They embedded into the wooden floor and the demon snatched them back, nicking Taig's ear in the process. He roared at the demon and forced him upwards, lifting his weight off him so he could get his wings out of the twisted position they were in. He pressed his feet into the demon's stomach and kicked hard, sending him smashing into the ceiling. When the demon fell, Taig was already on his feet. He grabbed Lealandra's attacker around the throat and pinned him against the white pillar beside the kitchen counter. The demon went to swipe at him with his claws. Taig used the points of his wings to stab through the demon's palms and fix them to the pillar above his head.

"Who sent you?" Taig growled, verging on surrendering to his hunger to break the demon's neck.

The demon struggled against him and Taig kicked him hard in his shins, putting an end to any thought he might have had about using his feet to fight. Extending his claws further, he pressed each point into the demon's neck.

"I won't ask nicely again."

He growled when the demon's eyes shifted away from his to look over his shoulder towards Lealandra.

His claws penetrated the demon's throat, spilling blood in thin rivulets down it.

"Last chance."

"Who sent you?" Lealandra's voice startled Taig. He looked down at her where she stood just behind him.

Her milk-white skin held a strange ethereal glow and her dark hair floated around her shoulders, writhing and swirling as though she was underwater, drifting across eyes the colour of blood.

And she was naked.

Taig stepped to the side to hide her body with his own. She surprised him by touching his shoulder. Excruciating pain erased the momentary burst of pleasure her caress brought as her power sapped his strength. He grimaced, struggling to remain standing as she drained him. What was she doing? If she kept this up, he wouldn't be in any condition to fight the demon and get the information from him for her.

He glared at her, his own red eyes meeting hers and silently asking her what she was doing.

She smiled, deep rosy lips parting to reveal sharpened teeth. Her gaze was dull and glassy, distant. Something was very wrong.

The mark on her chest pulsed brightly, sparkling dots of crimson dancing around each symbol and circle. He could see it without touching it. A shiver bolted through him. The ascension.

A red glow lit her face, strangely highlighting it. Her fingers tightened against his shoulder.

"Who sent you!" She turned on the demon.

Taig's wings slipped free of the demon's hands as his power ebbed away, stolen by Lealandra. His vision swam with darkness, wavering even as he tried to cling to consciousness.

CHAPTER 18

Lealandra caught Taig as he collapsed and she hit the floor with him. She cleared the hair from his now human face and furrowed her brow. She cursed herself for going this far, for taking everything from him when he had fought so hard to protect her. His power was the only thing able to stop the change within her and she needed to get answers from this demon. It hadn't been her intention to take all of Taig's strength.

She looked up at the blue demon and raised her hand. Rich red threads of magic encircled her fingers and she narrowed her eyes on the beast.

"Don't even think about moving," she ground out and with a flick of her wrist, pinned him to the wall with her power.

She laid Taig down on the wooden floor and rose to her feet, remorse weighing heavy on her heart. He wasn't going to forgive her for this. If he didn't wake soon or if he couldn't bring himself to help her after what she had done to him, she was doomed. The ascension had begun and without his help, she wouldn't survive it. The power she had stolen from him could only give her control over her magic for a short time. She could already feel it rising again. She needed blood.

Her eyes met the blue demon's yellow lizard-like ones.

"Know you will die by my hand. Speak now and I will take revenge on those who sent you to your death."

The demon's eyes widened.

His mouth opened.

Before he could speak, there was a cracking sound and he contorted, screaming as he writhed against the wall. Lealandra's gaze shot to the demon's legs and she frowned when she saw his body was petrifying from his feet up. A spell. Whoever had sent him, wanted him silenced. Permanently.

She muttered an incantation under her breath. Red ribbons of magic gathered around her hand and knitted into a tight orb. She cast it at the blue demon. The moment it hit him, a bright yellow symbol flashed on his chest. It was a mark that she recognised but couldn't quite believe she was seeing. Gregori. The leader of the coven was attempting to interfere with her ascension. A curse rolled off her tongue. He had always hated anyone who showed signs of achieving magic stronger than his own.

This time he had messed with the wrong person.

"Why did he send you?" Lealandra growled the words at the demon and pressed her hand against the symbol on his chest, determined to fight and put an end to it all.

Touching the burning mark on her own chest, she unleashed a fraction of the power inside her and channelled it into the demon, fighting the spell that was killing him. She couldn't let Gregori kill the demon before she had an answer. She ground her teeth tight together and focused, shutting out the pain and trying to gather all of her magic so she stood a chance of stopping Gregori's spell.

"Tell me why he sent you!" She couldn't hold out much longer. Fighting Gregori's magic was taking all her strength and each second that passed saw her power begin to take control. Her eyes widened when the demon's hands became stone and the spell swept up his limbs. She redoubled her effort, desperate to get an answer. The magic was too powerful to stop when she was fighting the ascension at the same time. All she could do was slow it down.

"Blood," the demon whispered.

Blood?

"Yours."

There were only two reasons why Gregori could want her blood and both of them chilled her. When her ascension had begun, it had triggered a constant rise in her power. Every day, she was getting stronger, heading towards the moment when her magic reached a peak, the point at which she would go through the final process and it would mature.

In that moment, her magic would be at a level that she would never attain again, not even after she had ascended. She was close to reaching it. If someone drank her blood from this point forward until the time when her power peaked during the final stage, they would temporarily become as powerful, if not more so, as her.

The other possible effect overshadowed that one in the frightening stakes. If a witch drank her blood, there was a chance that it would initiate their ascension. Was Gregori after her blood purely for the sake of a turbo boost on his magic or did he want to ascend too?

The latter sounded more like the effect he was after. He had held his place as coven leader for years and he would see her as a threat to his throne if she ascended. By taking her blood, he would have a shot at ascending himself and therefore having the strength to retain his position. If her blood didn't trigger the process, he would at least have the power to fight her and eliminate the threat that way. Whatever way the dice fell, it was her death on the cards. She couldn't afford to let him get her blood.

The blue demon cried out and dragged her out of her thoughts. Her eyes widened when she saw Gregori's spell had reached his shoulders. Her time was running out. She had to attack Gregori now while the spell still connected him to the demon.

Closing her eyes, Lealandra screamed as she forced her hand hard against the yellow symbol on the demon's scaly chest and sent the strongest spell she knew through it. The connection to Gregori shattered in sparks of twisted pain and the demon's body exploded into dust.

Lealandra stumbled backwards, panting and struggling to remain on her feet. She collapsed beside Taig. He was still out for the count, his face peaceful. There was no way he was going to look like that when he woke. Anger wasn't a strong enough word for what he would be feeling. Rage seemed more appropriate.

She pushed herself to her feet and her magic abated. She touched the ascension mark on her chest and frowned down at it. It had started, hadn't it? She thought that it had begun but now she almost felt normal again, her magic whiling back down to its usual level. Had the magic taken control in order to get answers out of the demons, in order to fight? Confused, she stooped and caught Taig under his arms. She grimaced and hauled him towards the couch, dragging his feet along the floor. He wasn't going to be happy with her. She wasn't happy with herself either. Fear had made her react on instinct and that instinct had said to use Taig's power to soothe her own and bring it back under control. It had worked, but she had hurt the man she loved. She was just like her mother, only at least her father had chosen to give his power to her. Taig hadn't.

It was a struggle to get him around the couch. He was heavy. Two hundred plus pounds of dead weight. She growled in frustration and wished she could use her magic but she wouldn't risk it. Not yet. It would drain the remains of her power and she wasn't sure if her spell had worked. The connection had broken before she could discern whether Gregori was dead. She needed to make sure that he was.

Taig mumbled something when she was halfway through getting him onto the couch, his legs dangling off it. A frown creased his brow and his lips parted.

"Taig?" she whispered, afraid of how he was going to react. She finished hauling him onto the couch and then brushed her fingers over his forehead. "I'm sorry. I had no choice."

"Do I scare you?" he muttered and his eyes slowly opened. She frowned. Scare her? She smiled at him when she realised that he meant his demonic appearance.

"Not at all." She stroked his cheek.

He raised his hand and frowned at it. "Hmph. Not a demon. What happened?"

Glassy black eyes met hers. He was still coming around. She gave him five seconds before he remembered that she had stolen all of his strength and then his mood would shift.

"You didn't frighten me when you showed your demon side." She skirted around answering his question.

His gaze searched hers.

"That's good," he murmured and then frowned again. "My head is splitting. I think my brain is falling out."

She smiled and ran her fingers through his hair. "Not splitting at all." She hesitated. "I am sorry... I really had no choice."

His frown increased, his eyes narrowing with it. "You took me out."

"I needed your power to control the magic."

"Did it work?" None of the anger she had expected laced his tone and only concern touched his beautiful dark eyes.

She nodded. "I don't think it was the ascension. I think my magic was just trying to protect me... us."

Taig smiled lopsidedly and closed his eyes. "Good. Now I think I need to sleep a while. Feels like I drunk half a bar and then got into a brawl with a Gargantuan."

Her smile faded. "There's no time to sleep. I know who's after me."

His eyes shot back open and he pushed himself up on his elbows.

"Gregori wants my blood. We have to go to the coven."

He didn't look pleased and shook his head. "You were barely in control, Lea, and I'm not exactly feeling up to a fight. If you flip again, if your magic takes command, I might not be able to protect you. We can't storm in there like this. We wouldn't stand a chance. We can go in a few hours when we're stronger."

Lealandra stared at him, considering what she was going to do. Taig wasn't angry now but he would be if she went through with it. Her magic was under control. It had to be now. Gregori knew that she was on to him and she was eighty percent sure that she hadn't killed him. He wasn't going to give her a few hours. He would send more demons or even witches after them. She had to go after him instead and turn the tables on him while he was weak.

An apologetic smile touched her lips and she cupped Taig's cheek. Awareness rippled through her. He had sensed her intent.

"No," he said in a firm voice. "You can't go there alone."

Lealandra took one last look at him and said the incantation, one strong enough to penetrate the back path in Taig's barrier. A black vortex opened and swallowed her. Only she didn't go alone. Taig grabbed her arm and the current sucked him through with her. They landed hard in the expansive lobby of the coven building, creating a crater in the pale grey marble tiles. Taig cursed and pushed himself to his feet. Lealandra blushed when she realised that she should have at least done one thing before teleporting out of Taig's apartment.

She should have put on clothes.

Taig pointedly raised an eyebrow.

"You wouldn't let me face demons naked but it's okay to drag my bare arse to a building full of witches?"

Lealandra clicked her fingers and a pair of black jeans and a black t-shirt materialised, covering him. A black corset and black trousers appeared on her, encasing her body. Another click and she was suddenly wearing a pair of black knee-high boots and Taig's heavy army boots were on his feet.

"Better?" she said with a smile.

"Guns?" He looked hopeful and boyish, charming.

She pulled a face. Materialising clothes was one thing. Weaponry was a bit more difficult. It took time to make complicated mechanical items appear in their complete and working form.

A sudden leap in her power told her that it was time that she didn't have. He would have to rely on good old-fashioned brute strength. It would be like the old days. Her with her magic and him with pure rage. Back when they had hunted together, he had often carried his guns but had rarely relied on them.

The sound of running feet rumbled through the building.

They were coming.

The room dimmed. Darkness flowed into her. A strong power. Gregori.

Lealandra grabbed Taig's hand and opened the vortex again, teleporting them higher up in the building to a refectory. Closer. She held on to Taig and teleported again. A barrier near the top of the building forced her to set down on the floor below in a pale corridor close to the elevators.

"Problem?" Taig rolled his shoulders, a black look on his face.

His power was returning. It flowed around her, a light mist that caressed her skin. She nodded.

"I can't teleport to the floor above."

Taig smiled. It quickly turned into a grin. "I guess we know where he is then."

Lealandra caught his wrist when he moved towards the emergency exit at the other end of the corridor.

"Wait." She focused above them, trying to penetrate the barrier and see just how many witches were waiting for them.

Gregori couldn't have everyone on his side. Some of them had to be against him, or didn't know about this. She cursed. Gregori had probably told them that a demon had invaded their building. They would all be on the defensive. A lot of them had headed downstairs to greet her and Taig. At least she could hinder the lower level witches who couldn't teleport.

Lealandra shifted her focus to the elevators and sent a wave of power that way. Her magic snaked through the gap in the elevator doors and moved into the shaft. She closed her eyes and felt the mechanics of the elevator, seeking out a way of stopping it. Her power moved down and became one with machine, running through the metal and into the electrics. A motion with her mind and all of the electrical wires snapped, leaving the elevators immobile. She released her hold on them and pressed her hand against her head.

Dealing with machinery always drained her and left a metallic taste in her mouth that reminded her of blood.

She glanced at Taig and her magic surged through her, demanding that she taste him and feed it. Not now. She pushed back against her power, hoping to subdue it, but it overwhelmed her. Her knees gave and she was in Taig's arms, cradled against his body.

"You're too weak for this," Taig said and she smiled faintly.

Whispered words crawled around her mind. Her gaze fell to his arm. Just a little blood. It would quell the magic and help her keep it under control. It would make her stronger. Taig moved and surprised her by running a dark claw-like fingertip down his forearm. Blood instantly filled the short ragged line.

She licked her lips. A little blood.

He brought his arm to her mouth and she moaned when she tasted his blood. Her hands moved of their own accord, tightly grasping his arm and clutching it to her mouth. She suckled deeply. Hazy warmth filled her, suffusing every inch of her right down into her heart, and her magic calmed, the darkness of its demands drifting from her mind. As Taig's blood became part of hers, her strength returned and she stopped drinking. She lay in Taig's arms, looking up at him. How had she ever been foolish enough to leave him when he was everything that she needed?

Taig smiled at her, tender and full of affection, and she closed her eyes when he brushed his fingers down her cheek and then opened them again, wanting to see him.

"Come on, sweet cheeks, let's go finish this." He stood with her, lifting her off the ground and then setting her down on her feet.

Lealandra nodded and headed for the door to the stairs that would take her up to the next level. She climbed them, wary and searching with her magic, trying to discern where the barrier started. They were getting closer. Taig followed behind her, the strength of his power radiating through her and calming the turbulent maelstrom of nerves within her. She was glad that he had tagged along. She had hoped that he would, either by coming through the vortex with her or teleporting himself here.

The instant she sensed the barrier, she raised her hand, her palm facing the invisible wall. It bent under her will but didn't break. Getting in wasn't going to be easy. It would take time that she didn't have. Gregori would be regaining his power by the second, getting stronger while she was getting weaker. The magic was pushing again, rising inside her as it began to take control. The ascension might not have started yet but it was coming. She needed to get this over with and get to her parents.

"Allow me." Taig wrapped one strong arm around her waist. "Hold on."

Lealandra did, unsure of what he was going to do. She clutched his shoulders and he pressed her close to his chest. Darkness swallowed her, pitch black and endless, and then she was back in the emergency stairwell.

On the other side of the barrier.

Taig released her and grinned. "Gregori needs to improve his security. Demons don't move physically through things like witches do when they teleport."

Lealandra didn't want to ask exactly what plane a demon moved through when they were teleporting. The darkness she had seen wasn't only an absence of light. It had a presence. It had felt as though it was the world between worlds, the one where evil spirits were born as shadows. Could Taig enter that realm so easily and without fear?

She shuddered and trudged on, not wanting to think about it. She stopped at the closed door for the nineteenth floor and reached out with her power to see what awaited her. Witches. Several of them and they were powerful. Gregori wasn't alone. Two stood just the other side of the door and two near Gregori. The ones defending him were the supreme mages judging by the strength of their magic as hers briefly touched it. The two nearer the door were high-level witches. Nothing she couldn't handle but they would prove a distraction and give the supreme mages and Gregori a chance to attack her and Taig.

Taig touched her arm. He motioned in the direction of the two weaker witches and then pointed at her. She waved a hand in Gregori's direction and then at herself. Taig frowned. She hadn't expected him to be happy about the prospect of her going after Gregori alone while he fought the weaker demons but she had to do it. Someone had to keep him busy while Taig evened the odds and she had to make sure that he didn't regain his full strength. Taig pointed to the weaker witches again and firmly thrust his finger towards her. Lealandra placed her hands on her hips and shook her head. He rolled his eyes and then a sigh lifted his shoulders and he touched her cheek.

She knew what he was trying to tell her. Be careful. She mirrored him, stroking his cheek, and smiling as she nodded. He had to be careful too. While he had completely regained his power, he still had a weak spot. Her. He would be worried about her during the fight. She would do her best, would fight without restraint so he didn't have to worry and wouldn't leave himself open to attack.

Taig gave her one last look and then burst into the large open plan room with a roar. Lealandra followed and immediately pinpointed Gregori, her gaze sweeping away from the bank of windows that formed the long wall opposite her. He stood to her right in the low-lit brown-walled room, near his office and the mahogany double doors to his master suite. She broke away from Taig and headed straight for Gregori and the supreme mages. Gregori was pale even in the dim light of the stand lamps and ceiling spotlights. Dark rings circled his hazel eyes, his face gaunt and hollow. His jaw-length brown hair was a mess, strands falling out of the ponytail, and the tail of his black shirt hung loose from his trousers. He stared at her with dark lifeless eyes. He was still recovering from her spell. Now was her chance.

The second she was within reach of firing a spell at Gregori, something hit her and flung her backwards towards where Taig was fighting near the couches and table at the other end of the long room. The world rushed by and she held her hands out. Red threads of magic wound around her fingers and she slowed. Such a simple attack wasn't going to stop her. She pushed her arms towards the supreme mages and frowned as she unleashed her magic, sending one of the older greying men flying backwards past Gregori, creating an opening.

She ran at Gregori.

The other supreme mage appeared in a swirl of dark blue material in front of her, the tails of his long coat flaring outwards, and backhanded her. The power behind the strike sent her smashing into the dark carpet and her entire side ached but she refused to give up so quickly. Before he could attack again, she shot a spell at him, a red burning orb that he ducked to avoid. It caught his grey hair, singeing it, and he cast a dark look her way and raised his hands. She barrelled into him, taking him down, and was about to unleash another attack when he cast his own spell and threw her off him. She tumbled along the carpet with the force of the bolt of magic and ended up near Taig.

The area was a mess now. One of the couches was broken clean in two and the table was kindling. Taig had already dealt with one of the witches. He hurled the other one across the room, sending him crashing into the far wall and the massive modern painting that covered it, and then held his hand out to her. She took it and smiled when he helped her up.

The guard attacked him. Taig growled and punched him hard across the jaw and then in the stomach. Lealandra ran back to her own fight at the other end of the room. Taig could handle the guard but she was beginning to think that she couldn't handle Gregori and his goons. She shot two spells at the supreme mages to incapacitate them and then launched everything she could at Gregori. Three spells in one. Bind. Silence. Pain. One big spell that drained her.

The two supreme mages deflected the spells she had hurled towards them but didn't move to protect Gregori. She breathed hard, weak and dizzy from using so much magic in one spell, and watched Gregori. He casually lifted a hand and waved her spell away as though it was nothing more than a gnat. She cursed. He had regained more power than she had anticipated.

She hadn't thought this through and she had placed both herself and Taig in danger because of it.

Taig was a blur of fury as he passed her. Her eyes widened when he threw the guard at the group facing her. The witch hit one of the supreme mages, taking him down, and Lealandra hit the other with a spell but they fired one back at her. She didn't have time to avoid it. It struck her and her hands snapped to her sides, her body encased in invisible chains that tightly held her. Binding spell. She swore silently and glared at the supreme mage who had fired it. Binding spells were strong and almost impossible to break without outside intervention from another witch.

The mage disappeared. Lealandra's eyes widened when she realised what was going to happen. This had been a terrible mistake. She should have thought it through.

A sharp pain in her neck sent rage pulsing through her and she struggled, fighting the binding spell and trying to lift her arms. Gregori stared at her from his place of safety, untouchable. Taig fought the second supreme mage, trying to get to her, his black t-shirt ripped to shreds and his face and arms bloodied from the fight. What had she done? She should have listened to him and to her mother. They weren't strong enough yet to fight and she had played right into Gregori's hands.

Her head spun but she fought on. Her magic rose, seeping into her veins and then out of her, creating an aura that shifted her hair, sending it floating and swirling. She growled when her teeth sharpened and the world changed. Her hands moved a millimetre and Gregori frowned.

The magic surged through her and took control.

With an inhuman cry, Lealandra shattered the bonds that held her and turned on the supreme mage. The needle left her neck and she tried to get it from him but it disappeared from his hand. She screamed and launched him backwards, sending him slamming into the brown wall and knocking him unconscious. She turned on Gregori. He waved the needle at her. She had been a fool.

Noises came from the stairwell. The others had reached them.

Lealandra set her sights on Gregori and ran at him, intent on finishing him off, her magic demanding his blood for what he had done. It controlled her, whispered the words for a forbidden incantation in her mind, one that she didn't know but recognised deep within her soul. Such a spell wouldn't only kill Gregori. It would kill everything within a mile radius. She couldn't do such a thing. Taig would die. She fought the magic but couldn't stop it. It wouldn't listen to her. She wasn't strong enough to command it now. The rage inside her, the desire for violence, was frightening. She no longer felt herself. She felt trapped inside someone else's body, unable to do anything. Unable to protect the man she loved.

Taig turned towards her.

Gregori smiled calmly.

She didn't see the spell that hit her. He lifted his hand and darkness descended on her. The shadows in the room came to life and the air turned to ice. She shivered and her magic withdrew, fearful of the things she could see, twisted shapes that crawled towards her. Spirits. He had sent her to that dark place that Taig had brought her through.

Lealandra backed away, casting glances around her at the encroaching shadows. Her breaths shortened. She pressed a hand against her tight chest and felt the pounding of her heart.

The black fog lifted enough for her to see Gregori smiling at her, his eyes full of darkness as he held the needle up. Her magic rose again at the sight of the blood he had taken from her and she took a step forwards, intent on reclaiming it. Another spell collided with her, wrapping her in a cocoon and then seeping into her. White-hot pain blinded her, bone-deep and threatening to steal her consciousness.

She doubled up, clutching her chest and stomach, and tried to expunge the spell, managing to force it away from her bones. It fought back, tearing at her flesh until she felt as though it was ripping her apart from the inside out.

Strong arms wrapped around her and the world brightened. A gust of wind hit her and then sound splintered through her mind. Silence followed with a cool rush of air over her body. Her magic pushed the remaining shreds of the spell from her body and the darkness left her. She leaned into Taig's chest and wrapped her arms around him as he cradled her, one arm under her legs and the other behind her back. She frowned and opened her eyes when she felt his wings and the strong beat of wind against her hands.

The world passed by below them, a myriad of twinkling lights in the silence.

She was flying again, floating in Taig's arms, and this time it didn't frighten her at all.

Lealandra idly watched the cars on the dark streets. It all looked so beautiful from up here in the night. Was this what the moon saw when it looked down upon them? How could a world so full of darkness look so beautiful from a distance?

"Hold on, Lea," Taig whispered and held her tighter. There was so much hurt in his voice. No, not hurt. Fear. He was afraid for her. "We'll be home soon."

Home.

She still liked the way he said that. As though his place was theirs.

She could see Central Park in the distance. Taig's wings beat heavily in the air, strong and taking away any fear of falling she had. He wouldn't drop her. He would keep her safe just as he had promised. She believed in him.

But could he protect her from Gregori?

He had her blood now.

Her only chance of defeating him was to make it through her ascension.

She had to survive.

She had to stop him.

CHAPTER 19

Taig sat in silence on the end of the bed, his elbows resting on his knees and his fingers forming steeples in front of his face. His eyes didn't move, fixed on Lealandra where she lay sleeping. Warm sunlight flooded into the room, casting a pale glow over her skin and marking that a day had passed since he had brought her home. He had tended her wounds, had done everything he could for her, and had waited ever since. It had been difficult, wore him down worse than any form of torture, but he endured it, knowing that she was regaining her strength little by little. His rage had quietened as she had improved and it was back under control now. She looked brighter at last. The greyness was gone from her skin. The sunlight made her look peaceful. Dead. Only the steady rise and fall of her chest beneath the deep red covers reassured him that she was alive.

Time crept on, the shadows slowly moving around, marking the passing hours across the black wall behind her.

Taig waited a few minutes more, willing Lealandra to stir and show signs of regaining consciousness. When she didn't, he stood and walked over to her. He pressed a kiss to her forehead, breathed in her sweet scent, and then grabbed a fresh black t-shirt and left the room.

The apartment was spotless now. He put on the t-shirt and walked across the room. The only sign of his fight with the demons was the dent in the far wall next to the long black side cupboard and a couple of holes in the pillar near the kitchen. He had cleared everything else away, including the remains of the demons. It had been the only way of distracting himself while he waited for Lealandra to come around. Now he had nothing to do to keep himself occupied. He paced across the room and came to a halt next to the picture of his parents. Without thinking, he reached out and picked it up.

Their happy faces smiled up at him. He stroked a finger over his mother's stomach. She had been so happy. His gaze shifted to his father. There was no lie in the demon's expression. He had been as happy as his mother. They had both wanted him. So why had they left him?

His demon surfaced along with his anger but again it didn't push for freedom. It lingered below his skin, one with him, called out by his need and his despair. He thought about what Lealandra had said to him. He was a man. Both his demon side and his human side made him who he was—a man who Lealandra loved, a man who was strong enough to protect her.

His fight against the demons and the coven had made him realise that without his demon blood, he wouldn't be able to protect Lealandra. It had been a difficult thing to accept and was only made harder by the fact that on some level he was glad now that he had demon blood. It was that which gave him the power to look after her, not only to protect her but to help her control her magic. When the ascension came, she would need his demonic power more than ever. It would be the key to her survival. If he had been born wholly human, he would have been useless to her, impotent in his desire to take care of her.

The smiling faces of his father and mother radiated affection up at him. The years he had spent with them had been full of tenderness and acceptance. They had both loved him and he was sure that they had loved each other too.

Were they really dead? Did he really want to go with Lealandra to find out what had happened to them? He had never wanted to venture into the underworld in search of them before but now he was considering it.

Meeting Lealandra's parents had made him think about how his would have reacted to her. His mother would have liked her. His gaze shifted to his father. Perhaps he would have been able to accept that his son loved a witch. After all, he had broken with the demon world to live with his mother and marry her, and have him. He had dared to love a human.

That was no less sinful than loving a witch.

Taig placed the picture down on the long black side cabinet and opened the cupboard below it. He chose a gleaming black-handled hunting knife and looked around the apartment. Where to start? He had to protect what was his, had to keep Lealandra safe. Gregori had her blood now but something told him that it wouldn't end there. Lealandra wouldn't let it and while she was alive and had a chance of surviving her ascension, Gregori would be after her. He would want to get rid of her.

Taig went to the door and ran his fingers over the marks on the wooden frame. The protection they offered was strong but not enough to make him comfortable. He took the knife and began carving symbols into the spaces on the wood, marking out the most powerful protection at his disposal—the protection his father had used on their home and had taught him as a child.

Nothing would be able to get within fifty metres of his apartment without him knowing about it, and, if they dared to attempt to enter by force, the enchantment would send them to the shadow world and trap them there with the evil things that it spawned. It wasn't a temporary or easy to break thing like Gregori's pathetic spell. It was permanent. The shadows would eat them before they could even think about trying to escape.

Over an hour had passed by the time Taig had finished scoring the protection marks on the door and window frames.

He ended up in the kitchen, leaning against the black glossy cupboards beside the red refrigerator. He toyed with his knife and tried to think of something to do now to keep his mind occupied. Humans moved in and out of the perimeter of the incantation. Nothing for him to be concerned about. He shifted focus to the bedroom when something moved. Lealandra. His heart said to go to her but she appeared in the doorway, holding a white robe closed around her, before he could move. The tiredness in her eyes spoke volumes.

She was still weak. Gregori had done a real number on her but Taig knew it wasn't only that which had sapped her strength. The ascension was close. She would be constantly fighting her magic now in an attempt to control it.

"Morning." She rubbed her eyes and yawned. "What time is it?"

Taig smiled and put his knife down on the black granite counter top. Her gaze moved to it and she frowned briefly before looking at the front door and the windows. The rise in the power of protection over the apartment would be significant enough for her to sense.

"You've been busy. We in trouble?" she murmured sleepily and padded barefoot across the living room to him. He rounded the kitchen island and helped her sit on one of the black stools. She leaned one elbow on the black granite counter and yawned again.

"You've been sleeping a while," he said and she looked at him. When she frowned, he took it as an order to expand on what he had said. "Over a day."

Her eyebrows rose and then fell again when she leaned her head heavily on her upturned palm.

"A day." She sighed. "Gregori has my blood."

"I know." Taig sat on the stool next to her, took hold of her hand and held it. It was warm in his, the feel of it comforting him as much as seeing her awake. "He can't get to you here. Not now."

She nodded. "I can feel it, you know, the barrier you've made. I couldn't before. I don't think it's your upgrade. I think it's close."

"The ascension?"

She nodded again and wrapped her arms around herself. "Real close."

Taig sighed, placed his arm around her shoulders and drew her towards him until she shifted and leaned her head against his chest. He held her in silence, memorising the way it felt to have her in his arms and to have her relying on his strength again to comfort her. His thumb started a soft motion against her arm through the robe and he stroked it while he thought about what they were going to do. If Gregori was after her, he would want her gone before the ascension hit. He wouldn't wait until afterwards, not even to see if she died during the process. Gregori wouldn't risk her becoming stronger than he was.

Lealandra was strong and just as stubborn as Taig. She wouldn't give in to the ascension and would fight to master her magic. It wouldn't defeat her. Taig wouldn't let it. If Lealandra needed all of his power, all of his blood, then he would give it to her. He would give her everything to ensure that she survived.

He placed his fingers under her chin and lifted her head. She looked up at him with round fearful eyes, their grey depths as stormy as the ocean. Taig lowered his mouth to hers and claimed her lips in a gentle kiss, one that he hoped told her everything that he still couldn't voice. He loved her and he wasn't going to allow anything to happen to her.

Lealandra was still a moment as his lips moved over hers and then she uncurled, her hands coming to rest on his waist and her mouth opening. She returned the kiss, as softly and slowly as he was, her lips barely meeting his.

He frowned when her tongue traced his lower lip and then brushed over his teeth and groaned when he touched it with his. She slanted her head and thrust her tongue into his mouth. One hand slid around the back of his neck and pulled him closer as her kiss turned fierce and hungry.

Their tongues duelled for dominance, drawing a quiet moan from her, and his brow furrowed. The hunger of her kiss was electrifying, shattering his restraint. It became a battle, a violent clashing of lips and tongues, full of desperation and need. Taig's breathing turned as choppy as the kiss and he dug his fingers into Lealandra's shoulders, clinging to her, holding her so she couldn't break away from him. His whole body tightened at the delicious feel of her fingers running down his chest. He moaned to encourage her and then frowned when she raked nails down over his pectorals. He loosed a muffled 'ouch' into her mouth when she clawed him again. Literally.

His tongue touched her teeth. Sharp. The taste of magic flooded his mouth, coppery in its scent, and then it felt as though it was crawling down his throat, infecting his body and sapping his strength.

Taig shoved Lealandra off him. She smiled, wicked and seductive. Dilated pupils darkened her bright red eyes.

He threw a cursory glance down at his chest. She had torn his black t-shirt to shreds. He went to touch it but Lealandra clicked her fingers and it disappeared. She was still smiling when he looked at her. Hunger flitted across her eyes as she stared at his body and she reached over and stroked her fingers lightly down his chest, following the marks she had made, and then took her hand away and licked each bloodied finger clean. She sucked them in turn, her eyes fixed on his, her moans making him breathless. He clawed back a little control over his libido and frowned at her.

"We have to get you to your parents." Those words didn't go down well.

She pouted at him and raised her hands. Red magic swirled around her fingers like ribbons in a breeze, her skin drained of colour and her eyes brightened, until the red began to bleed into the white.

"We really have to get you to your parents," Taig said, afraid that even his blood wouldn't be able to stop whatever was happening to her. Her magic was strong, flooding the room with a heavy feeling that pressed down on him, as though gravity had suddenly doubled.

"I refuse," she said in a voice he didn't recognise as hers and tilted her head to one side, her smile coy and seductive, and her eyes narrowing on him. He frowned when she reached out and ran her palms over his chest, trailing her fingers over his nipples and teasing them. His nostrils flared and his jaw tensed as he fought for control. Her magic seeped into him, stealing his senses and making his head feel light. Lustful thoughts filled it, urges so dark that they frightened him. His blood called for violence, for him to slake his thirst for Lealandra and have her, take her in ways he had only dreamed of. As a demon. "Everything I need is right here."

Taig growled and moved backwards, sending the stool toppling. He stumbled over it, regained his footing and growled at her again. Her eyes became dark red slits of anger and she stood. He swallowed when she shrugged out of the white robe, revealing the enticing curves of her bare body, and then snapped her fingers, ridding him of his jeans.

This wasn't going to happen.

He stalked towards the bedroom, intent on getting dressed again and getting Lealandra over to her parents. There was no way on Earth he was going to do what her magic wanted him to. He wasn't going to have sex with her like that. Lealandra was in there somewhere and he was as sure as Hell was hot that she didn't want it that way.

Lealandra snapped her fingers again.

His bedroom door slammed shut right in front of him. He tried the handle. It wouldn't give. The door didn't even have a lock. He threw a glare over his shoulder at Lealandra. She was still smiling, red-eyed and sharp-teethed. That wasn't Lealandra. That was her magic. The voice she had spoken to him with, her appearance, it was all her magic. It had taken control.

Taig stalked back to her and stared hard into her eyes.

A flicker of grey surfaced, pushing the red back for a moment and showing him nothing but pure fear. It laced her aura and sent a sickening wave through him that made him reach out to comfort her. He touched her cheek and the red began to seep back into her eyes.

Lealandra.

He had said he would do anything to help her survive the ascension.

He meant that.

Her lips moved, silently speaking what he could already see in her eyes.

Help me.

Red shot back into her irises.

White light engulfed the room.

CHAPTER 20

Lealandra's heartbeat shot off the scale as the world brightened so much that it hurt. She squinted and raised her hand to protect her eyes, afraid of what was happening. Was someone attacking them? Was it Gregori?

Her hand fell back down to her side when she realised that it wasn't an attack. It was her. Her power was doing it.

She swallowed, her heart fluttering in her throat, a frightened little beat that made her tremble. Too late. She had wanted to regain control and go to her parents so they could help her but her time was up. No one could help her now. Her mother's words came back to her. The symbol for blood in her ascension mark was about Taig. She had to be unafraid of taking what she needed from him, what her magic demanded, because she wouldn't survive the ascension unless she did.

Pain rushed through her, followed by the most incredible feeling of unrestrained power as every tether holding it snapped. She flung her arms out at her side, screaming at the ceiling as she lost all control. Her feet left the floor and threads of magic swept over her, weaving around her legs and arms, supporting her. Her eyes half closed and then snapped open again when something moved.

Taig.

The power sparked through her when she reached out to him, wracking her body and making her want to curl up in agony. Lealandra gritted her teeth and stretched her hand out to Taig again, desperate to reach him and regain control. She needed balance. Without it, the magic would completely take control and destroy her.

She screamed and bent over backwards when it surged through her, the pain so intense that she lost her senses and all awareness of herself. Her body melted away, becoming one with the light engulfing her, and she struggled to focus. It felt as though she was spreading outwards, losing herself to the very air in the room, and it frightened her. She had to hold on and hold herself together. She had to maintain her form if she was going to survive this. Her magic was one with the elements but she couldn't follow it into that ethereal state. She had to focus through the agony beating in her essence and hold on until she could reach Taig and save herself.

"Lea!" Taig called from somewhere within the white emptiness.

Her heart ached and she silently called out to him, unable to speak through the incredible hurt.

There was a sense of him being close and then the sound of something smashing.

"Son of a bitch." It must have been Taig.

Lealandra tried to speak, wanted to tell him that the magic wouldn't let him near her. She wanted to tell him to run and save himself. Forget about her. She couldn't control it. Her body trembled, weak and on the verge of collapse. Fighting her power in order to question the demon and then using it to battle Gregori had taken too much of her strength. Even with her borrowed power from Taig, she still hadn't been strong enough to hold the ascension at bay.

The world around her began to grey, fading slowly to black.

There was another spark and again the sound of Taig being thrown and smashing into something. She smiled at his persistence and wished she could find her voice to tell him to leave her while he still could. The magic was building inside her and she didn't know how much longer she could contain it. It felt as though it was going to tear her apart, rip through her to escape the physical prison of her body.

"Lea!" he shouted again and she screwed her eyes shut, her heart warming but breaking at the same time.

With a scream, she arched her back and flung her legs and arms outwards. A bright white shockwave rent the darkness and she could hear everything in the apartment smash and crumble beneath its power.

"Taig," Lealandra whispered, desperate to hear that she hadn't killed him.

She couldn't bear the thought of hurting him. She never should have asked him to help. She had known how dangerous it would be to be around her now when she was going through the ascension. Without her Counter-Balance, she had no way of fighting the power and getting it back under her command.

Another blast of power rocked her body and she frowned when it found resistance within the room. Whatever it was, it was powerful. Could it be Taig? Tears streaked her cheeks. Taig. How could she have turned her back on him all those years ago? How could she have left the man she loved? She should have fought him and told him that she loved every part of him, even his demon side. Seeing him as a demon hadn't frightened her. He had still been Taig, willing to sacrifice himself to protect her, doing whatever it took to make sure that she was safe. She had still been able to see him within his demonic appearance. She had been able to sense it was him and that he would never do anything to hurt her.

She screamed again when power ripped through her and blacked out.

Was this the end of her?

When she woke, would her magic be in command? Would it force her to do things that went against her will, her very principles, and make her suffer before she died? She didn't want that. She would sooner die now than succumb to the dark will of her magic.

When she came back, strong arms held her. More tears cascaded down towards her ears, drawn from her by the comforting feel of the embrace rather than the pain spiralling through every inch of her body. The arms pulled her close, cradling her gently and filling her with a sense of safety that made her want to give up the fight.

"Taig," she mumbled, her cheek pressed against his chest. She wanted to hold him but couldn't find the energy to raise her arms. Her power was a constant ebb and flow of pain through her tired body, stealing all her remaining strength.

Soon she would lose control completely and would cease to be herself. The power would take over and use her body as a vessel, a puppet to wreak havoc with before destroying her. She couldn't let that happen.

"Kill me," Lealandra whispered and opened her eyes. His face was hazy and blurred but she could make out the bright red of his eyes and his heavy frown.

"No." A flat refusal. Nothing short of what she had expected. He held her tighter. "Tell me what you need. Tell me how to help you. I'm not letting you go, Lea. Not again. I won't lose you. I... I can't... I can't lose you, Lea. Please... tell me what to do."

She smiled. Stubborn mule. Why couldn't he have been this stubborn all those years ago? The thought that they could have been together all this time broke her heart now that death was looming in front of her, ready to snatch her life and the beautiful dream that seeing Taig had brought into existence.

"Speak to me, Lea. Tell me what the fuck I need to do to stop this." Desperation laced his voice. It hurt her to hear it. She didn't want him to suffer like this because of her. Her resolve to fight came back, a desire to survive the ascension and be with Taig fuelling her. She raised her hand and grabbed his shoulder with it, followed by her other. Dragging herself up, she licked his neck and worked her naked body against his, silently telling him exactly what her magic needed.

His blood.

His body.

It was the only way for her to get enough power to control the magic and regain command.

He instantly moved her in his arms, shifting her onto his lap so she was straddling him. Her eyes widened when he bit into his wrist and then narrowed on the wound when he released his arm. Blood ran down his forearm, the crimson trail making her hunger rise and suppressing the fluctuations in her power.

He brought his wrist to her mouth and she moaned low in her throat when it pressed against her lips. She parted them and wrapped them around the wound. Pain tore through her when she sucked and the magic rebelled against the calming effect of his blood but she fought back, unwilling to surrender now. This was her body and her life. Her magic wouldn't defeat her. She sucked harder, swallowing down the cool metallic-tasting liquid and melting into his arms. She turned her head and pressed it against his chest, still suckling from his wrist, as he raised her up on his lap. A sigh escaped her when his hard length eased into her, making her ache for him and giving her back a fraction more control.

She went to move but his other hand tightened against her waist.

"I've got you," he whispered into her hair and then kissed it.

He moved her on his cock, a slow torturous rhythm. She wanted to writhe against him but she didn't have the energy. It was taking everything she had left just to keep drinking from him. She closed her eyes and swallowed down the next mouthful of his blood, regaining a little more control when its power radiated through her.

This wasn't exactly how she had imagined her ascension going. Charlie should have been here to absorb the excess magic and the coven should have used their magic to suppress hers. That was all she would have needed from them. Taig had to give her everything. His body, his power, and his blood. She needed it all. She didn't want to think about what would have happened if she had been alone when the ascension had hit. Either Gregori would have killed her or the magic would have.

She whimpered when new pain throbbed deep in her chest and began spreading outwards along every nerve.

Taig's arm encircled her, pressing her against him, moving her body against his.

"I'm here with you, Lea. I'm not going anywhere. Hold on."

Her eyes shot wide when he moved her so she was lying on the floor with him on top, his wrist still pressed to her lips, feeding his blood to her. His other hand pressed into the floor between her arm and her side, supporting his weight. She groaned when he thrust into her, filling her body with his own. The new pain grew more intense, white-hot and searing her body. It felt different though. Her power began to ebb away and she frowned when she realised that she could finally shut it down and restrain it again. She drank down another mouthful of Taig's blood and then released his wrist.

His face came into focus.

"You back with me?" He smiled but she saw right through it.

Lealandra had never seen him so worried before. She was going to answer him when he plunged deep into her core again and her reply became a breathy moan of pleasure. With renewed strength, she grasped his shoulders and dragged him down to her. He collapsed onto his elbows, his body sliding against hers, teasing her sensitised flesh and making her shiver with arousal.

His mouth covered hers and she rolled her eyes closed when he kissed her hard. His movements became as desperate and searching as that kiss, telling her without words how much she had frightened him and how much he needed her. Her fingers danced across his shoulders and he shuddered against her.

"Tickles," he muttered against her mouth a moment before his tongue tackled hers, tearing a moan from her throat.

Lealandra cracked one eye open and watched her fingers. They left glowing red trails in their wake as she stroked his skin. She smiled, her eyelids at half-mast, and Taig moaned and kissed along her jaw, hungry nips and sucks that spoke of his desire and need. Her eyes closed again and she leaned her head back, arching her chest into his. He slid one arm beneath her back, grasping her tight to him, and her body hummed with the feeling of his against it, moulding perfectly skin to skin, filling her with each long stroke. A groan rumbled in her throat and her lips parted as it came out as a sigh. Taig kissed her neck, devouring it while she traced patterns on his back and shoulders, lost in a warm sea of bliss and tranquillity. How did he do this to her? How did his blood and a physical connection to him give her control? There had to be a reason. She had never experienced anything like it with anyone else. Not even Charlie's presence had given her this much control over her power. It couldn't just be because he was a demon. She wanted it to be more than that.

She kissed Taig's cheek and then craned her neck so she could lick and tease the sensitive flesh of his throat. He moaned into hers and lightly bit down on it. His breath tickled her ear when he whispered words into it. Her cheeks flushed and her heart warmed. They were tender words, soothing ones that drew a wide smile from her. She really had worried him if she had reduced him to whispering sweet nothings.

The pain inside drifted away and strength surged through her, leaving her breathless, followed by a deep calm and a sense of peace.

Was it over?

The mark on her chest burned and she grasped Taig's upper arms, her fingers digging into his flesh. White-hot light burst through her, her power sending a shockwave through him and the room, and her hands blazed bright red.

"Taig!" she cried as she climaxed, her body trembling all over.

Taig reared up and roared, burying himself deep in her core, and then collapsed against her, breathing fast into her ear, his release filling her.

Her hands slipped away from his arms and she panted as her magic subsided, leaving her shaking beneath Taig.

When he eventually regained control and moved to rest on his elbows above her, their bodies still intimately entwined, she checked him over. He seemed all right, albeit a little dazed. Dull ebony eyes fixed on hers, his expression distant, but he didn't look as though he was in pain and he was in one piece at least. She ran her gaze over him. The scratches on his broad bare chest were gone. Not even scars remained. Her eyes dropped to his left arm where she had been holding him. They widened. Out of the corner of her eye, she saw him look down too.

There, emblazoned on his skin, was the intricate runic mark that they had given to her when the joint covens had recognised her as a witch.

It wasn't possible.

"What does it mean?" Taig eased back and kneeled between her legs. He pulled his arm around and frowned at the mark. She could only stare at the symbol. It was definitely her mark and it was definitely real, and no matter how long she looked at it, it wasn't fading or going away.

Her heart thundered. What did she tell him? It was hard to judge how he was going to react to the truth. Either he would be immensely smug, or incredibly angry.

She sat up, her eyes never leaving the mark.

It wasn't going anywhere, no matter how many times she told herself it wasn't possible. He was a demon.

"You... you're..." Lealandra couldn't get the words out. Taig moved closer to her, his hand catching her jaw and raising her head so her eyes met his. She blinked. Just a glance into his pitch black eyes left her breathless and turned her skin to goose flesh. There was such an aura of power and sensuality around him, of preternatural strength and otherworldly beauty, and most of all, of affection and concern. Her words left her automatically, sounding distant to her ears as she stared into his eyes. "You're my Counter-Balance."

Taig laughed. When her serious expression didn't change, the smile fell from his face and his laughter died.

"I'm not a witch. I'm not even human." Evidently, he was thinking along the same lines she had been.

She wracked her brain, trying to remember everything she had learned about the ascension and Counter-Balances.

She shrugged. "No one has ever had a demon as a Counter-Balance before, but there's nothing that says it isn't possible... I mean, what if my power needs someone stronger than a witch to balance it and provide me with control?"

Taig stared at her, blinked slowly, and then slumped into a relaxed position, his broad shoulders falling.

"What does this mean?" He glanced at his arm again.

She knew what he was asking. He wanted to know where it left them and what the future held.

"I need you, more now than I've ever done. Without you, I'll have little control over my power. Just your presence alone is enough to calm it. I can feel your effect just sitting here. Borrowing your blood would give me total control over the magic now." The thought of relying on Taig so heavily frightened her and she watched him closely for a sign that he would accept the burden that she had placed on his shoulders without his consent. She needed him.

Reaching out, she touched his cheek, her fingertips lightly resting against his cool skin. His eyes met hers again, dark and intense.

"The mark means you're bonded to me. I can't do anything to undo it. I'm sorry. I know I'm asking a lot—"

"A mark of bonding?" He cut her off, his deep voice full of curiosity.

Lealandra nodded.

It was the only way that she could explain it. Charlie hadn't worn her mark because she hadn't wanted to bond with him. She hadn't realised that she had wanted to bind herself to Taig though. The Counter-Balance was effective without her mark on his skin. Now she had tied him to her for everyone to see.

Had her fear of him leaving her driven the magic to claim him so she would never be without her Counter-Balance again?

Her heart hammered erratically in her throat as he stared at her, silent and distant, pensive. What was he thinking about? Her eyebrows furrowed and she wished she could bring herself to smile or say something stupid to lighten the heavy atmosphere between them and lift the tension from the room. Fear whispered malicious things in the back of her mind, making her believe that when he next spoke the words that left his lips would be ones to hurt her.

Taig looked down at his arm again, the black spikes of his hair obscuring his eyes. "It's not very fair is it?"

Lealandra's pulse rocketed and her chest ached. He wanted it off him. Her gaze followed his hand as he rubbed the mark. He didn't want to be hers. Her heart felt as though it was breaking all over again.

She frowned when he reached over his left shoulder, causing his muscles to tense and bulge, and pressed his hand against his back. His right hand caught hold of her left upper arm, clamping down on it and holding it so tightly that a sting of pain shot down to her fingertips. Before she could speak, searing heat scorched her skin where his hand touched her. She gritted her teeth and grimaced, flinching away from the fiery burning, fearing he was going to punish her for what she had done even as her heart cried out that Taig wouldn't do such a thing. He wouldn't hurt her. He loved her.

The flames subsided and he took his hand away. She immediately looked down at her arm, afraid of what she would see and confused about what he had been doing. There on her skin was a deep red tattoo of his mark.

He grinned. "Now we're even."

"But what does it mean?"

Taig smiled, stroked her cheek, and then pulled her into his arms and kissed the breath out of her.

Lealandra realised that was all the answer he was going to give her. She tried to break free but he wouldn't let her go. Her magic hummed with satisfaction at the taste of him. Was just kissing him going to placate it now and bring it under control? It was strange to think that she had bonded with him and that he was her Counter-Balance. She knew it wasn't because he had a human side. That side bore no magic and had no power. It was the demon in him that her magic had chosen as its balance.

She was going to have to visit her parents again to tell them about it and that she had survived her ascension. They would be thrilled to hear it and curious to know that a witch could have a demon as their Counter-Balance. Considering the bad blood between demons and witches though, she didn't see it catching on.

Taig stiffened and growled, pushing her away. He stared at the front door.

Lealandra turned to look there and her eyes widened when she saw the state of his apartment. She had decimated it. Everything lay broken around them and the wall to the bedroom was no longer there and neither was the kitchen. The red fridge still stood against the outside wall but the shockwave of her power had crushed it flat. She glanced at the windows and front door again. They were intact. Had Taig's power protected them? Had the marks he had scored on the frames stopped her magic from escaping and blasting a hole in the building?

Taig's power spiked, a black wave that warned of danger and sent fear surging through her.

"What's wrong?" She moved closer to him and stared at the front door. What had he sensed out there?

"We've got company."

CHAPTER 21

Lealandra jumped when someone knocked at the door. Her power stretched out, wanting to know who Taig had sensed. They knocked again, a double rap this time, and Lealandra felt their impatience and something else too. She knew them.

Taig stood, walked through the rubble to what used to be the kitchen and dug through it for his knife. Lealandra stumbled to her feet, winced her way barefoot over the mess, and caught his wrist. He looked down at her hand and then into her eyes.

"Wait." She frowned at the door, focusing her power there. Her eyes widened when she realised who was on the other side. They weren't here to harm them. At least, she hoped they weren't. Gregori couldn't have turned this person against her, surely? She stooped, picked up her dusty robe from the mess that she had caused and quickly put it on.

She snapped her fingers. Black jeans encased Taig's lower half. Another snap of her fingers and everything that littered the room began to fix itself. Lealandra focused hard to recall what it had all looked like before she had destroyed it. The kitchen popped back out, cupboards unravelling from the wall until they gleamed black again and the red refrigerator no longer resembled a pancake. The kitchen island rose up from the ashes and the white square pillar beside it reassembled itself.

Her magic fixed the bedroom wall next, reconstructing it and the bedroom beyond. The black coffee table and couch near her in the living room reversed through time until they were perfect again, and the huge flat screen television retook its place on the white wall.

The other walls repaired themselves around her and she turned at last to the long black side table that lined the one opposite the television. It pieced itself back together and a final sweep of her power told her that everything was back to how it had been.

Lealandra marvelled at the ease of it. Before her ascension, it would have drained her to perform such widespread and varied spells to undo the damage. Even fixing mechanical things like the television were simple for her to do now. She smiled when she saw the picture of Taig's parents on the sideboard. She hadn't needed to reconstruct that. It had survived unscathed, protected by Taig's superior power.

That was a godsend.

It was bad enough that she had wrecked his apartment and then bonded with him without asking. If she had damaged the photograph, Taig would have killed her. She glanced at her arm, the dirty white robe hiding the mark from view. What had Taig done to her?

Taig quirked an eyebrow at his apartment, picked up his black-handled hunting knife from the floor, and then pressed the flat of his hand against her chest when she went to move past him to the door.

"Where do you think you're going, little missy?"

She tried to get past him the other way but he blocked her again.

"It's safe." She took hold of his hand.

"It's a witch," he countered and tugged his hand free and folded his arms across his broad chest. His biceps bulged and his chest tightened. He frowned at her. "No witch is safe right now."

"This one is." Lealandra disappeared and reappeared by the door. Taig growled, grabbed her arm and pulled her back behind him.

"If you're so bloody insistent, at least let me answer it. It's my damn door."

Lealandra huffed and waved her hand towards the door. If he wanted to answer it, then it wasn't really her place to stop him. It was his apartment after all. She just hoped that the witch on the other side wouldn't make a wrong move. Her gaze fell to the knife clutched tightly in his hand. If Taig tried to harm her, Lealandra would have to intervene. She didn't want to see this person hurt. For all the times that she had faked her feelings when at the coven there had been countless moments more when she had felt true emotions towards this witch. If she could call anyone at the coven friend, it was her.

Taig stormed to the door and opened it. There was a quiet gasp from the other side. Lealandra could picture the sort of face Taig would be making and it was frightening, especially when his eyes were red.

"Can I help you?" he snarled and then rolled his shoulders, as though they were bothering him. His power rose, flowing through Lealandra, speaking of his irritation.

"Is Lealandra home?" A shy female voice echoed through the room.

Lealandra smiled at the sound of it—familiar and comforting, someone she knew that she could trust to be on her side.

"What makes you think this Lealandra you're looking for is here, kiddo?" Taig's broad form blocked Isabelle from view. Lealandra couldn't blame him for being suspicious but she knew how Isabelle had found her and it wasn't through Gregori.

"I followed my... er... magic. This might sound crazy but I'm a witch."

"No shit. You might not have noticed but I'm a demon and I could sense you a mile off. As far as I see it, there's only one way you're getting past me. You've just gotta tell me the truth." Taig shifted his shoulders again and Lealandra sensed the increase in his power, and his irritation. "Tell me how you found her and maybe I'll let you through. If you won't tell me or I don't like your answer, I'll eat you."

Isabelle squeaked. Lealandra smiled. Taig wouldn't eat Isabelle but it was just like him to throw his weight around.

"She shared a spell with me once. It's a sort of tracker. I got lost a few times when I first moved to the coven, so she let me use her as a beacon and then I could find my way back without a problem... so please don't eat me."

Lealandra covered her mouth to stifle her giggle. Taig looked over his shoulder at her and she nodded to confirm that Isabelle was telling the truth.

"Let her in, Taig, please?"

He rolled his shoulders again, frowning, and then stepped backwards.

He didn't let the woman pass him. He backed towards Lealandra, his strong shoulders tensed, the muscles in them clearly visible, and his fingers tightly clutching the knife. Something moved beneath his skin. Dark spots appeared on his shoulder blades.

Taig stopped just in front of Lealandra, his back still to her, and she reached up and touched his shoulders. The spots grew darker and rose into bumps. Two tiny points broke the skin. It was the only warning Lealandra had before Taig's dragon-like wings unfurled, so close to her face that air beat against her, and stretched across the room.

Lealandra smiled. He was protecting her again. When the demons had dared to attack them, he had done the same thing, using his wings to shield her. She touched his back between his shoulder blades and wings, silently letting him know that she was fine and that he didn't need to protect her from this person.

"Go cool off," she said and Taig looked over his shoulder at her again. The flames of Hell burned in his eyes. "I need to talk to her."

He didn't move.

"I'll be fine. Just give me a moment, okay? You'll know if I need you."

Lealandra jumped when his wings curled back up, shrinking down at the same time, and disappeared under his skin. The jagged marks healed, leaving his skin unbroken. It was fascinating to watch the process. He looked at her one more time and then walked into the bedroom. Her gaze fell on the slim young woman who had come to visit her. There was more fear in her green eyes now and a more wary air to her than when they had last met. It had been a while since Lealandra had seen Isabelle but she hadn't expected such a dramatic change. The bright youthful and carefree aura that had surrounded her was gone, replaced with a darker fearful one. Her mousy hair was as wild as ever, the waves loosely held back in a knot, strands of it falling out. She smiled but no trace of happiness touched her eyes. It hadn't in weeks.

"Lea," Isabelle said and moved over to her, her arms out as though she was going to embrace her. A growl from the bedroom stopped her dead and she frowned at the open black door. Her arms fell to her sides. "Your new man is a bit of an animal."

Lealandra smiled and sat down on the black couch. She patted the spot next to her. Isabelle sat and arranged the long trumpet sleeves of her black fairy-like top across her lap. Lealandra had always wondered how someone like

Isabelle managed with such long sleeves. She was rather accident-prone at times.

"He won't eat you, and he's my old man, actually." Lealandra glanced at the bedroom door. She could sense Taig stomping around it. He wasn't doing it literally. He was walking quietly. But she could feel in his mind that it was a definite stomp. A quiet stomp. He wasn't happy about letting another witch into his home and she couldn't blame him for being cautious. He only wanted to protect her. Her smile widened. He went into the bathroom and the sound of water running broke the silence. "And my Counter-Balance."

"He's a demon—"

"It is possible." Her gaze shifted back to Isabelle and she could see in her green eyes that she didn't believe her. It was a look that she recognised, one that another had been prone to giving her whenever she had said something they hadn't agreed with. "Our balance doesn't need to be a human bearing magic. Taig gives me balance like no other has, not even Charlie."

The room fell quiet and the air between her and Isabelle turned as thick as tar. Lealandra stared at her hands where they rested in her lap. They were dirty against her white bathrobe. She had fixed the apartment but had forgotten to fix her appearance. How bad did she look? She casually touched her hair. It was knotted and all over the place. She could still taste blood. How did it look to Isabelle? She probably thought that she was interrupting some sort of sex-fest. It probably looked terrible, especially after everything they had been through together.

"I'm sorry about what happened to him," Lealandra whispered.

Isabelle remained quiet.

Lealandra sighed and took hold of her hand. It was warm and she could feel Isabelle's magic rising within her, coming to the surface to meet her own power. Young magic that was weak compared to her old magic. Her power interlaced with it, giving strength rather than drawing it, as though it had felt Isabelle's need for stronger magic in her time of need.

"It was his choice." Isabelle's voice was low, her gaze not leaving their hands. "My brother always did like you. He was fairly set on being your Counter-Balance, even though he wasn't really strong enough for you."

Isabelle's gaze slowly rose to meet hers and then moved to the side, towards the bedroom. Lealandra knew why. Taig was there. She only hoped he was wearing clothes. A glance at him revealed that he was dressed in just his black jeans. The tight material clung to his powerful legs and rode low on his hips, revealing the full length of his abdomen and stirring hunger inside her.

"It's okay to keep talking. He really won't bite." Lealandra didn't take her eyes off Taig. He was an imposing figure when he wanted to be and was emitting a sense of danger that Isabelle's magic would pick up. Isabelle hadn't encountered many demons and Taig was far more powerful than the average type of demon she might have met in the field.

Lealandra's gaze rose to meet his. The black fathomless depths of his eyes spoke to hers, holding her captive and making her imagine them entwined again, as one with each other. Taig had been so sweet with her that she craved the roughness they had previously shared.

A seductive smile tugged at the corners of his lips. He leaned back against the wall, crossed his ankles and jammed his hands into his pockets. His torso tensed, revealing the delicious peaks and valleys of his body. The intensity of his gaze caused heat to rise up from her feet and scorch every inch of her.

Lealandra tore her eyes away from him. Isabelle was staring at him, a hint of colour touching her cheeks. She didn't think that Isabelle was particularly experienced with men. Charlie had been very protective of his little sister and had kept her away from the men in the coven as much as possible. When Gregori had suggested finding Isabelle a Counter-Balance, Charlie had petitioned against it, stating that his sister was too young for such things.

Charlie had been worried that Isabelle would fall for her Counter-Balance, just as he had fallen for his. Lealandra had never seen it before Isabelle had pointed it out to her barely half a year ago and after that, she hadn't known how to act around Charlie. She knew that it was common for Counter-Balances to fall for one another, but that wasn't what she had expected from her relationship with Charlie, and it wasn't what she had wanted. She hadn't wanted his love. She had only wanted someone to balance her magic.

Isabelle's attention slowly moved away from Taig. Her blush deepened when Lealandra met her gaze. She didn't mind Isabelle looking at Taig. He was putting on a display after all, but she could guarantee that he hadn't expected Isabelle to gawp rather than be afraid.

"Why are you here?" Darkness laced Taig's deep voice. Anger and mistrust swept over her in a wave so strong that she knew Isabelle would be able to sense it. "Unless you just came to catch up about old times and Charlie-boy."

Isabelle shot him a glare. The protective thing worked both ways. Isabelle had always been fiercely defensive of her big brother.

"I was out when I received a call," Isabelle said. "It was from Mariana."

"Mariana?" Lealandra leaned towards Isabelle, needing to hold her attention so she could see the truth in her eyes. The older witch was growing frail with the passing of years and the toll her magic took on her. Lealandra had often helped her during her classes for the younger witches at the coven. "Is she okay?"

Isabelle nodded. "For now, anyway. She told me that Gregori has gone insane. He's taken half of the coven hostage and the other half has agreed to work with him."

"He's going to come after me." Lealandra's eyes darted to Taig. Suddenly he didn't look so relaxed. The red was back in his eyes and the aura of danger had returned. His tension ran through her as though it was her own.

"I came straight here to tell you." Isabelle's gaze flickered to the front door. "It's a powerful spell you put on this place."

Lealandra shook her head. "It isn't my magic. I couldn't construct something like this, not even now. It's Taig's power."

Isabelle looked at Taig again, amazement written across her youthful face. He shrugged nonchalantly. Lealandra smiled at how uncomfortable he looked. She had always thought that Taig would enjoy such attention and would lap up this kind of awe, but instead he looked as though he wanted to leave the room.

"It was nothing." He pushed away from the wall, went into the kitchen, picked up his hunting knife and began toying with it. Nervous? She suppressed her giggle. It was new to see Taig shy about something. This was the man who was happy fighting naked and didn't give a damn about most things. A little bit of attention and praise had him almost blushing.

"Taig is very powerful. He's amazing," Lealandra said and he looked at her, eyebrows raised and eyes wide, as though she had shocked him by saying that. "He's not letting on but it took a lot of strength and skill to create this barrier, far more than we witches have."

He turned his back on her but not before she noticed a touch of crimson staining his cheeks.

Lealandra grinned at his back and felt warm inside. She had meant every word. Taig was far more powerful than she could ever be. Even now that she had ascended, she was no match for him if he unleashed his demonic side.

And the barrier was incredible.

Isabelle took her hand. Lealandra looked down at them and then at her. Isabelle was staring at their hands, a distant look in her green eyes.

"I... it feels different... your magic." Isabelle met her gaze. "Changed. Stronger."

Lealandra nodded. "I survived. I said I would, didn't I?"

Tears filled Isabelle's eyes and she brushed them away. Lealandra could sense her happiness and relief. Isabelle had been more worried than Charlie when Lealandra had revealed the ascension mark to them.

"He helped you?" Isabelle said with a pointed glance at Taig. Isabelle's gaze snapped back to him and she frowned. "He... you."

Taig walked back to the wall and Lealandra looked at him, and the place where she knew Isabelle was staring.

"You were right," Isabelle said. "He is your Counter-Balance, and you've bonded with him."

Lealandra smiled at the mark on Taig's arm. Her mark. Her Taig.

She placed her hand over her arm, over Taig's mark on her skin. Her gaze questioned him but he looked away to stare out of the windows. She wanted to know what it meant. Was it like her mark? Did it bond them?

"It's really quite disturbing." Isabelle's tone was deadpan. Both Lealandra and Taig looked at her.

"That I've bonded with him?" Lealandra said with a frown. She didn't think it was disturbing.

"No, the moon eyes you make at each other." Isabelle put her fingers in her mouth and pretended to gag. Lealandra rolled her eyes. Isabelle sighed and her look turned serious again. For a brief moment, the old Isabelle had been back. "You know, I always knew."

"Knew what?"

"That you were still in love with him and that you would never love my brother."

Lealandra blushed when she felt Taig's gaze burning into her.

"Did Mariana say anything else?" She wanted to deflect Isabelle's attention away from her love life. Taig continued to stare at her as though he was trying to read her mind. She would tell him. She would confess that she loved him.

When he confessed that he loved her.

Then she would know that he was ready to hear it.

"Only that Gregori is stronger now. I've been away for a few days. There was some sort of commotion I think and now Gregori has the ascension mark."

Lealandra's eyes shot wide and she tensed. It was as she had suspected. He had used her blood to trigger his ascension. With the supreme mages and half the coven helping him, there was a high chance he would survive. He had only taken her blood two days ago. His ascension couldn't be close yet. The quickest one known had been five days from when the mark appeared to when the ascension was complete.

"Your blood," Taig said and she nodded. Isabelle looked lost.

"Gregori sent two demons to take care of me and get my blood for him. I was so angry that, when the demons were dead, I went after Gregori. It was an idiotic thing to do. I thought he was weak but he was still stronger than me." Lealandra sighed and wrapped her arms around herself, chilled by the haunting memory of where Gregori had sent her. "He took my blood. The power in it must have triggered his ascension, just as he'd wanted."

"We have to put an end to this, Lea." The seriousness in Taig's tone scared her on some level. It wasn't like him to sound that way, not even when he was being serious. It hit home that she was still in danger. If Gregori ascended, she would be no match for him. His magic was older and more powerful.

"Our only chance is to hit him now, before he ascends."

Taig nodded. "Tomorrow."

"Why not today?" Isabelle said, fear lacing her trembling voice. Lealandra knew that she had never been involved in the kind of battle that was going to take place.

Neither had she.

But she wasn't afraid of it or Gregori, not anymore. She had to face him and this battle so she could survive and continue to live her life. So she could be with Taig.

"Lea needs to rest. You showed up barely minutes after her ascension completed. She isn't strong enough right now and I'm not letting her go into a fight when she's weak, not again." The resolve behind Taig's words brought a

Ascension

smile to Lealandra's lips. He really did want to protect her. He really did love her. He didn't need to say it for her to know, and she knew it was the same for him.

He smiled at her, cocksure and confident, typical Taig. The smirk suited him. The affection that shone in his eyes suited him even better though. That look could melt her. It warmed her heart to boiling point and weakened her knees. It was more powerful than any of his sultry gazes and seductive smiles.

"We'll come tomorrow," she said to Isabelle, aware of Taig's gaze on her. "Were you due back at the coven tonight?"

Isabelle nodded.

"Go as planned. Return and act as though you don't know what's happening. Tell the others that we're coming and we won't let Gregori harm them. I'll take care of him."

Isabelle looked nervous. Lealandra took hold of her hand and squeezed it.

"It will be fine. I promise. I'll come tomorrow night and finish this."

Isabelle nodded again and then rose from the couch. "I'm not a good actor."

"You don't need to be," Taig said and stepped away from the wall. "Just be yourself, kiddo. If Gregori frightens you, be frightened. Remember that you're not supposed to know anything."

She toyed with her long sleeves and walked to the door. Lealandra followed her and then pulled her into a hug.

"You'll be fine." Lealandra held her close, closing her eyes and hoping that she would. "I'll be there tomorrow night. Just stay with the others until then."

She felt Isabelle nod and then the young woman squeezed her. "Don't be late."

Lealandra nodded this time. She wouldn't fail her friend. She opened the door for her and Taig moved closer, coming to lean against the post at the corner of the kitchen nearest the living room. Awareness washed over Lealandra. She felt his hunger and her own need rose in response as his gaze roamed down her back and she itched to look at him, to touch him and feel his hard body against hers.

Isabelle gave her a little wave. She absently returned it and then closed the door. The second it clicked shut, she raised her hand and all the locks slid into place.

She cursed Taig for distracting her throughout her whole time with Isabelle. The young woman had deserved her full attention but it had been impossible with Taig standing there half-naked, temptation personified, making her want him.

She turned to face him, pressed her hands against his chest, and shoved him into the post.

He grinned at her.

She kissed him.

CHAPTER 22

Taig pushed Lealandra backwards, tightly grasping her upper arms. His chest heaved as he breathed and her gaze jumped to it, drinking in the sight of his taut muscles shifting under bronzed skin. He was gorgeous and she needed to feel his body on hers again. She tried to kiss him but his arms locked, holding her at a distance.

"Now who's the insatiable one?" He grinned at her, the smile touching his dark eyes and making them shine. She smiled back at him, a little embarrassed about the way she was behaving. When they had been together, there had been times when she had taken control and initiated things, like when they had been sunbathing, but those had been few and far between. Normally Taig had triggered their lustful interludes. He touched her cheek and grinned wider. "Not that I'm complaining, sweet cheeks. Always did like it when you played rough... just wasn't expecting it when company only just walked out the door... and when we've got a fight tomorrow."

"We never could keep our hands off each other after a fight... how about we start a new tradition?" Lealandra stepped towards him and he let her this time, his grip on her loosening. His black gaze fell to her mouth and he watched it in evident fascination as she spoke. "Preparation sex."

Taig quirked an eyebrow. "It sounds like a cream you put on something nasty."

She giggled. He was right about that but coming up with names for their trysts had never been her forte. Taig was far superior at it. He stared at her. She stared back. Waiting.

"Don't look at me." He shrugged. "The big head isn't doing the thinking right now."

Lealandra looked down at the bulge in the front of Taig's tight black jeans. He was right. She smiled. Just her kiss had him hot and bothered. That was Taig. Always ready for anything, especially her.

"Where were we?" he said with another grin and lightly ran his hands down her arms.

"Let's take it from the top." She placed her hands against his biceps, held on to him, and teleported them both to the bedroom.

Taig hit the bed first, collapsing onto it with her on top of him. His arms fell out at his sides and Lealandra pushed herself up so she was straddling his hips. The feel of his hard length pressing between her thighs made her ache to have him inside her.

"God, the things you do to me," she whispered and Taig frowned. She motioned across her mouth, pretending to zip it up. He never had liked it when she mentioned God, and he liked it even less if she mentioned the Devil. She ran her fingers over his chest, delighting in how perfect his body was, his strength and masculine beauty. "Mmm... you're the only god I need."

With a growl, he rolled them over so he was on top. She giggled again when he thrust against her and pulled a face of discomfort.

"Pinches," he muttered in a tight voice and shifted backwards.

No way was she going to let him leave her body for even five seconds. He was going to remain against her, just as she wanted him to. Lealandra snapped her fingers and Taig grinned when his jeans disappeared. Another snap of her fingers and the white bathrobe she had been wearing was gone.

"Start at the top you said," he whispered and then captured her lips in a searing kiss. She craned her neck, desperate for more, and thrust her tongue into his mouth. Taig ground against her. She moaned at the feel of his hard length rubbing her most sensitive area and the roughness of his kiss.

Lealandra relaxed into the bed as he kissed her, her body turning lax. She submitted to him, enjoying how his fingers pressed into her sides, stopping her from moving, and the hunger she could feel in him. His power placated hers, sending it deep inside her, until she couldn't feel it at all. She could only feel Taig and he felt divine.

She gasped into his mouth when one of his hands left her side and came to rest over her breast. He thumbed her nipple until it hardened into a painful peak desperate for his attention and then kissed along her jaw. She arched her back, hoping to encourage him to go where she needed him. She wanted to feel his mouth on her breasts, to have him suckling and teasing her nipples.

He kissed down her chest and around her breasts, torturing her with anticipation. She moaned and threaded her fingers into his black hair, desperately trying to guide him. His other hand came up and covered her other breast, cupping it. The weight of it against her was nice but she needed more.

He gave it to her.

She tilted her head back when Taig pulled her right nipple into his mouth, rolling it with his tongue and then lightly biting. She groaned and raised her knees, clamping them down against his hips. He ground his erection against her, teasing her clit and tempting her into thrusting against him to bring herself satisfaction, and tugged on her nipple, sucking it harder. Sparks of pleasure shot out from it, cascading over her body, and she wrapped her arms around him and held him against her, rubbing herself against his hardness and losing herself inch by inch in the moment.

Taig pulled back and she pouted before realising where he was going. She wriggled her hips and closed her eyes when he moved downwards, kissing a path from her breasts to her stomach.

Lealandra spread her legs for him and wriggled again, showing him just where she wanted him.

He pressed a kiss to the front of her curly mound and then tickled her with his fingers, tracing them down the length of her. She bit her lip when his fingers dipped in and then out, teasing and making her writhe. She needed more. He dipped in again, swirled his finger around her pert nub and then slid them downwards. She gasped and grabbed the sheets when he eased two fingers into her and began pumping slowly. Gods, she wanted his hard length inside her like that. She needed to feel him, needed to be one with him again. He moved inside her painfully slowly, taking her out of her mind. She tried to relax but couldn't. Her muscles tensed around him and she sighed when he found the spot that would have her climaxing in no time.

He withdrew his fingers.

She frowned and opened her eyes. They widened when he licked his fingers clean, his gaze locked with hers, intent written clearly in his eyes. He was going to have her and it was going to be as rough as she wanted it to be.

He motioned for her to roll over and Lealandra did it with a smile, happy to do his bidding when they were in the bedroom because she knew he would make it worth her while. Her eyes closed when he ran his hands down her back and over her bottom. They stopped there, massaging her buttocks and making her feel incredibly relaxed. He moved on, shifting her legs apart and dipping his hand back down. His fingers found her clit and she sighed as he circled it. It felt nice, but a little slow paced for her liking right now.

She wriggled again.

Taig growled, commanding and powerful, sending a thrill through her. Damn, she did like it when he took control.

His hands grasped her hips and raised them, so she was kneeling. Before she could even think about what he was going to do, his fingers had spread her open and his tongue was darting against her flesh, torturing her clit and stealing a gasping moan from her. She grasped the bedclothes and furrowed her brow as he licked her, swirling his tongue one moment and sucking the next. She wriggled her hips but he growled, stopping her from moving. Her mouth opened and she moaned with each brush of his tongue over her sensitive flesh and then groaned when he pushed two fingers back into her and began pumping her with them. She wanted him inside her. Needed him.

As if sensing that need, he pulled away. She had a second to breathe and then he was sliding his hard length deep into her core. Her grip on the bedcovers tightened and her knuckles burned white. Taig kicked her legs further apart and buried himself deeper, until his balls brushed her clit. She groaned and raised her backside into him. He growled again, grasped her hips so tightly that she could feel each point where his fingertips pressed into her skin, and began thrusting.

Lealandra raised herself up onto her hands and bit her lip. Taig pulled almost all the way out and plunged back in, groaning with each deep thrust into her. She tensed her muscles around him, intent on feeling every inch of his cock sliding into her, and moaned along with him. Her breasts swung with each hard thrust and her breathing quickened until she was gasping at air as choppily as Taig was. He held her tighter, his movements gaining speed, his balls hitting her clit with each meeting of their hips. She groaned and pressed back against him, desperate to climax.

One hand left her thigh. Taig grunted, reached under her, and then his fingers found her clit. He rubbed it, keeping tempo with the fast deep glide of his cock. She moaned and furrowed her eyebrows, biting down on her lip and tensing around him again. She wanted to climax. Was so close. Just a little more and she would be there, and she knew he would be right there with her.

His fingers pinched her nub.

Stars shot across the black of her eyes and she shuddered with her orgasm. Heat chased the tiny points of light, washing through her entire body as it convulsed around Taig's cock, clenching it. He growled, thrust deeper and harder for a few seconds more, and then came to a juddering halt. His hips pumped quick and shallow as he spilled himself inside her.

Lealandra moaned in unison with him and then collapsed onto her front on the bed when he withdrew his softening length from her. He hit the bed next to her, breathing hard and fast. Sweat beaded his brow and she smiled as she wiped it away. Her hand fell to the bed, her bones too limp to lift for any amount of time. Taig pulled her over to him, dragging her so she was lying with half of her chest pressed against his and her head resting on his shoulder. She sighed. She just wanted to sleep forever in Taig's arms, satisfied and content.

Taig's heart beat against her ear, the pace of it gradually slowing as he caught his breath. She sighed again and he wrapped his arm around her, his hand settling on her ribs. It shifted to her left arm and he stroked it. Her skin warmed beneath his fingers and she frowned when a deep sense of connection to Taig suffused her body. His hand came to rest over her upper arm. It burned. The warmth of it added to her sense of satisfaction.

She realised that he was touching the mark he had put on her. She looked up at him, her gaze tracing his noble profile, and willed him to look at her so she could ask him again what the mark meant and see the answer in his eyes.

"Taig," she whispered, not wanting to disturb him if he was falling asleep. He frowned. "What does it mean?"

He smiled.

He wasn't going to answer her. She curled up against him and focused on the weight of his hand on her arm. His mark. She smiled. He was staking his territory in a permanent way. That had to be it. Taig had bonded with her.

She grinned at the thought.

"What is it?" Taig murmured and opened his eyes, squinting at her. "I'm trying to sleep here."

"Bonding," she said and he raised an unimpressed eyebrow.

"You still on that?"

"It's a bonding symbol." Her grin widened. "We each wear the other's mark. It's practically like being married."

"Whoa, there!" Taig shot bolt upright. "No one mentioned anything about getting hitched. Demons have no place marrying humans."

"I'm not human," she countered and sat up too. His words hadn't offended her. She had said hers to get a reaction and they had done just that. She pouted and stroked the mark on his arm, continuing to toy with him. "And I thought you would want to marry me. I mean, all the unprotected sex... I thought you wanted us to have a little baby and get married, and settle down together in a house with a white picket fence and a yard."

"Now I know you're not being serious," he said with a frown. She frowned right back at him, wondering what had given her away. It wasn't the baby or the marriage part. She wanted both of those with Taig and knew that deep in his heart he probably wanted them too. He pulled her to him and pressed a kiss to her forehead. "You'd never want a house with a picket fence. Suburbia just isn't you."

"Oh, really. Then do tell me what is 'me'." Lealandra rested her head against his shoulder. He fell back onto the bed again, his arm around her, and sighed at the ceiling.

"Let's see, sweet cheeks." His hand left her side and he stroked her hair, running his fingers through it and untangling the knots.

Lealandra looked up at him, studying his face as he thought. He would make beautiful babies. She didn't care that they would have mixed genes and would be part demon, part witch, and part human. She didn't care what people would think and she would make sure her children grew up knowing that their parents loved them and there was nothing wrong with them, because they were perfect, born of love and happiness.

She was getting ahead of herself, but she couldn't help thinking about her future and the part she wanted Taig to play in it. He would make a good father, would make sure that their children would understand their demon side and accept it at an early age. He wouldn't make any mistakes with them, not like his father had with him, and she would help him teach their children everything they needed to know about demons, witches and humans. They would both make sure that their children knew they had a place in this world and were a part of it, and they would both protect them and keep them safe.

"The countryside." Taig untangled another knot, unravelling her thoughts at the same time and bringing her back to him. She liked the feel of his fingers in her hair. It was soothing.

"Just the countryside?" She liked this conversation too. They had never talked about their future before, and she got the feeling Taig was doing just that, and that he had put a lot of thought into how it was going to turn out.

"No... English countryside... somewhere near a little village full of old thatched buildings. A small manor with a beautiful rose garden and a fountain. Not too big. Cotswold stone and with pillars at the entrance. It would suit you just perfect."

Lealandra frowned. He wasn't talking about a dream place. He looked at her, his eyes open and full of honesty. She had never pieced it together before now. The way Taig spoke sometimes, he didn't sound American. His accent sounded mixed and the words he used weren't right for her country. She remembered the picture of his parents. They were in a garden. A beautiful rose garden. A chill swept over her.

"That's a real place," she whispered, holding his gaze so she could see the truth in it when he answered.

"Actually, that's a real place that I own."

Her eyebrows rose. "You grew up there. You're British!"

He smiled. "You're not going to hold that against me are you, sweet cheeks? Don't tell me you can accept the demon thing but not the ex-pat side of me?"

She laughed and shook her head. "Not at all. I just can't believe that I didn't realise before now… and… you really want to go there with me?"

He shrugged and she frowned at him. For a moment, she had thought he was being serious about their relationship and the things he was saying. He smiled again, reached out, and brushed the backs of his fingers down her cheek.

"Of course I want to go there with you." His expression shifted to one of wariness. "But I haven't been back since my parents—you know. I left there, wanted to leave my past behind me, but now I feel I can return… and besides, the place really is perfect for you. Quiet, beautiful, and full of old witches that could help you with your magic."

"Old witches?" That piqued her curiosity.

"Ancient." He stroked her cheek again. "Their magic keeps them going. They have a strong relationship with it. I figured you might want to learn from them. They used to know my mother. I'm sure I could put in a good word for you."

"Your mother knew witches?"

He nodded again. "My father didn't quite see eye to eye with them so they only came to the manor when he wasn't around, but my mum went to see them every week. I think she wanted to learn magic. She wanted to be different, like my father."

Lealandra smiled and closed her eyes. She was different, just like Taig, and he was right about meeting with the old witches. She wanted to see them and see if they could help her develop a stronger relationship with her magic.

"So, you want to come with me back to my old place?" Taig said as casual as anything but she could feel the underlying nerves in him. Was this like his version of asking her to go steady with him? It was a bit late for him to be asking that after they had both marked each other with a sign of bonding.

She wrapped her arms around him. "I'd love to… and then we can get married."

He laughed. "You are insatiable."

"That wasn't a no."

"No... it wasn't a no." He pressed a kiss to her hair. "It wasn't a yes either."

Lealandra rolled her eyes. It was as close to a yes as she was going to get out of him for now, and that was enough for her. It was nice to have him opening up to her at last. He felt so different since he had shown his demon form to her—comfortable and calm. Had he finally accepted that part of himself and her love for him? Wasn't he going to fight her anymore? She finally felt as though things were serious between them and he had let her into the fortress that protected his heart.

Taig held her in silence for a few minutes, the air between them comfortable, and then he tensed.

"What's wrong?" she murmured against his chest, gradually drifting off to sleep.

"Something's been bothering me."

"What?" She pushed sleep from her mind and looked up at Taig.

"How easy would it be for someone to pretend to be someone else, to sound like them?"

"Using magic?"

He nodded.

"Easy, sweet cheeks," she said in his voice, a perfect imitation of him.

He shuddered and glared at her. "If you ever do that again in the bedroom, I'm leaving."

She laughed. He didn't.

"You're thinking about the phone call Isabelle got, aren't you?" She thought about everything that Isabelle had told her. It made sense that Mariana would want to warn Isabelle and any witch outside the coven at the time that they would be in danger if they returned, but then what Taig was implying made a whole lot more sense. Gregori wanted to finish her off. What better way than to have her come to him?

"It's a trap." Taig's expression remained serious.

"I know." She laid her head back down on his shoulder and placed her hand against his chest. "Gregori wants me to come to him. He doesn't need to invite me. I was already going."

Lealandra closed her eyes and held Taig. He wrapped his arms around her and rested his cheek against her head. If Gregori wanted a fight, he was going to get one.

The moment they woke tomorrow, they were going to arm up and head out. She wouldn't fail Isabelle or anyone trapped in the coven. She was going to fight for them and for herself. She was going to fight for her future.

She was going to kill Gregori.

A sense of dread filled her.

She only hoped this wouldn't be the last time she laid in Taig's arms.

She wanted that dream he had for them, more than anything.

CHAPTER 23

Witches.

Taig growled, grabbed the man who had attempted to tackle him, and threw him across the expansive room in the coven building.

He hated them.

Well, there were a few exceptions.

He glanced across the fray at Lealandra. She was fighting hard, backed up by three female witches around her age that were strong, and Isabelle. He could never hate Lealandra, and he couldn't hate her parents, not if he was going to remain on good terms with them, and he didn't mind the witches back near where he grew up, but other than those, he hated them.

Give him demons, shadows, angels, any of the nefarious creatures residing in the underworld, any day of the week, and he would be happy to scrap it out. But witches.

They fought dirty.

His head spun as a spell slammed into him, knocking him off his feet and sapping his power. The drain was weak and temporary enough that it only pissed him off. The witches they were fighting right now weren't a threat but their half-assed spells were beginning to get on his nerves.

He roared at the group of young male witches who were casting the spells and stormed towards them, making his way past the toppled dark red couches and the overturned tables of the huge open living area. The lights were low, half of the standing floor lamps broken in the raging storm of battle happening all around him.

Casualty numbers were rising fast and their group of witches was dwindling. They were already down around half their number, almost forty dead, but nearly one hundred littered the room and the corridors around it. It was all taking its toll on Lealandra. He could see it each time he looked at her. She hadn't wanted so many to sacrifice themselves, but this was a war, a revolution, and that meant some paid with their lives for the freedom of others. Everyone here had chosen to come and to fight. Those who had been afraid, too young or old or too weak magically were hiding on the lower levels where they would be safe. Every floor from the end of living quarters upwards was a war zone. Lealandra's group had teleported straight to the eighteenth floor and into the stronger witches, but they still weren't fighting the highest level ones. Those waited on the floor above with Gregori.

A broken window in the long bank that lined the outside wall allowed a chill breeze to blast through the room, carrying the scent of cinders and blood. The world outside was dark, a myriad of twinkling city lights swallowed by sheer silence. This high up, the world didn't make a sound.

Three stronger male witches followed him towards his next prey, his back up but annoying nonetheless. He didn't need an entourage. He had told Lealandra that until he was sick of hearing it himself but she hadn't budged. She was worried about him and that meant he was stuck with three dark haired young men who looked as pleased about the situation as he felt. When Lealandra had pulled out the puppy dog eyes, it had been game over. He never could turn her down when she looked like that.

The man in the middle of the group of four witches he was storming towards backed off a step. Taig grinned. He had just elected himself the first one to die. The world sped by in a blur as Taig crossed the room in a heartbeat, appearing behind the man and snapping his neck before he could even realise he was there. The remaining three turned to look at him, their wide eyes reflecting the horror Taig could feel pounding in their veins. He slammed his fist into the pretty face of the young man to his right, sending him flying across the room head over heels and barrelling into another group of witches. Lealandra shot Taig a dirty look. He winked. She blasted the witch with a spell that Taig didn't like the look of. The moment it hit the man, he convulsed. Taig flinched when the man's limbs twisted in grotesque ways and then he went still. Dead. Taig noted not to get on Lealandra's nerves too much during the fight. He didn't want to end up playing contortionist too.

A spell whizzed past his head, narrowly missing his ear, and Taig growled at the man who had thrown it. He backed away, right into one of Taig's entourage. The man touched his shoulder, their eyes met, and his foe fell lifeless to the floor.

What kind of witches had Lealandra dumped him with?

Another of his men touched the remaining witch and he too fell to the floor.

Necromancers? Taig shook his head. No human had found a way to govern the spirits. They refused to listen to them and their magic. Perhaps these men were just more powerful than he had given them credit for. He had underestimated them. Well, he grinned to himself, they had probably underestimated him too. Demons weren't the only ones who didn't recognise the strength of the power in him when they met him, not until he unleashed it.

Taig stood still, surrounded by chaos on the empty floor, eyes locked with the men on his team. They were sure, confident, and bordering on cocky as they stared at him with empty eyes, no sign of feeling in their features. They were mocking him. Silently challenging him. Taig tilted his chin up, coolly held the leaders gaze, a man who looked around the same age as himself, somewhere in his mid-thirties, and with equally dark hair but very pale skin. The man's blue eyes stared impassively back at him. Taig would show him just who was stronger.

Witches attacked them but the other two men on his team handled them with ease, touching them and sending them to whatever dark place it was that they had some dominion over. It wasn't death and it wasn't the shadow world. These men weren't strong enough for that sort of magic.

Taig smiled, a small one that tugged at the corners of his lips and reflected his surety.

He unleashed his power a touch, just enough for the three men to feel it. He wanted them to know who was stronger and in charge here. The way they were heading, it wouldn't be long before they started getting ideas above their station, started trying to command him, and he would be dead before that happened.

The male witch's expression didn't change.

Taig released it a little more and then, with a smile, said, "Let's make this fight more interesting, eh?"

The man frowned.

Taig stared deep into his eyes, focused all of his power on the barrier between worlds, between Earth and the shadows, and nudged it a little. It didn't take much. Just a slight push in the right place. A demon way of shifting realities. A witch would go in head first, firing off their strongest spell to disrupt the worlds. All it took was a little poke in a weak spot and it tipped them off balance.

The already dimly lit open area grew darker, the shadows distorting and the air turning so cold that the witch's breath was visible. Taig continued to smile. The witch started to look nervous. His eyes left Taig's, darting around at the encroaching shadows that shifted and moved, contorting into new shapes that had long broken claws and fractured bodies.

The male witch backed away a step and cast a glance at his two companions. Their faces no longer spoke of confidence. Emotions skittered across them one after another, a shifting wave of fear and awe.

Taig grinned and folded his arms across his chest, causing the black t-shirt he wore to stretch tight over bunched muscles.

They were impressed.

"Taig!" A sharp voice rang out across the ever-darkening room.

Taig winced and cautiously looked across it at Lealandra.

She wasn't.

With a cheeky smile and shrug of his shoulders, he healed the breach between worlds and gave her his best innocent look.

"Not the time for games," she said and then her anger shattered, a small but relieving smile briefly touching her lips, "but you can show me how to do that later."

Maybe she was impressed. It wasn't every day that someone brought the shadow world to this one. Normally people sent their victim there and normally it took a lot of power to do so. He preferred to take the less draining route of bringing the shadows to him. Once here, brought by him, they would obey a command in the hope of a chance to taste human flesh.

The room brightened as the shadows melted away.

The three witches in his escort still looked wary. Good. Maybe now they wouldn't piss him off as much. Although, he had been in a foul mood since teleporting Lealandra into this situation. They had geared up back at his place, both dressing in their usual black but this time both choosing tight jeans and a black t-shirt, fighting clothes, and had brought guns with them as back up should they expend all of their power. He had dropped Lealandra right where she had wanted to be, although it had been by chance. He didn't know where Isabelle's place was in the building so had been forced to rely on guidance from Lealandra's power. She worked pretty good as a navigation system. They had landed right on Isabelle's couch, smashing it to pieces and sending Isabelle flying across the room. Several other witches had been present. It hadn't taken long for more to come, called telepathically by Isabelle. Now they were here, in what looked like some sort of open living area, a gathering place for the witches in the building.

A scream off to his left caught his attention and his head snapped around. Isabelle was clutching her arm, another female witch with long curly brown hair helping her move back from the frontline of Lealandra's fight. Isabelle had been radiating waves of fear since they had come crashing into her apartment. The girl was a liability—too weak to fight in this level of battle and too much of a distraction for Lealandra.

Taig leapt over another of the broken red couches, sidestepped around a long low wall with smashed potted plants on it, and came up beside Lealandra's group. He launched an arm out at a female witch as she appeared out of nowhere right beside him, her hands raised ready to cast a spell, and backhanded her across the face, sending her to the ground. One of the men behind him took care of her. He continued on, determined to remain close to Lealandra now so she would be more relaxed. He would protect anyone who Lealandra desired him to, anyone who would set her mind at ease, but ultimately he would sacrifice everyone for her safety.

Two male witches appeared in front of him. One grabbed him before he could react and the other hit him solidly across the jaw. Taig growled and yanked his arm free, throwing the first man into the second. His three witches moved forwards to fight the others that were surrounding them. A spell hit Taig hard in the gut and sapped the strength from him, making his stomach turn and his head spin. These witches were stronger.

The one further away unleashed a barrage of spells, glowing green orbs that were small and fast, hard to dodge. Taig did his best, stepping left and then right, ducking and leaping, and twisting in mid-air to avoid them, but they were faster than he was. The first hit him in the shoulder, sending him turning the other way, and then two more hit him on the right side of his ribs and his right thigh. The drain on his power was tremendous. He growled and his shoulders ached, his wings ready to come out and his demon itching for freedom. He held it inside, determined to save it, to store up his anger until bursting point and unleash it on the strongest witches they were yet to face.

Ascension

Somewhere above them, Gregori waited. Taig was waiting for them too. Gregori's party would have the pleasure of facing him while he was in his true form, and he would rip them to shreds.

Taig hit the floor. The three witches serving as his escort crowded him, fending off the enemy with magic that made the air smell of sulphur. Hell. It smelt like the underworld. He knew that smell, knew the heat of the world below his feet. His world.

No. He pushed himself up onto his feet. His demon shifted below the surface of his skin, one with him, fighting with him at last, not against him. He smiled ruefully. It never had been against him. He had been the one who had fought all this time, battling against it, his true nature. His demon blood gave him the strength to protect those he loved, and he was finally thankful for it, not ashamed of it. He was a demon and he belonged in this world with Lealandra—with the woman he loved.

With a roar, he flexed his fingers, his dark brown scaly claws shredding his skin. His hands grew, the skin on them peeling away to reveal the thick ridges of his real fingers, of the demon he was.

Lealandra blasted one of the witches away, sending him flying through a window. The glass exploded outwards and a cold wind gusted in, bringing the smell of earth. It was raining somewhere.

Taig grabbed the other witch around his throat, hauled him off the floor, and throttled him. The witch's eyes bulged, his face turning red. The three witches with Taig moved off to handle the few remaining enemies on the floor with them. Taig closed his fingers tighter around the man's throat, until he clutched at his hand, desperately trying to prise it off him. Taig stared into his eyes.

"You chose the wrong bloke to attack," Taig said and tightened his grip, until the witch's feet jerked and he went still, and then dropped him.

"Taig," Lealandra said and he was by her side in an instant. He frowned at her cut face, the smooth paleness of it marred by nasty dark bruises and red streaks. Strands of her black hair had fallen down from her long ponytail. He swept them back out of her face and then she smiled at him when he lightly wiped away the blood that had dripped down from a cut on her cheek. "You okay?"

He smiled back at her, staring into her grey stormy eyes. "Am I okay? You need to see what you look like, sweet cheeks."

"You could probably do with a mirror too." She reached up and touched his jaw. It stung like a bitch. He brushed her hand away and rubbed the spot she had touched, feeling the blood and the gash there, and the angry bruise that was waiting to make itself known tomorrow. She was right, he probably did look like hell but it was worth it. It had been a long time since he had been part of a fight this big and it was stirring his blood and his lust for violence like nothing else before it.

"We're gonna need some serious victory sex after this one... although I might be a bit tired." He grinned wide and imagined her taking care of him, riding him into oblivion just as he had dreamed of back in his apartment. They had done the slow and steady thing. Lealandra had shown him that she liked the rough stuff just as much as he did, and he did love it when she took command.

"Taig!" Lealandra slapped his arm and pointedly glanced at the witches surrounding them. He shrugged. He didn't care if they were listening. He probably wouldn't care if some of them wanted to watch. Actually, he would. No one but him got to see Lealandra naked.

"The floor's clear," one of his men said and Lealandra nodded. Her cheeks were scarlet, betraying the thoughts he could feel in her. Her power spoke clearly to his, as hungry as its owner and himself for the connection that came with sex.

"Let's move. We'll go up via the emergency stairs. Half of you head that way." She pointed to the far end of the room and then at the exit nearest them. "I'll go this way."

Lealandra walked a short distance and then stopped and looked back at him. Taig nodded and signalled his men to follow him. He followed Lealandra to the exit. She didn't need to ask him to go with her team. He wouldn't leave her side now. He would keep his oath and protect her. The future she had talked to him about was one that he wanted too—taking her to a place where she could learn to be one with her power, marriage, and maybe one day in the future when they were ready to settle down there would even be little Lea's running around. He wanted her and he was going to fight to be with her.

They headed up the stairs as silently as possible. The cool air in the stairwell was musty and stale. Through it came a sense of power, a strength that flowed down from above. He stared up the centre of the stairwell. It wasn't only power that he could feel.

He was tired and so was everyone else. He could feel it now they were closer together, packed into the stairwell. The energy that had been there at the start had died away, their strength stolen by the fight and by seeing their friends fall at the hands of their enemy. Everyone was on the brink of collapse but they had to keep going. They couldn't stop now. They weren't only fighting for Lealandra's survival. They were fighting for freedom, and to win that, they had to fight to the end.

Lealandra threw a blast of energy at the door of the next floor. The two sides of the door ripped off their hinges and exploded into the room beyond. They suddenly shot to the side, as though they had met with resistance, and then a wave of incredible power hit Taig. Lealandra froze. The whole group right down the stairs became still, chilled by the strength of power washing over them.

Taig stepped forwards past Lealandra.

Ascension

His eyes met the man's who stood before him, only a short distance away, a dark figure against a backdrop of long windows and the silent world outside.
Gregori.
Taig smiled and clenched his fists.
He was going to beat the crap out of him.

CHAPTER 24

Lealandra came to her senses the moment Gregori moved his arm around in a sweeping arc. Taig flew across the room, so fast he was only a blur, and slammed hard into the dark brown wall at the far end, creating an impact crater. Plaster rained down on him. Lealandra shot a glare at Gregori. He smiled at her.

She clenched her fists.

He looked better than he had the last time they had been here in this room, facing off against each other. His clothing was immaculate. The long black buttoned coat of his standing had never suited him better. It lent him a mysterious and dark air, one that enhanced the strong aura of power radiating from him, flowing across the room and winding itself around her like a poisonous snake.

He was ready to strike.

She wouldn't let him get in the first punch. Every sense of preparation she felt in him was a mirror of what she felt in herself. Her body was tense, alert, her attention fixed solely on him so she could notice the split second he moved.

Gregori stared at her, his hazel eyes impassive and emotionless, void of any feeling or any glimmer of intent.

Lealandra stood her ground.

Gregori didn't frighten her anymore. Neither did his two supreme mages. They stood flanking him in the low-lit room. The dark brown walls sapped the light out of the place but didn't hide that it still bore the scars of their previous battle, and it didn't hide the group of witches stood off to her right, waiting for their master's command to attack.

Lealandra's power spread through the vast room, sensing everything, mapping it out in preparation for the fight. The walls remained fractured in places and a lot of the furniture that had previously been in it was gone. Only a few scattered couches remained and some art on the rear wall. They had fixed the window. The closed broad mahogany double doors behind Gregori's witches to her right hid the master suite from view but she could still sense the size and shape of it. Her magic sharpened until she could sense every fibre in the dark carpet and sense every twitch of Gregori's body.

Behind her, hearts beat in rapid unison. Fear crawled over her skin. Not her own but theirs. Most of the witches she had brought with her hadn't faced someone as powerful as Gregori. Only a few of the necromancers that she had assigned to Taig had fought witches that were stronger than themselves, or fell creatures that could have killed them in the space of a heartbeat if they had wanted it.

Creatures like Taig.

Lealandra could sense that he was holding back. She had never noticed it before but now she did. She was more aware of everything about him and could sense that he wasn't using his full strength, and he never had. He hadn't even used it in his apartment when the two demons had broken in. Would he ever unleash such godlike power on Earth? It would be devastating.

It would be more destructive than her most powerful spell, the one her magic had wanted her to release when she had last been here. He could level a city with his power, not just a few blocks.

Lealandra stared at Gregori. Waiting. Gregori remained still, unwavering in his intent gaze and his focus. He had all of his power fixed on her. No one else in the room concerned him. Not even Taig.

That was his first mistake.

Taig hated it when someone ignored him in a fight.

Dark power rippled through the room, sharp in its feeling and full of deadly intent. Lealandra's magic whispered to her, making her further aware of Taig's strength. It reached to him, drawn there, desiring his power, and she released it enough to make contact with Taig. Tendrils of her power entwined with his and the boost in her strength was tremendous. The magic rose inside her, spiralling through her body and her mind, suffusing every inch of her until she felt invincible.

A blur shot past her and suddenly one of Gregori's supreme mages was gone. A moment later, the window behind Gregori shattered. The same window Taig had smashed to save her.

She didn't look. Didn't take her eyes off Gregori.

She didn't need to in order to know that Taig was evening the odds in his own way. He roared, disappeared, and reappeared right beside the other supreme mage.

"Let's dance, fancy man," he said and then he was gone, and so was the other supreme mage.

Gregori's right hand shifted.

Lealandra stepped forwards, disappeared and reappeared in front of him. She shot her hand out, grabbed him by the throat, and screamed as she hurled him around and sent him flying across the room. He smiled and disappeared. The room erupted into pandemonium as Gregori's witches piled forwards, rushing hers. The door at the other end of the room opened and the rest of her force came in. They had lost so many already and she knew that they would lose more before the end of the fight. The thought of them dying filled her heart with cold pain but it had been their decision to make and she had to accept that. It didn't lessen the feeling of responsibility that pressed down on her.

Spells hurtled past her, bright coloured flashes that punctuated the fight, filling the air with strange smells of fire and brimstone mixed with honey and other sweet things. Screams and cries filled the room and she blocked them out, focusing on her own fight so she would survive and be the victor.

The other supreme mage reappeared, long dark blue coat shredded by the broken glass of the window. He shot a spell towards Lealandra. She raised her hand and deflected it towards the ceiling. The spot it struck turned dark and bulged downwards. The black shape moved and wriggled, as though something was growing inside it. They were playing with shadows.

"Taig!" She unleashed a glowing red bolt of magic and blasted the supreme mage back out of the window, and then ran towards Gregori, away from the forming shadow.

Taig whirled to face her, his hand clasped over the head of the other supreme mage. "Bit busy, sweet cheeks. Not a good time for telling me how much you love me."

He grinned at her, dragged his arm around, and smashed the mage into the floor, pinning him there by his face.

Lealandra deflected every twisting blue orb of magic that Gregori threw at her, forcing him backwards towards the far wall where there was more space. She needed to keep her fight with him one on one and that meant keeping him away from the other end of the room near the master suite where everyone else was fighting.

"We have a problem." She ignored Taig's attempt at humour. This definitely wasn't the time she was going to choose to confess her feelings for him. Things weren't that dire yet. She nodded behind her.

Taig looked there and his expression instantly darkened. He tossed the supreme mage into the group of three male necromancers that had been acting as his back up and stalked towards her.

"Let daddy take care of the kiddies." He grinned again and then his eyes brightened, the fires of Hell filling them. Lealandra lost focus, drugged by the flow of his power through her as it rose and tangled with her own. It was intoxicating to feel such strength in her veins. Her magic swirled inside her, contented by the surge in power it gained from Taig.

Darkness slammed into her stomach, knocking her off her feet.

Taig growled. Her head spun. She tried to get up but the world shifted and twirled, spinning around in front of her eyes. A strong hand hauled her to her feet and set her down. Taig smiled at her. She shook her head and glared at Gregori. He stood far away at the other end of the room, a row of witches acting as a wall around him. He looked smug. Her eyes narrowed. She was going to wipe that look right off his face.

"Little more careful. Can't look after you all the time," Taig whispered and then released her. He was gone before she could respond. An ungodly cry filled the room a moment later. A strange sense of icy emptiness flowed over her like mist, the same feeling she'd had back in the void that Taig had travelled through with her. A shadow had been born in this world.

Angry at the idea that Taig thought she was weak and needed protecting all of the time, she severed the connection between them and forced her magic to focus. It darkened within her, irritated by her actions. Good. If it wanted to feel the connection to Taig again, it was going to have to help her.

Lealandra raised her hand and focused on Gregori.

The witches blocking her way to Gregori shifted and parted, leaving her path clear. They tried to move back again but she held them at bay. It was too easy to move such weak witches. Raising her other hand, she signalled her side to attack. They rushed past her, down either side of the invisible path she had created between her and Gregori.

Gregori raised a hand and smiled at her. His hazel eyes shifted, the colour in them draining and then red surfacing. So that was how he wanted to play the game. Dirty. Lealandra released her focus and hold on her magic, allowing it free rein. It surged through her, claiming a fraction of control. She sensed the moment her eyes changed. It was the same moment that the voice in her mind joined with her own. Gregori was playing a fool's game. He hadn't ascended. His power was nothing compared to her own.

Red ribbons of magic curled around her fingers, lacing them together, and spiralled up her arms.

The fierce fight around them drifted away, inconsequential noise, a buzzing of flies that didn't concern her. Gregori's eyes melted completely to red. He was surrendering total control to his power.

A fool's game.

She could sense how close he was to ascension. Surrendering to the magic now was risking it destroying him. It would seize control and act out its own will. He was taking a huge chance by believing it would want her dead.

Lealandra ran at him, raising her hands and feeling the incantation at the same time. Three spells in one again. Bind. Silence. Pain. Only this time, they wouldn't drain her and leave her open. She was stronger now. She could use high-level magic without fear of weakening herself. The magic around her hands turned blue and she launched her right hand forwards, sending the spell shooting towards Gregori. With an idle flick of his wrist, he dragged one of his supreme mages across the room and into the path of the spell. The man fell to the floor, twitching and screaming in agony. Lealandra made a noise of frustration and threw the second spell. Gregori looked at the window. Lealandra could sense the second supreme mage there. Gregori's magic dragged him across the room, throwing him in front of the spell. He dropped to the floor too.

Lealandra growled and began casting another spell.

Gregori rushed her. He was across the room in an instant and slamming into her stomach. The force of the impact knocked the air from her lungs. Her arms flung forwards as she flew backwards. She didn't hit the floor. There was a momentary darkness and then the sound of wind rushing and the chill night air surrounded her. The breeze threw her long black hair around and the cold brought goose bumps out over her flesh.

She cast a quick glance around her new surroundings and got to her feet. Gregori had taken her to the roof. He stood on the far side of the helipad opposite her, his coat tails flapping in the wind and strands of his hair flying free from his ponytail. The low spotlights around the perimeter of the round helipad cast strange shadows on his angled face, forming dark hollows in his cheeks and around his eyes. Their red depths burned into hers.

A split second later, a twisting spike of bright blue flew towards her. She rolled to one side to dodge the spell and then back again to dodge another. Gregori hurled two more spells at her, bigger this time, huge bright orbs of yellow that came at her fast. She stepped towards them and then the wind shifted and she was ten feet closer to Gregori, past the spells. They shot off into the distance behind her. Her magic rose and, without thinking, she cast a silence spell at Gregori. The second she sensed his intent to move out of its path, she hurled another spell. The binding spell hit him square in the chest, constricting his arms against his sides. He stared at her, frowned, and then raised his arms with considerable effort. His eyes brightened and his arms came free.

Lealandra sent another two pink orbs shooting his way and then ran, casting faster smaller spells that he wouldn't easily be able to avoid. He disappeared and reappeared quickly, each time dodging one of the spells. He winked in and out of existence so fast that Lealandra couldn't keep up. The ease with which he avoided the spells made her cold. He was far more powerful than she had believed. It was almost as though he could sense them even as he was moving through the vortex opened during teleportation.

She hurled more spells, low grade binding ones that wouldn't stop him but would slow him down long enough for her to get a better shot in. He disappeared and the hairs on the back of her neck rose when wind blew across them. Behind her. She turned but wasn't quick enough. Gregori's fist slammed into her cheek, sending her mind spinning and her toppling to the ground. Before she could hit it, she opened the vortex and fell inside. She reappeared above Gregori and roared as she hurtled towards him, her foot outstretched, aimed for his head. He caught her foot, twisted it, and flung her across the roof.

Lealandra bounced along it, tumbling and turning, and barely managed to stop herself from falling over the edge of the helipad to the roof below.

Her entire body ached and protested when she pushed herself up. Physical fights weren't her style and they weren't Gregori's either but he would easily best her in one. She dragged herself to her feet and resumed a fighting stance.

Two bright pinpricks of purple shot towards her, so small she could barely make out their centres and so dazzling that they hurt her eyes. She didn't recognise them but her magic did.

It whispered words of death at her and she ran, skirting the edge of the helipad. The wind rushed against her, slowing her down, and she cast a frightened glance over her shoulder at the twin spells. If one hit her, she would survive. It would take both to impact in order for the spell to be effective. They shifted course and shot towards her, tracking her. She ran harder, her heart exploding with panic. They were closing in.

Glass smashed in the distance.

Lealandra tripped.

The helipad came up at her in slow motion and then the wind changed course. It shot downwards and she shot upwards. Below her, the two purple dots of light moved course again, heading up with her. Wind beat down on her, strong against her back. A firm arm held her tight against him. Taig.

Lealandra raised her arms in front of her face as the spells closed in, so bright that she couldn't see anything but them, but her inevitable death.

And then they stopped.

She stared wide-eyed at Taig's extended hand. His human skin was gone, replaced by dark brown scaly claws, their tips longer this time and gleaming. His palm faced the two orbs and his dragon-like wings beat the air to keep him stationary. Taig moved his fingers and darkness grew around the twin spells. More than an absence of light again. Lealandra could feel what was on the other side, what waited there, eager for the power that Taig was sending them. The spells dulled, growing faint as though the darkness was sucking the light out of them, and then they winked out.

Taig clenched his fist, his long pointed claws curling around.

The darkness disappeared.

"I leave you alone for a second..." Taig muttered in her ear and wrapped his other arm around her, holding her close. "I said to be a little more careful."

Lealandra nodded, rested her head against his chest and let her magic latch onto his power. They slowly descended towards the helipad and Gregori. He was watching her, waiting, reminding her of the dark things that lived in that other world that Taig could so easily command.

Taig set her down. She readied herself, her focus split between Gregori and Taig.

Taig backed off a step and stood motionless at the edge of the helipad behind her. She frowned, surprised by his actions. Gregori wasn't stopping him. He was keeping back, letting her fight by herself, as though he had sensed her need to be the one to end it with Gregori. She smiled inside at that. The magic must have communicated it to him. Taig's presence was a comfort though. He wasn't only her back up but her pillar of strength too, the one person she could rely on to give her what she needed without judgement and with affection. He would give every last drop of his power to her if she needed it. She knew that without asking, and she might just need it.

Gregori's eyes brightened, until the red completely filled his eyes, absorbing all of the white.

His power rose and hers followed suit, intent on being stronger than his was.

Lealandra took a deep breath and then ran at Gregori. He came at her, throwing spells in quick succession that she dodged by leaping and stepping on the air itself as though it was a physical platform for her to use. The magic continued to rise inside her, guiding her and giving her an inkling of just how far she could go now. She could walk on air, could step great distances without the need to open a vortex. The feel of the wind against her, the cold silence, was comforting. It gave her peace as she moved without thinking, avoiding everything that Gregori was throwing at her. His face darkened and he snarled at her, revealing sharp teeth. She had to stop him before he became too powerful. If the magic controlled him completely, she wouldn't be powerful enough to stop him, not unless she drained Taig of every drop of his power.

She raised her hands and rained fury down on Gregori, whizzing red spells that slammed through the air like bolts of lightning. They struck true and Gregori jerked backwards with each collision. The spells sapped his power but it rose again, until a dark red aura surrounded him. He was losing control. She launched herself at him, cutting through the air towards him. Her eyes narrowed on him and she drew her hand back, readying the highest level binding spell that she knew.

Gregori smiled at her.

Before she could release the spell, he slammed into her, his hands against her chest, sending them both up into the night air. Bright green light filled the space between them and then it felt as though a bullet train had hit her. Her ears rang, her body felt heavy, and her mind felt numb. Gregori disappeared.

Lealandra fell backwards, her hair streaming upwards as she dropped downwards. Her arms hung limp in the air above her and she could only stare as the side of the building appeared beyond her feet. An odd sense of calm filled her as she fell, dropping down through the cold night air. She didn't feel the rush of wind or hear the sound of it as her hair fluttered and flapped. She felt nothing but peace and an overwhelming sense of tiredness.

Something sparked in her mind, a quiet voice that said to teleport, to get her backside back up to the helipad. The voice had an aura of fear around it, panic lacing through it. Hurt. And something else. Love. Overwhelming love. A shiver raced down her spine. Taig. Her eyes widened when she realised that she was falling. The top of the building was so far away now. The floors rushed past her, a blur that she couldn't keep up with. She didn't have the strength to teleport to the roof and she couldn't clearly make out a floor to teleport onto. Panic filled her and she reached up, silently stretching for Taig.

She didn't want to die.

Her magic burst through her, taking control for a split second at the exact same moment that she hit something hard. Not the pavement. It dropped with her and then she was going up again. Fatigue engulfed her and she leaned against Taig's chest. The feel of his arms around her, holding her close against his chest, and his warm scent soothed her, stealing away her fears and restoring her balance.

"Thank you," she whispered and tried to stay awake.

Whatever Gregori had hit her with, it had drained her strength but not her magic. That was hurtling around inside her, furious about the spell that he had cast on her and pushing for control. She closed her eyes and surrendered to it. Her only way of winning now was to fight Gregori with everything she had, and that meant letting her magic take control, just as he had done. She had to trust that it would surrender control to her again when the fight was over. She had to trust that it wouldn't dare utter a spell that would harm Taig or anyone other than her enemy.

Taig pressed a kiss to her hair. The top of the building passed her by. She looped her arms around Taig's neck and claimed his lips with her own, kissing him softly and drawing strength from the love she could feel in him. She wouldn't let him down again. She would defeat Gregori and then they could be together, just as she knew he wanted them to be, just as they should have been all this time. They belonged together. A mismatched but perfect for each other couple. Nothing in this world would separate them again. She wouldn't let it.

Taig moved her so his full length pressed against hers and then he lowered her to the floor. The moment her feet touched it, she felt the net that Gregori had spread over the area, a tangled web of magic that would feed his senses. She looked at him out of the corner of her eye, her hair causing the image of him to stutter as it blew across her eyes.

Lealandra crouched and held her hand out above the ground, feeling the threads of magic he had woven over the helipad. They were strong and tuned to her. She released her magic a fraction, letting it steal more control from her, and the change shocked her. Strength surged through her, erasing the fatigue she had felt and filling her with a sense of invincibility that ran bone-deep and bathed every fibre of her being.

Taig moved back again, her sentinel, always there if she needed him. She knew he would help in a heartbeat if she faltered. He wouldn't let things go on so long this time. He wouldn't allow her to endanger herself again.

Lealandra stood and faced Gregori, readying herself. It all came down to this. One moment that would decide both of their fates. Their magic was in control now, guiding their destiny, choosing whether their carrier should live or die.

Her mind receded but her consciousness remained, joined with her magic, one with her power at last. All of her faith, all of her trust, was with the magic and its reaction surprised her. It didn't snatch control or fill her mind with dark thoughts this time. There was no sense of threat about it. It truly was one with her, a part of the same being, joined in a common purpose.

Eradicating the man that had dared to hurt them.

Gregori raised his hands. Black wires of magic twisted around his arms, sucking the light from the area surrounding him. Lealandra's eyes widened.

She knew what she had to do. The moment she realised it, her magic began the process. It burrowed into her flesh, dark red ribbons that sank into her, going down into her bones, into the depths of her body and her core. It fused with them, with her, and in her mind she heard the words, heard the magic's will and intention. Revenge.

Her magic reached out to Taig but it didn't have to reach far. His power was right there with her. She latched onto it, absorbing as much as he would let her so she could cast a spell beyond her dreaming, beyond her abilities, and beyond her knowledge. It was a spell that her magic knew, one that only a powerful demon could help her cast. She needed Taig's full strength to summon the incantation, all of his dark power and his connection to the underworld. The words jumbled together in her mind, weak and fading.

A spark, a tiny leap of electricity bridged the gap in the connection between her and Taig and then immense power coursed into her through the bond, mixing with her own magic. Power so strong that her magic wrapped around it, entwined itself with the invading force and drained the strength from it. Her magic used it to grow and become stronger, until it was powerful enough to form the words in order and to bring about the spell that she needed to cast.

The stilted wires around Gregori's hands grew wider, jagged, menacing as they writhed against his flesh. His eyes darkened to black. The wind rose, sending Lealandra's hair floating upwards and her power rose with it. The words fell into line in her head and she raised her hands. Red magic seeped out of her skin, soft smoke-like ribbons that wound themselves around her arms, illuminating the darkness.

Her mouth opened and silent words fell from her lips, each landing heavily in the air and shaking the world.

A dark void opened around her, chasing outwards from her back, from where Taig stood immobile, her bridge to the world that she was calling. It was his power that allowed her to do this, that would see her end this fight and become the victor. It was his strength all along that had helped her, through both the ascension and also through what lay ahead. She would always need him and his power, his support and guidance, but most of all his love and devotion.

She needed him as she needed no other.

And she knew he felt the same.

The darkness swept past her, covering the helipad and focusing on her enemy. Gregori's magic stuttered, faltering and shrinking away, growing small and weak, tiny strings that hid on the far side of his forearms. His eyes lightened to red.

Lealandra focused, using all of her remaining strength to control the world that she was opening, a world of darkness and shadows where spirits were born and fed upon those who strayed into their land. A place where Gregori would become a feast, his magic drawing the creatures to him, his power his downfall.

Ascension

"No," Gregori hissed and backed away but it was too late.

The shadows moved around him, taking form in the darkening night. The stars winked out of existence above them and nothingness blanketed the lights of the world. Not an absence of something but a presence, a joining of worlds, a shift that Taig had made possible.

This wasn't a weak version of the shadow world as Gregori had created and used to torture her, and it was stronger than the form of the world that Taig had opened before. This was the shadow world brought to Earth in its entirety so the strongest darkest creatures that inhabited it could come forth and it was difficult to contain, even with Taig's power flowing through her and controlling it.

Twisted shapes rose up from the shadows, contorting into new forms, jagged creatures that she could see through and that she feared. She held that fear inside, knowing instinctively that if she showed it, they would turn their attention to her too.

Lealandra glanced over her shoulder at Taig. He stood behind her in his larger demon form, dark brown scaly skin covering his muscular bare body, his thick arms folded across his broad chest. He snarled, exposing his sharp teeth to the gum, and narrowed his eyes on Gregori. They burned brightly, flickering in time with the flames that danced at his back. The inferno silhouetted his massive dragon-like wings and reflected off the twin horns that curled from the back of his head. Hell. It stood there for her to see, a fiery pit of despair and destruction that caused a chill to creep over her skin. A place she had promised herself that she would go to in order to find Taig's parents. It frightened her now that she saw it but she would still go there, for his sake, to heal his pain and end his uncertainty.

Beyond the flames, there was infinite darkness. The shadow world. The unspeakable horror that Taig had helped her call to this world.

Taig's power wrapped around her, masking her presence with his own and rendering her invisible to the creatures. Her magic would be just as alluring as Gregori's. She turned back to him. No matter how much her skin crawled or how deep her fear went, she had to remain calm and within Taig's reach. She had called this world to her own. She had to face it and see what it was that she had done.

The shadow spirits wound themselves around Gregori's legs. He blasted them with spells, one after the other, but to no avail. Any shadow that he hit divided and became two, and those two rose up to bring him down, clawed black fingers stretching for him, scratching at his clothes and dragging him down into their waiting mass.

It was as though the night itself was swallowing him. He fought hard, desperate bright coloured blasts of high-level spells that drained him. She sensed his magic recede, felt the moment it gave out and left him no more than mortal, watched as the shadows dug their claws into his shoulders and pulled him down, covering him, drowning him, and then she turned away and buried her face into Taig's chest, hiding there as Gregori's scream rent the still night air.

Strong arms folded around her and then there was silence. Warmth suffused her as Taig's wings closed over her back, completely surrounding her, and he pressed a kiss to her hair. The twisted dark connection within her to the shadows snapped and she sensed the air lift, her world returning to fill the gap she had created in it.

Her magic relinquished control as Taig's power left her and she collapsed against his dark scaly chest. He held her close and tightly, protecting her in a way that would always make her smile and make her feel safe. She held on to him in return, her hands against his bare ridged back. The feel of his demon skin beneath her palms didn't frighten her. She clung to him and felt the love in his strong embrace. She could never fear Taig. She only feared losing him. The skin beneath her fingers smoothed and warmed, and she knew that he was changing back, regaining his human form. The darkness within her faded, stealing away the evil words that had danced around her mind and the sense that she was drowning in the shadows along with Gregori.

She looked up at Taig to find him smiling at her, a cocksure one that barely tugged at the corners of his lips.

"You can come out now, nothing frightening out here except me."

Lealandra didn't let him go. She held on to him and stared deep into his eyes, watching the way they flickered red like flames. Her eyes half-closed when Taig touched her cheek, lightly brushing his fingers over it, and smiled wide. It didn't alleviate the worry she could feel in him, or the hint of it in his eyes.

"You okay?" he said with a small frown. She nodded.

"More than okay." She rested her head against his soft chest. He unfurled his wings and they shrank into his back. The chill night air washed over her, calming her. Looking around, she saw no sign of Gregori or the shadows. They were gone. She didn't know where to and she didn't want to know. Whatever gate Taig had opened, it had been to a place far worse than where Gregori had sent her. She would never see him again. It was over.

The twinkling lights of the city grew dim in the distance where the sky was lightening. She could sense the sunrise coming and it drained the remaining strength from her. Turning back to Taig, she held her smile inside when she saw that he was naked, standing unabashed and watching the sunrise as the wind tousled his dark hair. He really was divine like that but she didn't want others to see what was for her eyes only. She clicked her fingers and his black jeans encased his legs, his boots reappeared, and his black t-shirt moulded itself back onto his delicious broad muscular torso.

Taig shot her a smile, lifted her into his arms and unfurled his wings again, tearing through the t-shirt she had so carefully constructed. She pressed a hand to his chest to stop him from leaving with her. She couldn't leave yet. She desired nothing more than to sleep in peace with him, to recover her lost strength and power, but she had unfinished business. She couldn't leave the coven without a leader and they would look to her now.

"Tell me you're not staying." Taig frowned and she smiled and rubbed her thumb between his eyes, smoothing away the crease it had caused.

"Never. I don't want to be their leader, but I can't leave right now without making sure that everything is over and that they'll be okay without me." She could feel that the war below her feet had ended, that the witches had felt the loss of their leader and stopped fighting one another, and that it wouldn't be long before some of her side came to the helipad to see if it was true. She would wait for them here in Taig's arms and then together they would decide what would happen to the coven now.

She owed them that.

Taig rolled his eyes. "And the victory sex?"

Lealandra smiled up at him and looped her arms around his shoulders. "As soon as you're ready mister."

He grinned. "I'm always ready for a fight or a f—"

Lealandra cut him off with a glare. He gave her an innocent look, his now black eyes twinkling with it. He could pull that face all he liked but it wasn't going to change her mind.

"I want more than that," she said and he frowned again.

"More than what?"

"Than screwing."

Taig rolled his eyes again but she knew he wasn't unnerved by what she was asking or about to refuse any kind of commitment. He lowered her back onto her feet and touched the mark on her arm, staring at it. It tingled. There was such heat in his look but so much love and tenderness too. He was happy that she wore his mark.

Lealandra moved his hand away and stroked the intricate red lines of the mark. It still looked like a heart to her. She stared into Taig's eyes.

"What does it mean?"

"You're mine for everyone to see... just like our deal stated."

Her gaze fell to the mark on her left arm again. It was petty revenge for what she had done to him. Typical of Taig. Or wasn't it revenge? The things he had whispered during her ascension came back to her and her cheeks blazed and heart burned. Maybe he was using marking her to make them equal as an excuse to claim her as his. That was definitely just like him.

"It's permanent." He stroked the mark, his touch so light it tickled and a warm shiver raced through her. "I guess we're stuck with each other... a demon hunter and one of the World's most powerful witches. We make one hell of a combination and one hell of a team. Not a soul in this world will like us."

He hesitated.

Lealandra's eyes locked with his ebony ones. She had waited for this moment for six long years and she wasn't going to rush him now that he was on the precipice of saying what she wanted to hear. The black spikes of his hair drifted across his forehead, tousled by the chilly morning breeze, and an awkward look settled on his face for a moment before his expression turned serious.

"You know I'm crazy about you, sweet cheeks. I know I can be hard to handle sometimes and I can tell you now that it won't be easy, but how about all that stuff we talked about the other night?"

Lealandra fought to keep her expression blank and expectant even when she wanted to smile over what he had said. It was his way of telling her that he loved her but she wasn't about to let him get away without saying it straight.

"I think you can do better than that."

His look turned boyish and then his lips curved into a sexy smile that had her heart galloping and her legs trembling.

"I love you," he whispered and took hold of her hand. His thumb swept over her knuckles.

Lealandra smiled into his eyes. "I love you too."

Taig pulled her into his arms and kissed her. Her eyes closed as his lips played against hers, a slow sensual dance that had her body heating through and aching for him. She leaned into the kiss, eager for more and desperate to feel him against her, here in this moment with her.

Six years ago, she had found her balance with him and so much more besides. If she hadn't been so convinced that a demon couldn't be her Counter-Balance, she would have recognised Taig was her true other half back then. She smiled against his lips and wrapped her arms around him, holding him tight and swearing never to let him go now that she had him. Taig was her balance, the other half of her soul, the only man strong enough to love her. Now they were together again and she thanked fate for giving her a second chance with the man she loved.

Breaking the kiss, she looked deep into his black eyes and touched her mark on his arm. His hand covered hers. He smiled at her, sinfully handsome and making her heartbeat quicken as he always did.

She was finally home again, back with the man she loved, and she couldn't wait to spend some quiet time with him at his estate in England, settling into her new life. First, she wanted to learn more about her power and find a deeper harmony with it, and something told her that the witches Taig had spoken of could help her do just that. Once she was more in control of her power, at one with it, she was going to drag Taig's backside down into the underworld to find out what had happened to his parents. Deep in her heart, she was sure that they hadn't chosen to leave him, and she hoped that they would be alive and that she could reunite Taig with them.

They would make it into Hell and back again without a problem. Taig would be able to hold his own in the underworld, she had no doubt about that, and she was a lot more powerful now. He was right. They did make one hell of a combination and one hell of a team, and not a bad guy in the world up here or down there was going to be safe from them.

With devastation surrounding them, a dark and bloody history behind them and an undoubtedly exhilarating future ahead of them, Lealandra's world felt strangely balanced at last.

"So, how about it? You up for a little trouble?" Taig stroked her cheek, his dark gaze holding hers, mesmerising her.

Did she want to partner with a sexy, sarcastic demon who she was crazy about and throw herself into the path of danger every night for the thrill of hunting?

It beat the hell out of sitting around a coven waiting for something to happen.

And victory sex was fantastic.

A slow smile teased her lips and she looped her arms around his neck, drawing him in for a long heated kiss.

"I wouldn't have it any other way."

The End

ABOUT THE AUTHOR

Felicity Heaton is a romance author writing as both Felicity Heaton and F E Heaton. She is passionate about penning paranormal tales full of vampires, witches, werewolves, angels and shape-shifters, and has been interested in all things preternatural and fantastical since she was just a child. Her other passion is science-fiction and she likes nothing more than to immerse herself in a whole new universe and the amazing species therein. She used to while away days at school and college dreaming of vampires, werewolves and witches, or being lost in space, and used to while away evenings watching movies about them or reading gothic horror stories, science-fiction and romances.

    Having tried her hand at various romance genres, it was only natural for her to turn her focus back to the paranormal, fantasy and science-fiction worlds she enjoys so much. She loves to write seductive, sexy and strong vampires, werewolves, witches, angels and alien species. The worlds she often dreams up for them are vicious, dark and dangerous, reflecting aspects of the heroines and heroes, but her characters also love deeply, laugh, cry and feel every emotion as keenly as anyone does. She makes no excuses for the darkness surrounding them, especially the paranormal creatures, and says that this is their world. She's just honoured to write down their adventures.

To see her other novels, visit: http://www.felicityheaton.co.uk

To read more about the Vampires Realm series, visit the official website: http://www.vampiresrealm.com

If you have enjoyed this story, please take a moment to contact the author at author@felicityheaton.co.uk or to post a review of the book online

Follow the author on:
Her blog – http://www.indieparanormalromancebooks.com
Twitter – http://twitter.com/felicityheaton
Facebook – http://www.facebook.com/feheaton

Printed in Great Britain
by Amazon.co.uk, Ltd.,
Marston Gate.